REDEMPTION

MICHAEL L. TYLER

Palmetto Publishing Group
Charleston, SC

Redemption
Copyright © 2020 by Michael L. Tyler

All rights reserved
No portion of this book may be reproduced, stored in a retrieval system, or transmitted in any form by any means—electronic, mechanical, photocopy, recording, or other—except for brief quotations in printed reviews, without prior permission of the author.

First Edition

Printed in the United States

ISBN-13: 978-1-64111-837-8
ISBN-10: 1-64111-837-7

*I would like to dedicate this book to my wife Marie,
as well as thank her for coming up with the title.*

*She has always believed in me and has always made me feel as though
I had the aptitude, and the talent to not only write a novel,
but to excel at it.*

is defined as *feeling sad, repentant, or disappointed over something that has happened.* It is a sense of guilt and sorrow for hurting yourself or, usually, someone else. The part that is not defined in the dictionary, however, is how to deal with it, how to get over it, and how to live with the consequences. How to look at yourself and know there may be nothing you can do to resolve the guilt and shame and self-blame you feel. Regret, more often than not, is not about what you did, or what you said, or who you said it to, but rather what action you took when you had the chance for redemption.

A NEW FRIEND

John Jacobi had come to love how great it was at the city park near his house. He could walk to the park stopping maybe only once or twice to catch his breath. He seemed to be stronger and more energetic ever since he'd started coming to the park a year or so ago. The walk seemed to keep him in shape, and kept him healthy—and also kept his girlish figure, as he had jokingly told others. He was told on a regular basis how good he looked for his age, and he attributed it all to the two- or three-block walk that he took to the park each way every day, or at least almost every day.

John had a favorite bench that he walked to every morning. Its paint was chipped here and there, but it was a really nice wrought-iron bench that was in just the right spot, perfectly centered in the middle of the park. The bench offered shade from the huge century-old Cypress right behind him that kept the sun from beating down on the top of his wrinkly old hairless head. He got to sit in the center of the hubbub of the jogging and biking traffic, as everyone either walked or ran or pedaled by him, and at times he had to laugh at some of the characters that he noticed. Some even had wheels on the bottom of their shoes that kept John laughing even after they'd gone by. A big grin would spread across his face when he saw one speed by. *There was never anything like this at the car hop when I was working on roller skates*, he thought to himself. But his days of roller skating and performing all of the dangerous stunts that he'd witnessed from his perfectly stationary bench were over.

John enjoyed seeing his regulars walk by. Most said hello, or would offer the tip of a hat or a salute on the days when he had his Korean War cap on. He usually took it off once he was under the protection of the Cypress, but there were the times when he forgot and sat there on the bench for a while before removing it. He loved to engage with people, and to the ones that conversed with him, he loved to tell stories from the old days that were as vivid in his memory as if they'd happened last week. Most mornings, though, he was lucky if he just got a nod of the head. People were in too much of a hurry nowadays. They didn't have time to hear a story that was more than a few seconds long. He felt bad for this generation of isolation and ignorance of history, people these days only listening to soundbites on Google. He knew that not every young person had that stamped on their resume, but he knew from just observation that a lot more did than did not.

John was a never-ending book. He had stories that left you in awe, and then others that left you about ready to weep, and then of course the ones that had people saying, "We don't say that word anymore." But no matter what story he was telling to whomever would listen, it was a very interesting story, especially the way he told it. He was animated when he talked about the days on the farm, or the way he'd thought he had hit the lottery if there was actual meat on the chicken bone he was given for dinner. He thought it was a shame that he got to tell fewer and fewer stories as the days went by. He figured that the regulars didn't want to hear the same old boring stories from back on the farm anymore. If truth be told, he knew that most kids nowadays weren't interested in hearing about things that they had no way of relating to. It made John feel very sorry about what the future held.

John took out the bird seed that he brought every morning from his bag of goodies he brought, almost every day. and started throwing a few seeds down here and there. Before long, he had his usual friends swooping down to peck at the cobblestones and eat their fill. The jays and the pigeons and the starlings were eager to get their beaks full, and on some days he was pleased to have even a few doves stop by and say hello. He thought of them as his friends, and he was delighted to see them each morning.

As he watched the frenzy for the bird seed ensue, he took out his tattered crossword and word search book from his bag he got from Trader Joes. He liked this bag, because it had handles that were easy to carry. He liked Trader Joe's because their stores were much smaller than the grocery stores which killed his aching back.

He opened it to the page where he'd left off. His pencil was not new—it was chewed up as if a ravenous chipmunk had gotten ahold of it—but it was him who gnawed on it during those times when he couldn't figure out the word that was probably sitting right in front of him. It seemed as though he took all of his frustrations out on this poor pencil.

John was always looking up and greeting passersby as well. He said hello to the girl who was training for the half marathon. She has such a pretty smile, he thought. She seemed to always be happy, but at the same time, she was also focused on the task at hand. He assumed that she worked in some business park, always dressed to the nines, trying to make partner. He hoped she wasn't trying to sleep her way to the top, because as he'd learned from so many shows that he had watched, that scenario never worked out. Someone usually ended up dead, or a family was ruined. Or at least that was what happened in his shows.

John Jacobi was the type of guy who would look off into the vast openness of the park and enjoy the view as the maintenance man mowed the grass and pulled out the gas-powered trimmer to sharpen up the landscaping around the young and old trees, trying to make the park look as respectable as possible. He watched as the old man painstakingly used all of his efforts to trim the hedges, mulch the flower beds, and prune the flowers, until everything in eyesight was truly a sight to behold. He got so much enjoyment from watching the old man rake a few leaves or prune a tree, turning a messy area into a gorgeous one.

He liked to see the kids being walked to school up the street by their parents. He was not an old pervert, but some of the mothers were very good looking, and watching them walk by was not a problem with him at all, he thought most days. He would tip his hat in greeting to the mom and the young kid. They were usually four or five years old, some shy and reserved, while others would come right up to him and say, "Hi, what's your name?" and ask a hundred other questions about how old he was and why does he come here every day, and why doesn't he wear socks, and what was the weather like a hundred years ago when he was a kid? John got the biggest charge out of some of the unique and blunt—very blunt—questions that he was asked by these kids at times.

John looked up from his book just in time to see one of his regulars, a mom and her son who was about four or five years old, who walked by almost every day. She smiled, and the boy just hugged his mother's thigh as he scooted on past. He had a slight limp, so John figured that he was probably withdrawn, because more than likely he was teased because of it. He knew a little bit about being teased. When he was a kid, sometimes he got nervous and stuttered, and the flurry of jokes soon followed. He was mortified in class when Miss Jacobs called on him and someone else, some freak, used his voice and started talking. Someone who couldn't put two words together without a roar of laughter ensuing behind him. Those memories were ones that he could do without reminiscing about, though. He did not force the kid to interact with him. He just tipped his finger to his brow and said, "Morning, folks."

As they passed him by, John tried to piece together who these people were. Were they rich, or poor? Were they down to earth or complete snobs? And how did people see him, in turn? Did they see him as a nice old man sitting on a bench making sure the birds were fed, or some poor old bum who doesn't have anywhere to be? You could see it in the eyes. The sadness was so evident in their eyes. The appreciation for feeding the birds was just as evident, too. He could see that most eyes were in the category of "oblivious." They didn't care about anything or anyone, really, especially an old fart sitting on a bench feeding a bunch of feathered rats. He kind of felt sorry for them, but at the same time he connected with them, because he had been that person before his body had gotten so old. Now that old age had finally caught up with him, he wished that he'd paid a little more attention to the old farts he had passed in his lifetime.

He wished that he'd done so many things differently. His life was an Olympic-sized swimming pool filled with *Maybe I should've* and *I wish I had...* He caught himself saying it more and more as life went on. He knew he couldn't change anything about the past, but at the same time, it was nice to just think about *what if* and the *if only*. John could see in the eyes of the people who were nice enough to give a minute or two of their time that they were thinking it, too. He figured everyone did.

On most days, nothing much was usually said, if anything, just a "hi" or "how are you?" And then they were off to their own lives. There usually wasn't much time for anything that would resemble a real conversation. The joggers were busy and focused on everything but jogging, he figured. Their brains were focused on the contract they had to peruse when they got to work, or whether or not they were going to meet a deadline. You could see in their eyes that they were miles away. The busy mothers usually didn't register a reply, nor did their children. They just walked by and went about their hurried lives. None of the mothers would engage him on their way back from the school, either, but it was okay, he thought. Not everyone grew up with an attachment to others, including him.

His folks spoke with old man Munley all the time. John didn't remember his name, but he remembered that everyone called him Buddy. He wasn't sure whether that was his actual name, or just a term of affection. His parents made John acknowledge people. They believed that it was the polite thing to do. You didn't have to invite them home for dinner, but you did say "hi, sir," or "hi, Ma'am," as you walked by. John kind of missed those days now, even though he didn't stick to the philosophy himself as a young man. Today's world was all about solitude and privacy and separateness. It was a "*you stay over there and I'll stay over here*" mentality, and it was very sad to John. These young people were missing out on so much with that way of thinking. He wished he had followed his parents' teachings.

Another regular walked by and did not look down. He too stayed in his own world, his own reality, and then he too was gone as quickly as he had arrived. John gave him a glance for a second or two and then went back to finding the word that had been eluding him for the last minute or so.

John was jostled out of his focus on the word *tiny*, which to him was like trying to find a needle in a jumbled-up haystack. Someone was suddenly sitting next to him. This was a rare occurrence indeed, he thought. He knew he wasn't prim and proper and shaved and hair-combed, but at almost ninety, who cared? He knew for sure that he didn't. *If they care, then let them move on,* was always his way of thinking.

He watched as the other old fart sitting on the bench alongside him pulled out his thermos and poured something into a small cup. He assumed that it was tea or coffee. At their age—which was eighty plus, easy—John figured their drinking days were so far in the past, you would need the Hubble Telescope to see them. John wanted to say hello, but at the same time, he didn't want to be rude—if the man wanted to just be left alone, he should let him be. But then it dawned on John that if the man wanted to be left alone, there were other benches to sit on. Unless this was indeed the perfect bench, and it was not known only to him. It had the perfect amount of shade, and on a day like this—a nice sunny day—this would be the optimal chair to park your carcass. He went for it. "Beautiful day, isn't it?" he said cheerfully.

The other old man took a second to finish sipping his green tea with honey. "Yes, this is a beautiful day indeed," he said. "There are only a few days like this in the year, but this is definitely one of the better ones. It's sunny, but the sun is warm, but is not melting your face, ya know? And with just a hint of a breeze blowing every so often. Nice day indeed."

John hadn't attended M.I.T., but he was smart enough to recognize a kindred spirit, someone who just wanted to sit and bullshit the day away. "So, I haven't seen you around here before," he said.

"I've only been here a few times, but I always sit on that big rock down the path a piece. It looks out over a really nice piece of Charleston. Its right on the outskirts, but the smell of food coming from that block are heavenly. Down-home cookin', as they say."

"I can't speak for the cooking," said John, "but even with this bad nose of mine, I can smell the honeysuckles and the gardenias floating in the air around here. The groundskeeper must have mowed recently, because on my way here this morning, I could smell nice fresh-cut grass. I used to love that as a kid. Summer is the best time in the world in these here parts. I can't wait for April to get here so that I can start coming down every morning and seeing the new flowers first come in to bloom. It is an actual sight to behold."

"Oh, yes," continued the other man, "I used to love that, too. The honeysuckles and the rose bushes bring all kinds of butterflies and birds around, and I used to sit there and watch them for hours. Definitely a picturesque site. I' am sure it is just as beautiful over here."

"I'd like to think so." John figured that using words like *picturesque* meant that this guy was a learned man, with probably an expensive education. Unlike him, who only had a tenth grade education and a tiny understanding of the world outside Charleston, South Carolina. Other than his short period with the United States Army, he had been pretty much rooted in the same zip code for the past few decades. He loved it there, though. One of his kids was there, his wife was buried there, and his old friend that he was sitting on at the moment was always there when he wanted to see it.

"Excuse my manners," the other man said. "My name is Anthony, what's yours?" Anthony gave a big broad, welcoming smile.

John placed his book down and creakily swung his knee up onto the bench so that he could be facing his newfound friend opposite him. He looked the man over quickly. He was a tall, slender man, with an obvious shiny bald head and, surprisingly, not a ton of wrinkles weighing him down, as John's body did. "My name is John, John Jacobi," he said. "I'm glad to meet you, Anthony." He didn't say Tony, which furthered John's belief that this was a learned man who took pride in his achievements. "So, you live here in Charleston?"

"I do. I moved here a while back, but when I found this park, it became my favorite part of the city. I found myself coming down here more and more. Even in the colder months, I found myself bringing a lawn chair and sitting over there and just watching life unfold. You can see all kinds of things, even when there are a few inches of snow on the ground." Anthony pointed to the area past the trees down the path a bit. "I used to come here and sit in my chair and take a nap, or grab a chili dog from Trish's meals-on-wheels truck. Her chili dogs are worth fighting over. I'm sure you've had one."

John got a chuckle out of Anthony's exuberance. "Yeah, I've had one or two. When my son Peter used to live down here, he was always saying not to, but my old saying is that I'd rather die from it than die from wanting it. You know?"

Anthony nodded vigorously. "At our age, what is more likely to kill us is boredom, not a chili dog," he said. Anthony held his stomach as he rumbled with laughter.

John got a big smile on his face from watching the old man crack himself up. "Yeah, I guess you're right." He didn't know what to say, but he knew for sure that he wasn't going to crack up laughing and fall on the ground like this guy was about to do. He grinned and thought, *That may have been exaggerating quite a bit, but not by much, and besides, his joke was way better.* "Nowadays, I sneak a chili dog or a burger or anything I damn well please." *Now that was funny*, he thought to himself.

"I hear you, John," said Anthony. "It's not going to kill you if it hasn't by now."

"And if it does, I'm okay with it," continued John. "When my number is called, I've got all my bags packed, and I'm standing in the express line ready to be checked out."

Anthony and John both laughed together as if they were sitting front row at the Apollo. Anthony put his arm on the back of the bench and turned so that he could look at John more directly, and he said, "For an old fart, you've got a good sense of humor."

"I'd like to think the candle still has a wick," said John.

"I like that," said Anthony. "I might use it, if you don't have any objections?"

"Knock yourself out, Anthony."

"You said you had kids. Does Peter have any siblings?"

Was this guy being nosey, John wondered, or just trying to get a dialogue started? John figured it was the latter, so he tapped his finger on his stubbly chin and said, "There's Peter, God rest his soul, and there is John Junior, and Nikki, the daughter everyone—I mean no one—would want to have, and then there's Marcus, the pain in my butt. He also lives in Charleston." John cleared his throat. "I shouldn't say that, really, because he has done very well for himself. He was an engineer for N.A.S.A. before he retired last year, and has done quite well in the loving family department as well, even if it is a bit unconventional."

"So, why is he a pain in your butt? I mean, does he not like your quick wit or your word search puzzles or something?"

"No, more like political and traditional differences, if truth be told," John admitted. "I always had to stop him from alienating us from the neighbors and the family and almost anyone else who wasn't a left-wing nut job."

"Are you a full-fledged patriotic Republican?" asked Anthony. "Is that where you fall?"

"I would say Republican moderate, I guess. I do think that the Democrats do have a tendency to want to save the whole damn world, but if your thing is guys and that is what makes your heartbeat flutter, than you go for it, boy, but it's just not my thing."

"So, what's wrong with that? I guess Marcus is batting for the other team?"

"Homerun on the first swing there, old man," John confirmed.

"Well, if you say it's okay with you, then why is he a pain in the fanny? I mean, it sounds like you could care less if he is gay."

"Well, it's like this, I guess," said John. "I think he always felt that he had to prove that the little Nancy boy could hit a ball or kick a field goal with the best of the girl-loving boys, and in retrospect, it got his ass kicked a lot. He cared too much about what other people thought, and that really hindered him from having some close relationships with anyone who wasn't in his bubble of friends."

"You?" asked Anthony.

"Oh yeah, definitely me, among others. I was one of the 'beat it out of him' dads. I was sure I could beat the gay right out of him, but for some reason, it just made us grow very far apart."

"For some reason?"

"Yeah, I know, I know." John tilted his head back and watched the memories fly past his face in supersonic speed. "I know now, but at the time, I was sure I was doing him a favor. He used to come home with a bloody lip or a bruised cheek, or even a black eye. How can you help your son if he doesn't want to accept reality for what it is?"

"So, what happened?" Anthony was indeed interested in his life. He knew why he was sitting on a park bench all alone, but he wanted to know why this shabby, worn-down, and worn-out looking old man was there every day. It was obvious that he needed a good shave and a long shower, and some clothes that didn't look like they'd been ravaged by a swarm of hungry moths.

"Well, in the sixties, people were not very cotton to his kind in most parts," John said, "so he ran off right after school and went to college in a more understanding environment. He got away from this place and all the bigotry, racism, and the plethora of uneducated hicks that lived around here. I don't blame him, but it also made us kind of drift apart as well." John sighed heavily. It had been a long time since he had taken that trip down memory lane.

Anthony could see that his newfound friend was on the verge of crying all over his crossword puzzle, so he changed the subject. "I guess Peter and Nikki and John Junior were not of the gay persuasion? They stuck around?"

"It's funny you say that. You would think that, but actually, running Marcus off to San Francisco kind of made them all mad at me—made them hate me, I guess—for not accepting Marcus the way he was. They were all older than Marcus and took up for him no matter what he did. It kind of left a big hole in all of our relationships. Before Peter passed away, and after, I guess, it always felt like me against the kids, and I only received messages about newborns or major achievements through my wife. God bless her, but she never was able to fix this problem, even though she fixed all of their internal squabbles. Me and the kids just never got right with each other."

"Do you ever see them?" asked Anthony.

Sarcastically, John replied, "Oh yeah, they come by from time to time, every decade or two or five." John changed gears. "Marcus unbelievably took a job near here a few years ago, and he stops by every blue moon or so. I know that I could call the rest of them at any time and say, 'hey, I need something,' and I'd have it. I think. Maybe? Probably not."

"Loving and being loved by your kids is great," said Anthony, "but not feeling like you are their friend or their best friend stings." Anthony said this as though he likely had a bit of experience in the area.

"Like a bitch." John felt a bit like he was on the couch of a psychiatrist. He decided to put a halt to the "why did my life turn out this way?" crap. "So what about you?"

"Oh me? I don't have any gay kids."

"And?"

"And, I guess me and my kids are like every other family on the planet," continued Anthony. "There are some days when I want to kick the shit out of them, and then there are some days when I want to hug them and never let go."

"So, where are they now?" asked John.

"Oh, geesh, they're all over the place, all over the world. Tammy, my youngest, is jet-setting all over the place, running after whatever new story is going to have her on the eleven o' clock news. Fred is retired and living about two hours away, but he's always going to some new exotic place with his wife. My other kid, Trevor, is mostly just running around, handling his business and his own life, I guess. They call me every once in a while, but I leave them be. I try to be there when they need me, but not in their face, you know?"

"I do," John said with a nod. "I try not to get in my kids' business too much. Junior used to let me know when something was going on with him and his kids. I guess he hasn't had much news to share in the past decade or so. I heard from Marcus that he got divorced and his ex took the kids to Chicago, and then nothing, really. I try to give Nikki what she needs over the phone, but without my wife, it's just a quick howdy and not much more before I hear a dial tone, unless we talk about money and how much she needs."

Anthony smiled and nodded his head, indicating that he understood very much. He changed the subject. "Were you in the army or anything?"

"Yeah, I was in Korea, and got out the minute that they'd let me," said John. "I hated it over there. Everything about that place and that war. I wanted to just go home. I was a snot-nosed kid trying not to get killed. I slept in fear, I ate in fear, I took a shit in fear."

Anthony coughed to hide the fact that he was laughing at his last remark, even though it was delivered with obvious pain. "I'm sorry, but that was funny."

"You try taking a shit with bullets tearing up the same leaves you were about to use as toilet paper. To this day, every time I drive by a Korean restaurant, I have to go take a shit."

Anthony couldn't help laughing. This guy had a great sense of humor, and it was becoming easier and easier to like him as the stories were told one after another. "That was it?"

"Yeah, I guess so. I got out and stayed out. I thank the kids nowadays for their service, but if they were anything like me, they were itching to be rid of that uniform. To me, it was like wearing a wool sweater in August. I don't envy anyone living that life, and voluntarily choosing to do so. Did you?"

"No, I just kept my head down, and they walked right on past me," said Anthony. "I'm just kidding. Actually, I wasn't living in the States when that particular war was going on. I was too young to be in the big one and too hyped up on living and seeing the world when I was young to be in Korea. I biked across France all the way to Rome. I lived in a little village outside Paris for a while, and just soaked in what I called life. I never worried about what was going on unless it was at my doorstep or in my mailbox. I didn't care too much about the day-to-day lives of others, unfortunately."

"You sound like a pretty selfish prick," John said. Then he cleared his throat. "I'm sorry if that hurt your feelings, but I call 'em the way I see 'em."

Anthony started to grin a bit, but after John's obvious confusion, Anthony remarked, "John, I don't care if you call me a selfish prick, because I *was* a selfish prick. People were just a nuisance to me when I was twenty. They were always in my business or asking me to do them a favor. I preferred to be left alone."

"Sounds like you were decades ahead of your time, because that's how everyone—and I mean *everyone*—is now," said John. He wasn't sure whether his first instinct about Anthony was accurate. He now seemed more like a pompous, self-centered, *I am the universe* type of guy.

"I guess that's one way of looking at it. I tend to veer toward *youth is wasted on the young*. It wasn't until I met my dear departed wife that I found that there was actually a human being in this world that was worth talking to."

"Sounds like you miss her a lot," John said sympathetically.

"Times ten, times a hundred." Anthony's smile said it all.

"I can relate," said John. "I miss my wife Betty every day, sometimes every minute." John released a heavy sigh. It was obvious that he was missing her at that very moment.

Anthony, too, gave a reciprocal sigh indicating that he too was in the moment. "Yeah, my wife and I had one thing that we both agreed on," he said. "I treated her like a queen, and she in turn treated me like a king. It was a long and very happy marriage. I miss her laugh, and I miss the way she would act like it didn't matter, so I would say it was okay, which is what she wanted to begin with."

"Oh my God, yours did that too?" said John. "Betty was always saying stuff like 'I don't need that dress,' or 'That is too much money,' knowing damn well that that would make me pull my wallet out and buy it just to show her that the money wasn't an issue. At the time, it used to bug me, but if she was here now, I would buy her a whole store full of dresses, and anything else that she wanted."

"What I miss most is the food. Oh my, could she cook!" Anthony exclaimed. "I mean, there were times when I came home from work and I could smell it before I hit the porch. The smell of her pork chops made the hard day's work worth it. When the kids came along, it was not so many one-on-one dinners, but they grew to be a family event, which my wife took very seriously. Your hands had better be washed and your butt better be in that seat when the food was placed on the dining room table."

"Same here. Betty would crack your head like an egg if you were caught messing around at dinner," John said. "The kids were to set the table and make sure that the younger kids hands were washed, and if your hands didn't smell like soap, she got this look as though you were an intruder at her table."

"That look is very familiar to me, too," said Anthony. "Unfortunately, nowadays, I bet that look is gone with the dinosaurs. The meals of this century are carry-out, TV dinners, and delivery. Those are the only dinner choices you have now. it's a shame what this country and this planet are turning into." Anthony was serious about feeling sorry for the youth of today. The family bond was as strong as a piece of Bounty paper towel, as he'd said so many times. He really did feel sorry for today's kids.

"I hear you," said John. "My choices are to pay someone to cook for me every day, or learn to cook. Guess which one I chose to do?" John made a face that conveyed that he was no cook by any means.

"Let's see, you chose to cook?"

"Wrong, sir," said Anthony. "I choose to go to the Time Café down the street and let them make me a nice bowl of vegetable or potato soup. It sticks to my ribs and keeps my stomach quiet during the middle of the night." John and Anthony shared a laugh at the same thought. Who would learn to cook when you could have someone just plop it down in front of you? It's what they had gotten married for, after all.

Anthony pulled a memory out of the far recesses of his brain. "My favorite was when she would cook me two eggs, some home fries, and a piece or two of bacon, and it found its way in front of my face at dinner time. There was something about having breakfast for dinner that just made those eggs taste so much better than at any other time of the day."

John nodded his head in agreement. He too knew that dish. "Yes, Lord, that was one of the best meals of the week for me, but unfortunately without Betty, it's just bacon and eggs now."

"You're so right," said Anthony. "Without my wife putting that tablespoon of love on it, it's just breakfast food."

John looked over and saw the mother returning from dropping her kid off at school. She didn't look directly at him, and that was okay. He gave her a nod, acknowledging her anyway, and let her just walk past. It did bring to light that the two had been bull crapping for an hour or so, though. "There goes the mother of the kid who has the limp, so it must be going on nine. We've been sitting here shooting the shit for an hour, Anthony. Don't seem like it, does it?"

"No, not at all. I think geezers our age have more to talk about than what's on Facebook or on the internet, or what new text you just got on your smart phone. They are stupid phones if you ask me, because they just make everyone an idiot."

John had his own ideas about people and their phones. "Any jackass that walks out of the bathroom with his head buried in his phone and doesn't see someone else trying to get in should be shot," he finished emphatically, "and then put on display and their phone shoved in their ear for all to see."

"Bitter?" said Anthony with a grin.

"Damn right," said John. "More than once, I've had one of the kids over and they would uh huh me while concentrating more on that damn phone than on what I was saying to them. I used to want to take their damn phones, even though they were grown adults, and tell them they could have them back when they grew the fuck up. It used to irk me so much."

"Really? You hide your anger towards the phones very well."

"I was never mad at the phones," said John. "I was mad at myself, because I thought I—or we, I should say—had raised our kids better than that, is all. So, if I'm mad at anyone or anything, it's definitely me."

"But you're over it now, right?"

"I think in another twenty years or so I might be."

"Do you plan on living another twenty years?" asked Anthony.

"Hell no," said John. "I'm ready to go now. The problem is that they won't let me."

"Your kids?"

"No, the damn doctors. They keep telling me I'm in great shape for a man my age."

"You really want to check out, then?"

"I don't want to die," John said, "but I don't want to just hang out at home doing nothing all alone for years until someone says that John is finally at peace."

"I hear that," Anthony agreed. "I don't want that for myself, either. As long as I can get up, dress myself, feed myself, and wipe my own ass, then it's a good day. Other than that, why hang around?"

"Right," John said with a nod. "I don't necessarily want to go, but I damn sure don't want to stay if it means someone is wiping my ass and drool hanging on for dear life at the end of my chin."

"You seem to be okay at the moment. I would suggest maybe a shave and some clean clothes from this century, though."

"What's wrong with the way I look?" asked John.

"Uh, where do I start?" said Anthony. "When I first saw you, I thought you needed a piece of cardboard and a magic marker."

"Screw you, fella," said John, but they both knew that it was meant in jest. John couldn't care less what people thought of him and his disintegrating T-shirts. They could kiss his you know what, as far as he was concerned. "Are you offering to go out to the store and get me all the things that I need to look like you?" asked John.

"You don't have to look like me," said Anthony. "You just have to look not so homeless."

"What if I was?"

"Then you definitely already look the part."

"Screw you sideways," John said.

Anthony got a good charge out of that one. "I've been told off many times, but never sideways. I will have to use that one."

"You should get out more."

"Nice. Very nice."

"I thought so." John was in his element when he could just be the cantankerous old curmudgeon that he had morphed into. The older he had become, the more negative his disposition had become. Instead of seeing fluffy white clouds in the distance, he saw potential rain clouds. Instead of seeing people for honest good people, he saw them as wanting his money. It was something that at times he wished he could change, but unfortunately, he was unable to transform. He just couldn't help it.

REDEMPTION

Anthony just sat there and just smiled at the old geezer. He was rough and a bit ornery, but he had that "I have seen shit, I have caused shit, and I damn sure won't take no shit" kind of person.

"Is my mascara running or something there, kind sir?" asked John. "What the hell are you looking at?"

"I just like your sense of absurdity and wit, okay? Is that a damn crime where you come from?" Anthony just smiled even harder.

"It's not a crime, but I'm assuming you're staring at my captivating blue eyes, and not some creeper. Below my belly button is off limits, fella." He repositioned himself on the bench. "You aren't a creeper, are you? I mean, I don't have to get a beat cop to come over and thump you, do I?"

Anthony repositioned himself as well, so that he could look at John, and then he stared hard at him. "I am not a creeper, you jackass. I am not a creeper, I'm not eyeing you up like candy, and I'm not even sure why I'm still sitting here, actually. You are a mean old fart."

"You almost had me, until the last part," said John. "I may have been some eye candy a hundred years ago, but now I'm some wrinkly ass milk dud."

"You are a saggy sweet-tart," Anthony agreed.

"A flagellant Fig Newton." John liked his comparison better.

"You are a mean old Milky Way."

John still thought his was more creative. "Your comparisons need some work."

"So does your face," said Anthony.

"Better, but still needs a little more effort." John enjoyed the banter. Usually, he just sat there by himself and watched as life walked by. The passersby had bags in their hands and lives to get to. For him, it was more of a spectator sport, and he was not much of a participant anymore.

Anthony's smile faded quickly, as he could tell that his new friend's mood had gone somber. "What's up?" he asked.

John looked at Anthony and then at the trees and then at the flowers. He scanned the area and saw a lady walking past like she was late for a meeting or like she'd left the stove on and needed to get back home. He saw a young man jog by looking as though he had not a care in the world.

He saw an old lady being pushed around in a wheelchair by some young man in a white outfit. It was then that the thought struck him.

"John, what is the problem?" Anthony was saying. "Are you having trouble with something?" Anthony looked a bit worried and also perplexed and his bench mate's new demeanor.

John watched as the old woman was wheeled by him almost in a slow-motion act. He saw every line on the old crone's face. As she slowly passed the bench and the two men sitting on it, John looked over at Anthony and said, "Nothing wrong that not getting any older won't fix."

"Huh?" asked Anthony.

"That old woman is my next step," said John. "I am on that train bound for some young punk pushing me around so that I can go take a piss. Why can't we just get to a certain point and then slip away one night after watching our favorite television show? Why do we have to live this life?"

"I take it you don't want to end up having a hairy nurse sponge your balls?"

"When I can't wash my own balls, Anthony, it's time to check out."

"Let's not get too dramatic, John. Just have faith that everything will be fine."

"Not dramatic," said John. "I'm just telling it like I see it." He paused and looked up to the cloudy sky. "Faith is for the people who want to escape the fact that corruption and famine and disease are out there and that it's very real. They hide in their little book and tell themselves that it's going to be okay and that it won't happen to them. Truthfully, though, if there was a God, I mean if he really does exist and loves us like we are all told in Sunday school, he would let us just go to sleep one night when it was time and just cross our arms and he'd pick us up from this mud ball."

"Not into God, are we?" said Anthony.

"Anthony, don't be one of those guys, please."

"One of what guys?"

"Don't play dumb, Anthony. One of the guys who has signed up for the final exam."

REDEMPTION

"Final exam? That sounds like you can actually study for something that supposedly doesn't exist." Anthony paused for a second and then went on. "I thought you were one of those cattle-eating, wife-loving, kid-rearing, and God-loving Republicans, I mean Americans?"

"I take it you're one of those salad-eating, folk-singing, shacking-up and God-hating Democrats, I mean Americans?" John smiled and went on. "If you're one of those Americans, what are you doing believing that some old guy is going to be sitting there waiting for you to come by and just swish you off to some heaven where all your family is, and all the dogs you've had all your life are sitting there wagging their tails waiting for you. You're crazy, and you deserve everything you get."

"Why aren't you a believer, John? It's what your party lives on, after all?"

"Anthony, for a learned man, you've got to be kidding me, right?" John was actually pretty surprised, which didn't happen too often. He was sure that this guy would be on the other side of the universe than those fanatical believers.

"I just asked why, John, that's all? It's just a simple question, really."

"None of it makes sense," said John. "Why would you think that your deeds in life did anything? Where is the proof? If you truly—and I mean truly—believed it, would you think people would do half the garbage they do in this world?"

"I think you are mixing up a god with a babysitter," said Anthony.

"Do you think He is a good father if he doesn't teach his kids to be good? We're taught that being bad has consequences, but I don't see any proof of that, either."

"Were you always a good father?" Anthony felt sorry for someone who didn't believe in something even if it was very minor to most, but John seemed to be one hundred percent negative. He assumed that he hadn't started off this way, but over time it became the pit of misery sitting in front of him. It was a shame that he had morphed into this, thought Anthony.

"I don't know what the hell this has to do with what we were talking about," said John, "but if I were to be honest, hell no, I was a terrible father."

"If you think God is a bad father, then maybe you need to reflect on your own parenting in order to understand his."

"He is a God, he doesn't make—or isn't supposed to make—mistakes, right?"

"Why?" asked Anthony.

"Why do you keep saying 'why,' you old fart?"

"Why don't you just answer the question?"

"Why don't you just mind your own fucking business?" John replied sharply.

"I can do that. I can change the channel." It was obvious to Anthony that he had touched on a sensitive subject. He backed off.

"Thank you," said John. "I think it's time for me to go home and get some lunch, and maybe take a nap."

"What's for lunch?" asked Anthony. "Maybe I want some."

"Today is probably beef stew. I think I still have some left that Mrs. Wiggins made me."

Anthony stood up just as John stood up. "How about we accidently bump into each other again sometime?" he asked.

John wasn't exactly sure whether this guy was his cup of tea or not, but it was better than talking to the birds at his feet. "I'm here almost every day at eight," he said. "I have my coffee and my muffin, and by that time, the park is open and teeming with two-legged and four-legged life to watch. Maybe I will see you again sometime." He started walking past the trees and the trash can and turned on the sidewalk that led to the small apartment he rented.

John didn't like dredging up the past, but that guy really did make him think about a few things that he would prefer to have stayed buried. He knew that at some point he was going to have to deal with this fifty-pound sack of guilt that he was carrying around everywhere he went, but for now it was all he could do to eat a bowl of soup and maybe watch a few episodes on the Game Show Network, which he was excited to get back to.

JACK SPARROW

Danny was running around the kitchen trying to get breakfast ready. It was a big occasion today, as Marcus was starting his new job and he needed a good breakfast to fuel that big brain of his. He threw some chopped onion into his omelet and finished it off with a nice piece of cheddar to melt on the top.

Danny pulled the skillet off the flame and placed it on the chopping board next to the sink. He ran over to the stairs leading to the second floor that adjoined the kitchen and stopped at the bannister. He yelled, "Marcus, are you coming down or not? I'm going to eat this stuff if you don't want it."

Marcus stepped out of the bathroom to yell back, "I will be down in a second. I have to brush my teeth and then I will be there, I promise."

"You better. I'm not a maid."

"Maid, concubine, it's your choice."

"I got your concubine right here, Marcus," Danny yelled almost at the top of his lungs.

"Where?" replied Marcus from upstairs.

"Right here."

"Where?" Marcus started laughing and stopped yelling to spit his toothpaste out and rinse his mouth. He wiped his hand on the small towel hanging next to the sink. He paused to make sure that he didn't have any residual toothpaste on his chin.

Danny just ignored him and went back to what he was doing. He placed the omelet on a plate and placed it where Marcus usually sat at their breakfast nook. He had his orange juice and toast next to his plate of eggs when Marcus spun around the threshold.

"It's about time," said Danny.

"I have to look good on my first day. So, how do I look?"

"I guess you won't scare any of the kids." Danny thought Marcus was still a good-looking man, even at his age.

"Wow, that hurt me real deep," said Marcus.

"Hey, that's what you said last night." Danny started laughing at Marcus' obvious fake attempt at looking hurt.

"Maybe twenty years ago, but it definitely wasn't me saying that last night."

"That wasn't you saying that last night? I wonder who that was then?"

"Can you be honest with me, Danny? Did you add 'pool boy' on the grocery list right after a dozen eggs and a pound of roast beef?"

"Um, I guess you caught me." Danny let out a lively laugh.

"I think you've been sniffing too much Pam cooking spray." Marcus paused for a second and then continued, "Uh, Pam, that is."

"When are you going to stop doing foghorn leghorn," said Danny. "It's not relevant anymore. No one knows what you're doing except for you and maybe two other people on the planet, if you're lucky, and shit, I guess I'm one of those two."

"You love my foghorn, or you used to." Marcus swung around the kitchen island and gave Danny a light peck on the cheek so that he could grab a piece of bacon without being discovered.

"I saw that," said Danny, "so go sit down and stop dicking around."

Marcus did as he was asked. He plopped his butt down on the seat and looked at the beautifully prepared breakfast in front of him.

Danny watched as Marcus gobbled down another piece of bacon. "Don't fart around eating like a five-year-old. You don't want to be late on your first day."

"How long do you think it's going to take to get there?" Marcus responded. "It's a fifteen-minute drive at the most, and I don't have to be there for almost an hour. Calm yourself down." Marcus was excited about helping out with the kids at the Charleston Boys Club during the school vacation. He could show them a thing or two about shooting pool and maybe how to play on the shuffleboard table. He'd used to be quite proficient in both.

"You have a tendency to screw around and then run around and expect me to find your keys, and your head," said Danny.

Marcus just let out a heavy sigh. "Okay, okay."

"So, what are you doing after work?" Danny knew, but he wanted to hear this foolhardy plan one more time.

"I'm going to stop by and see Dad after work, just stop in and say hi for a minute."

"Still going with that, huh?"

"What?" asked Marcus. "I am going to see my dad and make sure he is okay. That's all." Marcus knew that Danny was not a huge fan of his father, but he hoped that Danny could understand why he needed to do it. "You have to let this crap go," he said. "He is not the issue."

"He *is* the issue, Marcus. We've been together for more than twenty years, and not one day has he ever looked at me, or you with anything other than disgust and hate."

"I don't think that's completely accurate," said Marcus. "I think he hates me way worse than he hates you."

"Horseshit!"

"Whoa there, Seabiscuit."

"You know damn well I'm right. Why do you do this?" Danny turned and put the dishes in the sink so that he didn't have to be looking at Marcus.

"I'm not doing anything, babe. I just want you to understand a little bit, is all. I don't want any regrets in my life. I don't want to have anything weighing on my shoulders. Why can't you understand that?"

"I understand that just fine," Danny began, "but that man treated you like shit your whole life because you didn't see the world like he did, and he treated you like there was something wrong with you. And now you're forgiving everything, like it never happened."

"First of all, hon, I know exactly what that dick did to me my entire life. Not allowing me to be me, not accepting me, pushing me away from everything I loved. I know exactly who that old fucking bastard is. I know all too well."

"Then why are you—"

Marcus interrupted Danny. "I don't have any kids, I'm not a young man anymore, and he is almost ninety. I don't want a bunch of regrets being recited to me in the mirror every morning, okay? That's all. They say that all this is treasures in heaven."

"Who the fuck are you, Jack Sparrow?" asked Danny.

"Really, Johnny Depp, you know he's my weakness."

"First of all, our kind isn't welcome behind the pearly gates, remember? And second, it's a better reference than your foghorn leghorn—at least the *Pirates of the Caribbean* movies are from this century. Pirates, treasure, it makes more sense than most of your lame jokes that no one under sixty even gets."

"First of all, I will be welcome if God turns out to be a woman like I think, and two, I only have to make you laugh, so bite me." Marcus scarfed down his last bite of eggs and pushed the plate to the other side where Danny was standing with a disapproving look on his face.

"The one thing you said that I agree with is that we aren't young anymore," said Danny. "Shit, you just retired, and I'm going to be retiring soon, for God's sake. We shouldn't have to put up with old bigoted farts who think that just because that was what they were taught a hundred years ago, that it's okay today. All it shows me is that they can't think past their little peters."

"I agree with you," Marcus began, "but the truth is that I don't see him like you do. I know who he is, and I see all his flaws, but I also see a guy who is reaching the last chapter, and he knows it. I see him every time he sees me, he is eaten up with guilt at the choices he made in life, and I see him as an opportunity to make myself feel good by forgiving him. I need to lose my burden just like he does, hon."

"Boo fucking hoo," said Danny. "Okay, you go ahead and unburden, but the shit he put us through when we were dating… He can kiss my old pimply ass."

"Okay then," said Marcus. "I think we're done here."

"I'm sorry, babe, but I hate the fact that he doesn't see you as a son. He sees you as a gay guy who could have been his son if only you had just learned to suck on a tit instead of a shlong."

"I know, hon, I know." Marcus quickly changed the subject, "Oh yeah, Nikki and Johnny are coming up in a few weeks to visit, and I think they just want to stop by and say hi to us. And Johnny wants to stop by and see Dad, either to say hi or spit in his face, I don't know which one. Just in case he won't get to say it again."

"They're both coming all the way from Maryland?" asked Danny.

"Yeah," said Marcus. "Ever since Nikki moved in with Johnny, I think they do almost everything together."

"It is a fifty-five or older community of two people."

"Pretty much."

"Don't bring that gold-digging bitch around me, Marcus," said Danny. "You know I love Johnny, but Nikki can go screw off."

"You have to let all that shit go too," said Marcus. "We are too damn old to be worrying about what other people do and what they let people do to them." Marcus stood up and reached for his keys hanging on the hook. He knew that this conversation never went anywhere, and that Danny would never see his father or Nikki as anything but throwaway items.

"I know, but you know damn well that that bitch is only living at Johnny's because she's too damn selfish and too lazy to live on her own," said Danny. "She's been divorced more times than I have fingers, and Johnny is just the next man to take care of her."

Marcus said sharply, "And what can I do about it? My brother is the oldest, and he has always felt this responsibility to take care of us and pretty much the rest of the world. If he decides to let her stay with him, eat up all his food, and go through his bank account dollar by dollar, then that's his business."

"He can't be that stupid, and you can't be that damn stupid," said Danny. "She only wants to come up here so she can see if your father has any money or any antiques she can hock the second he is in the ground, and you know it." Danny knew he had to calm down, as he always got too emotional over this crap. He was so glad that his last bit of family was all the way across the country. The drama was limited to very rare get-togethers.

"If he is, it's his choice, though, babe. I can't make him see her for what she really is. He has to see it, and even if he does, then what?"

"He could kick her out and make her take care of her damn self, that's what."

"Okay, let's say he does," said Marcus. "How does he benefit while watching someone he loves suffer?"

"Suffer?"

"Yes, Danny, suffer. How much do you think she can make being an uneducated old bitty who has always been taken care of and never took care of anyone besides herself? Her kids barely speak to her, and if her kids won't take her in, then how will she survive? Hell, her kids might be even worse than she ever was. No one is going to want her old ass as a wife."

"That should not be Johnny's burden to bear. That should be *her* burden."

"I know you love Johnny, and I know you love me, but after twenty some years, you'd think you would get past what my sister or my brother or even my father thinks. I don't care if they accept me. I don't care if they like me. I care that you love me and that you accept me." Marcus was trying to inch toward the door, because these conversations were becoming more and more exhausting—and more and more redundant.

Danny walked Marcus to the door, and even though both were in their sixties, they had taken pretty good care of themselves over the years. Marcus looked good for sixty-four, and Danny, being younger than Marcus, was still amazed that he was able to be with someone as loving and as good-looking as Marcus was. His salt and pepper hair and those brown eyes and the five o'clock shadow drove him wild some nights. There were times when he wished they were in their thirties again, back when they still had a little bit of energy after dinner. He definitely considered himself a lucky man. "Please have fun," he said, "and remember that I'm heating up the pot roast for tonight, so don't fill up on junk."

"Yes, sir," said Marcus. "I will be home about five, I guess and we can finish this conversation if you want, but for now I've got to get going. There are kids waiting to receive my sage advice."

"See, that was closer to a joke, very good," said Danny. "And about continuing this mundane conversation, I think I'm done. I just have to remind myself every once in a while that my beliefs and standards can't be everyone else's. I love you for wanting to help the old fart, even though you know he would not ever do the same for you, if the roles were reversed. You are a good man, Marcus Jacobi. You are a very good man."

"Thanks, babe," said Marcus. "Now I'd better get out of here before the kids think the old man lost his way getting there." Marcus left the apartment and walked down the hall. After pushing the security door open to leave the building, he turned right and turned right again at the corner of the sidewalk so that he could jump in his cool Prius parked at the curb and zoom off like it was a race car.

Danny watched from the window as Marcus got in his car, and after making sure that he was seat-belted and comfortable, he could hear the almost inaudible car come to life and start backing up and merging onto the street. He was glad that Marcus had gone back to work. It was obvious that after his retirement that he was getting restless just sitting around watching the grass grow in front of their building. Danny hoped that getting out and helping these kids would get Marcus out of the funk that he'd been in lately.

Danny turned and went back to the kitchen. He wasn't ready to stop being pissed off about his so called in-laws. He loved Marcus, but he couldn't fathom how he had turned out the way he did after undergoing that kind of upbringing. Other than Marcus's mother, there wasn't much to choose from as far as free liberal thinking in that family tree.

To Danny, it was a black and white and right and wrong kind of decision, and gray was just a color of a horse you bet on. Except for Johnny and Peter, maybe, he didn't believe that the family deserved Marcus's loyalty. It burned him up that his husband continued to put himself in these situations. He shouldn't have to help his grown-ass sister, who was in fact more of a succubus than a sister.

As he threw the clean and now dry dishes back into the cabinet, he closed the cabinet slowly and said to himself, "What are you doing, you jackass? Why are you letting this stuff bother you so much? Why can't you stop being such a drama junkie? The choices that Marcus or anyone else make should be theirs and not yours. Just be there for Marcus when that old dick lets him down again. That's what you should be concentrating on." He couldn't really figure out why he let it bother him so much, other than the fact that he hated when Marcus was upset, but that was something that he was going to have to let his husband deal with on his own.

It was obvious that Marcus was trying a new forgiveness path, and Danny all of a sudden felt bad that he kept diverting him from that path, even if he didn't completely agree that John Senior deserved it. He needed to let this stuff go, and he promised himself as of today that he was really going to try.

WHAT'S EATING YOU?

Marcus stood and watched as the kids played foosball and shuffleboard or just sat in the corners bullshitting with each other. He watched as the other adults worked with the kids. It was he and two other much younger adults trying to help these kids from becoming the next eleven o'clock news headline. He felt really proud to be involved. He'd been waiting for something to do, and maybe this was it. Maybe helping these kids three times a week was his next thing, the next thing in his life that he could be proud of.

He sat and watched but did not want to be too pushy with any of the kids too hard or too fast. He was an observer, and he figured one would jump out to him eventually that looked like he needed a friend. He knew in his heart that there was a kid here who would need a shoulder or need an ear, and if all he did was listen, he figured it would be a good day.

Marcus knew, being a gay man, that he would hear a bunch of stereotypical hatred towards gays, so he knew not to egg it on by being too pushy. He knew the news would get out eventually, and he also knew that the universe would show him what, where, and when, and now all he had to do was wait. He didn't want the kids to feel awkward, nor did he want the parents to get in his face. He just wanted to help some kids and go home, nothing more.

His eyes scanned the room. There were at least fifteen or twenty kids, varying from twelve or thirteen all the way up to seventeen or eighteen. They all had smiles on their faces, and they all seemed to be really close with Tom, the director. Marcus presumed that Tom probably knew everything about them, from their favorite color to the majors they were planning to choose in college. Tom just struck Marcus as that kind of guy. He was caring and genuinely kind. Marcus felt very fortunate to be here, and maybe he'd be able to help some of these kids. According to Tom, some of these kids had some nasty stories.

He found the giant room in pretty good shape compared to what he'd been expecting. It didn't have Danny's flare for color patterns, but it was not falling apart. The walls were not all marked up with holes punched in them, cigarette butts littering the floors. The ceiling was lit up and not encrusted with dust. It was a really nice room, Marcus thought. He was glad that he would be able to help keep it that way. It seemed as though Tom ran a pretty tight ship. Marcus figured that the kids who got out of hand were probably put back in line by the other kids and Tom, too, but the kids probably took care of their own.

As he watched the kids having fun, he couldn't help but let his mind wander. It jumped from questions about why certain drapes were chosen, to what color a wall was painted, to thoughts about not having kids of his own and what would it have been like if he'd walked a different path and had kids. He had been thinking about it ever since he accepted this job, really. What kind of father would he have been? That led him to thinking about his own father. He had mixed emotions. He hated his father like no one else. He'd hated him all his life, just about, and he wondered if it was a good thing he never brought a kid into that kind of hate.

His thoughts continued to wander from one thing to another. Would a kid have grown up okay with a parent with that kind of hate in his heart? Would a child have been able to love him differently than his father loved him, or didn't love him? Why did his father hate him just for being different? Why did he not just give him away to someone who wasn't burdened with such an ignorant mind? Why didn't he just love him? I am a damn good person, he thought. Why was my father such a colossal dick?

Marcus snapped out of his daydream when he was approached by one of the kids tugging on his sleeve. "What's going on, Mister?" the boy said cautiously.

"Oh God, I'm sorry. I'm Marcus. What was I doing? Was I drooling or something?"

"No," the boy said. "You had a look, that's all."

"A look? What kind of look?" Marcus wiped the imaginary cobwebs from his head with his palm. "What's your name, son?"

"My name is Scott, Scot Thomas, but everyone calls me Scotty. You had a look like you were, I don't know, it just looked like a look like you get when you want to cuss someone out."

"Really?"

"Really. I get that look sometimes."

"Like when?" asked Marcus.

"When I want to take a baseball bat to someone's head," said Scotty. "In my case, usually my father's head."

"Wow," said Marcus. "You saw that in my eyes from way over there?"

"I see it every morning in the mirror before I go to school, and after a while, you can see it on others. Who do you want to hit with a baseball bat?"

"No, I was just sitting here thinking."

"About whooping someone's ass?"

"No, I was just thinking." Marcus was amazed at how well Scotty had picked up on that, or maybe he was just very obvious in his facial expressions. He wasn't sure which, but either way, he was looking at his first patient of sorts. "Why do you want to smack your father upside the head with a baseball bat?" he asked.

"Because I don't have a tire iron, duh." Scotty smiled.

Marcus liked this kid. He could tell that he was smart. Most quick-thinking, quick-witted people were, which left him out. "Okay, then. No, heavy metal objects for you then, Scotty. But for real, what's going on at home?" Marcus walked over a few steps and sat down on the second step of the old staircase leading upstairs. This would be his area to get away from the noise. He now claimed this area to be his psychiatrist's office. Marcus smiled at the thought of where he would hang his shingle.

Scotty followed and waited for the old man to sit down. Scotty seemed to have come over more because he thought that this guy needed to vent, and not the other way around. "Let's just say my dad is a first-class dick," he said. "Does anything else really need to be said after that?"

"I guess we do have something in common, then. We should start a club or something."

"I knew you wanted to bash someone's head in," said Scotty. "I just knew it. It was your dad's, wasn't it?"

"No, I don't want to bash my father's head in, or anyone else's. I just wish he wasn't such a—"

Scotty whispered bluntly, " A real dick. That's the word you're looking for."

"Yeah, I guess so. My dad is a dick, and so is yours, I guess. Why is your dad a dick? I mean, why does your dad upset you so much?"

"I came over to talk about you. I wasn't the one leaning up against a wall muttering."

"First of all, you are fifteen at best, and please don't think you know what's inside my head. Secondly, even if I disliked my father, I would never want to do anything bad like give him a concussion with a bat. I will tell you my 'I hate Dad' story if you tell me yours." Marcus put "I hate Dad" in air quotes with his hands.

Scotty wasn't one hundred percent sure about this guy. He seemed nice enough, and Mister Tom had told them last week that he was one of the good guys and that they could go to him with any problem. He figured what the hell. "Okay, but your story better be a good one."

"I bet it's better than yours." Marcus gave Scotty a big broad smile.

"Did your father put cigarettes out on you when you talked back? Have you ever gotten knocked out, I mean knocked out?"

"Scotty, have you told someone about this?" Marcus said, concerned.

"For what? So that some guy can come to my rescue and be able to sleep at night knowing that he helped some poor black kid get help by putting me in the state system where it's ten times worse? I don't have a mom, and Pop's all I got. No one wants a fifteen-year-old kid with baggage. No one, no thanks, Mister. Now, how about your story?"

Marcus was silent. This kid reminded him of a dog who had been beat, beat bad, but their personality was just the nicest, most loving temperament no matter what. He didn't know what to say. The only thing he wanted to do was hug the kid and not let go. He fought the urge. "Um, I—" he began.

"Come on, you promised me a good story," said Scotty. "Now, do you have one or not?" Scotty was about to bounce. This guy was getting lamer by the second.

Marcus grabbed Scotty's arm before he could disappear. "Okay. I've got a story for you. It's about a kid who never understood why his father hated him so much, never understood why his father couldn't just simply love him."

"I'm with you so far." Scotty stood up against the wall and then slid down until his knees were almost in his face.

John let go of the boy's arm. He motioned for Scotty to move over a bit closer. He didn't want to have to scream his story for others to hear. Marcus moved up one step to the third step leading to the upstairs portion of the house. He assumed that it was the office area of the organization, but he hadn't been shown that area yet. He didn't hear any noise from upstairs when he peeked his head up the steps. He wanted to know if anyone might overhear this story. "Come here, Scotty, and listen," he said. "I mean really listen to what I am about to tell you." He waited until Scotty was in position at the foot of the steps. How far down this rabbit hole did he want to go?

"Okay," said Scotty eagerly. "What is this great story?" Scotty was like any kid, and he loved hearing a good story, even if it was about a bastard dad.

"My father was a first class, real jerk for as long as I can remember. I don't know whether he was born that way, or if he just morphed into it, but nonetheless, he was a real piece of work. He and I never bonded. Never had anything in common."

"Why?" asked Scotty.

"I just didn't think like he did. I didn't have the same belief system, let's say, so that led us down different paths."

"Was he racist? Did you date a black chick or something?"

"Among other things, but no to the dating thing. He never looked at me like we had anything to say to one another. I remember as a real small kid, he used to play with me and help me with my bike, and he'd help my brothers and sisters with things. But then one day it kind of just stopped. I never really knew why, when I was a kid. I figured he was pissed about something and that it would blow over. But after almost sixty years, he's still the same guy I ran away from."

"You ran away from home?" Scotty had thought about doing that many times, even dreamed about it. He just didn't know how, didn't know where to go, or even what was worse. He'd heard so many stories about kids having to sell themselves just to eat. To him, he had to stay. If he left, his kid brother would have to deal with that bastard. He just couldn't live with himself throwing his little brother to the wolves.

"No, I never ran away from home," said Marcus. "My older brothers and sisters kept me sane until I was old enough to move out, get a job, and continue my education without him."

"Did you?"

"Did I what?"

"Get an education?" asked Scotty.

"Sure did," said Marcus. "I worked my but off, and sometimes worked two or three jobs at a time just to buy books and get through college. It was tough, but I never asked my father for a cent. I did it without him, and because I did, I never thought I needed him for anything." Marcus stopped for a second and then continued, as if he had something important to say on this particular subject. "Pulling up to my father's house, a man who I at one time worshipped, and showing him that I did all this, that I had a great job, a great car, had money in my pocket and didn't need him to get it, is about the most satisfying moment I'll ever have in my life. And don't ever think you can't do it too, Scotty."

"So, what did you end up doing?"

"I became an engineer for N.A.S.A. I worked on some great projects over the years, and I retired not too long ago. That's kind of why I'm here helping you guys. I got bored sitting at home just watching the paint peel."

"Why us?" asked Scotty. "I mean, why didn't you help someone else?"

Marcus reflected for a second. "I met Tom at a function, and we started talking. He made it sound like something I'd be interested in. I mean, I don't have my brother Johnny's 'save the world' thing going on in me, but since I never had kids, I guess this was a way to help."

"That sounds cool, I guess," said Scotty. "I mean, most of us here are heading down one of two roads, and we are mostly hopping on the bumpy one. It's full of pot holes and speed bumps, but life is life, I guess."

"You can change it if you want," said Marcus. "Don't ever doubt that."

Scotty raised a hand that told Marcus to save that thought. "Save it. I'm the wrong color, I'm on the wrong side of the tracks, I don't get all A's in school, and I don't see myself breaking the cycle like you did. My complexion is just too dark, and my brain is just not built for it."

"Nonsense. You will have roadblocks, I won't bullshit you and tell you that you won't. But the idea is to put all that crap aside and find out what you *do* want. What do you want besides to sit here and bitch and whine about how hard life is? How can you change it?"

"I could grow whiter skin," said Scotty with a sneer.

"Stop giving me horseshit, Scotty," said Marcus. "Any farmer will tell you that horseshit is to be dealt with, not stared at. No one is going to tell you that it's not tough, and I'm not going to sit here and say that I know how it is to be black, or how it is to be in your shoes. What I *can* tell you, though, is that everyone falls short of something. Everyone has some kind of pain, some kind of Achilles heel that makes them think that they can't do something. Whether you are black or white, or Mexican, or handicapped, or old, or gay, or even living on the wrong side of town, everyone—and I do mean everyone—has a story to tell. Yours is no different. One person may have trauma one way, and someone else may have it another, but we all have our stories."

"So, what is yours?"

"Mine?" Marcus thought that it might be a little too early to be showing Scotty his homosexuality membership card. "Mine is like everyone else's, or a lot of kids, I guess. I grew up with two brothers and a sister, and a parent who didn't love me, and another parent who did. Most of my life, I felt like screaming, and the times I didn't scream, I cried. I hated myself, I hated everyone around me, and it wasn't until I left home and many years later that I met someone who made me see things in a 'what can be' kind of way instead of a 'what was' kind of way. I am sixty plus years old, Scotty, and I'm still haunted by what was. You're not going to ever be rid of those demons until you face them, and a bat doesn't work against these kinds of demons. That's one reason why I'm going to see my father today, and no matter what he says or does, it's me who controls my path. Do you know what I mean?"

"Not really," Scotty admitted, "but I guess you never hit him in the head with a baseball bat, huh?" Scotty liked this guy's story. He may not have known him a long time, but he could tell the guy was alright.

"My father is almost ninety, and I go see him from time to time. I can tell every time I go and visit him that I feel better about myself and less and less angry. A few years ago, I would have said that you were silly to even think of me doing such a thing."

Marcus enjoyed talking with Scotty. He liked to think that maybe he helped this kid out, maybe just a little, while helping himself out, too.

"I can't say what your life is going to be like in a few decades," Marcus said, "but if you hold onto the hate and anger and resentment, I can guarantee that you will never be free of your father. No matter how far you run, no matter how hard you try, no matter how much money you make, he will always be looking at you and telling you in that mirror you look in every day that he owns you, and that he always will."

"What if he died?" asked Scotty.

Marcus definitely didn't like the sound of that comment. It was almost as if Scotty had a plan that he was mulling over. "It would be ten times worse," he said. "You would never be able to look him in the eye and tell him to his face that he does not own you. He cannot break you, and you don't feel broken, no matter what he says, no matter what he does to you."

Scotty wasn't sure what this guy's deal was, but the one thing he knew for sure was that his father had fucked him up good. He knew it as well as he knew his own name. "I guess," he said.

Marcus leaned back against the banister and looked at the other people through the railing. "Okay, so you heard my story, now how about yours?" he said.

Scotty stood up against the wall in front of Marcus. He had to think for a minute. What was his story, other than that he wanted to take his kid brother Andre away from there and away from everything else that was fucked up in their lives? There wasn't much to it other than that, really, he thought. "Okay, I got it," he said. "I will give you a rundown of a typical twenty-four-hour period at my house."

"Okay, sounds good," said Marcus, but he knew he wasn't going to like what he had to hear.

"When I get out of school, I take my little brother Andre over there so we can play a few games of pool and shit. I mean stuff." Scotty produced a smile.

"Is he here?" asked Marcus.

"Yeah, that's him over there with the pool stick and the black shirt with the swirly symbol on the front. He's twelve."

Marcus looked at the boy who Scotty had pointed out. He looked to be scrawny, maybe ten or eleven. He definitely was not a well-fed boy by any means. In fact, neither of them were, he realized after looking at Scotty again. Neither had new clothes on, nor full bellies, but both seemed to be wearing smiles. To Marcus, it was like finding one of those rare gems that you find on the beach or something while you were looking for something totally different. He equated the two of them with that kind of story.

"After we leave here, we go home," Scotty continued, "and I help my father up so he can go to work, and clean up the beer cans and stuff." He wanted to say shit, but this time he caught himself. "I wake him up, remind him that he has to get to work, and help him get into the bathroom to get the stench of beer off of himself. He usually pushes me away, but I know he couldn't do it without me. It's the only thing that keeps me from cracking his skull."

"Knowing that he knows he needs you?"

"Yep." Scotty punched his other palm. "He knows he would have been fired a long time ago if it wasn't for me getting his ass neat and tidy. It's like he knows, too, so it's a tradeoff. I help him and he leaves us the fuck alone. I mean, he leaves me alone, and Andre."

"So, you plan on doing this until you grow up and move out?"

"It's not as bad as me and Andre getting split up. It's not as bad as having to fight for scraps every day with a hundred other kids."

"How do you eat?" Marcus was amazed that the boys were still alive. It didn't sound like their father cared about them at all.

"Before I wake his drunk ass up, I usually take a few dollars out of his pocket," Scotty said. "Then I go get groceries from the convenience store run by the nice Korean lady near our house. I wait until the fucker leaves, and then me and Andre go shopping for dinner, and breakfast too if I can get enough money out of the dick. Then I wake up, and get Andre and me out of the house before he wakes up and starts his beer drinking all over again. I guess that would be where you would say 'the end.'" Scotty air-quoted "the end."

"Well, wow." Marcus had to take a second to let everything he'd heard soak in. The story had been delivered in speed talk, but after absorbing it all, he knew one thing was true. "Okay," he admitted, "your story is worse."

"I told you," said Scotty. "Not that your story isn't messed up, and I'm sure you left a lot out of yours, as did I. But I don't need your sympathy, Mister Marcus. It just felt good to vent a little bit, so thanks."

"Anytime, Scotty, anytime. I pray that you and Andre get out of this with the smiles I see you wearing today."

"Please, for the love of you know who, leave God out of this," said Scotty.

"I'm not religious, but why? Did he abandon you?"

"He took my mother away from me, so he can go screw himself, is the way I feel," said Scotty. "He let her fall down the steps and not my father, that's why. God doesn't give a shit about you or me or anyone else, and if he did exist, I would tell him to go screw off, because that is exactly what he told me to do."

Marcus recognized Scotty's rage. He knew that it was in there hiding behind those smiles. He knew it like he knew his own fake smiles. He figured Scotty's rage was more real, but he knew in his heart that both he and Andre were good kids, and were trying to stay that way. "Well, I won't tell you that God did me any favors, either," he began, "but hating someone even if they are fictional is no better than hating a flesh and blood person."

REDEMPTION

He knew all too well about the bullshit he'd heard about God's plan. God's plan sucked ass, as far as Marcus was concerned. "Scotty?" he asked.

"Yeah?"

"I can't tell you that everything is going to be great," he said. "And I can't tell you that your life won't suck at times. But what I can tell you is that you can count on me, and Tom, and the other volunteers here. We are here if you want to vent, run away, or just get a meal in your tummy and not rely on peanut butter and jelly to make the meal, okay?"

"I hear you, Mister Marcus," said Scotty. "I hear you." Just another grown-up who thinks that grabbing hold of our feelings instead of your balls is the answer, he thought. Scotty knew that grabbing your balls and manning up was the only way to get out of these situations. "Do you want to meet my brother and shoot a game of pool or something?" he said. "I have time for one quick one."

It was almost time to get home, and Scotty was also tired of this conversation. It was nice of Mister Marcus, but reality soon set back in, and he knew that to stray away from reality too far, or for too long, came with consequences.

YOU AGAIN?

John sat and did his crossword puzzle, occasionally looking up at evidence of life running past him, walking past him, and being wheeled past him. No matter how it was traveling, he knew that his life was passing him by. He saw his past jog by, as well as his future being wheeled by. Some days, it looked like everything was going at jet speed.

John looked up when he heard the clearing of a throat. As he looked up, he saw his new acquaintance, Anthony. "You again?" he said.

Anthony replied, "Would you like me to find another bench to sit on?"

"Did you just meet me or something?" said John. "You have to learn to take a joke."

"Well, actually, I did just meet you, and a joke is something that's actually funny. Was your joke funny?" Anthony pulled his thermos out from inside his bag.

"It was, to me," John began, "and if you had a sense of humor, you would have laughed. I'm not sure I can talk with anyone who doesn't find my hilarious jokes funny."

"Well, I'm waiting."

John produced a big smile for Anthony. "Okay, so now that we have established I am funny."

Anthony said, "We have?"

"I thought we had."

"Okay, well, I think the jury is still out on that, but please continue." Anthony poured his tea into a tin cup and then acted as though he was all ears to hear what important comeback John would have.

"As I was saying," John began, "now that we've established that I'm funny and that you're a stalking fan, what have you been doing the past few days since I saw you last?"

"Oh my," said Anthony. "I've been doing all kinds of things."

"Like what?"

"Like, um—" Anthony thought for a few seconds. "I wrote a few letters to the kids, so I'm hoping that they'll now shoot me a line back. I watched a bit of politics on television."

"Full blown liberal, I assume?"

"Not crazy liberal, but yes, I guess I do lean towards helping people as opposed to walking past someone in need. I think that I have many of the things I have now because of my life choices. I've helped a lot of people, so I receive a lot of help in return when I need it. It's not the solitary accomplishments that I remember more than anything. It's the ones that I did *with* someone. A friend, or my wife, or one of my kid's faces is what I remember when I look back on the golden memories."

John knew exactly what Anthony meant by that. Certain memories with Betty were the last memories he lingered on before drifting off to sleep. The nights when they would sit out on the porch and not really do anything, but she let him hug her and squeeze her and sit with her to watch the stars while the kids were sleeping. It was one of his best memories in his life. "They seem so distant, though," he said. "It gets harder and harder to remember the details."

"Positivity isn't your strong suit, is it?" said Anthony.

"When you don't have a wife, and your kids don't want to have much to do with you, the positivity is lacking, I guess," John confirmed.

"Well, your wife and son are dead, and they aren't coming back, but your other kids are still here. Why not create new memories with them?"

"What, memories of them helping me see the beauty all around me?"

"Positivity, John."

"It's too late for all that. You can forgive, but you can't forget."

"No one is asking you, or even them, to forget anything. What you are asking for is a dinner, a walk, a visit, and for God's sake, stop building a wall before they get a chance to build one."

"I appreciate your advice, Anthony, but I think I know my kids better than you do. I think I know what they are willing to do for me, and what they aren't."

"Can I tell you a story?"

Anthony took a sip of tea while John said, "Can I stop you?"

"You can," said Anthony, "by getting up and moving to a new bench, or you can sit your butt there and listen." Anthony figured that John wasn't the only funny person there at the park.

"One of my kids, Tina, was a daddy's girl," he began, "but one day, when she was about seventeen, I guess, we got into this big fight because I would not help her with getting a car. It wasn't that I didn't want her to have one. I just didn't want to help her. I wanted her to work, pay for it, and have pride in getting it herself. Well, she didn't see it that way."

"Kids always want it handed to them," said John.

"Are you done?" said Anthony. "Because I wasn't close to being done with my story."

"Sorry, go ahead."

"Well, she puffed her chest out and stuck out her upper lip and acted like a shit for a long time. Five years had gone by, and neither of us really budged. I knew I was right, but so did she."

"But you were the dad." John knew the feeling all too well.

"Damn right," said Anthony. "There comes a bit of respect with that title." Anthony took a deep breath and swallowed all the pain. "I knew that if I caved in, she would be able to bitch and whine her way into getting anything she wanted, so I let her walk past for a bit. But on her eighteenth birthday, I got her not a car, but a lesson that life sucks sometimes but is also sometimes necessary. I got her a boot in the ass."

"Whoa," said John.

"Whoa is right," said Anthony. "I told her that she was more than welcome to stay, but she needed to get a job or go to school. She wasn't an honors student, nor did she like the thought of getting a job at the car hop or anywhere else. It wasn't like it is now. Kids didn't have a hundred different choices of fast food restaurants to choose from to make money flipping burgers. It was slim pickings, and the more she whined about not being able to find work, the more I was on her ass about it."

Anthony took another deep sigh and smiled at a fleeting memory. "I wasn't going to put up with one of my kids eating my food and watching my television and then walking past me like I wasn't even there. No sir. So, to make a long story a bit shorter, she moved out with one of her friends, and it was another four years or so before we ever really got anywhere."

"So, what happened?"

"Well, I guess a few things happened," continued Anthony. "I felt that my kids were good kids, so what did I do to turn Tina into someone who didn't like me? I sat down and asked her just to talk. No arguing, no back and forth mud-slinging, just talking. We kind of put the past behind us without trying to decide once and for all who was right and who was wrong. I wanted to know what was going on in her life, and I wanted to know what she had done since we'd last spoken. I had heard bits and pieces, but it was like seeing previews for a movie, and I wanted to hear the whole thing. I wanted to hear it from her lips, and not my son's or my wife's. I wanted to know if she was okay, and I wanted to know whether her life had turned out the way she wanted it to be."

"So, you just buried the past and started over," said John. "Doubtful." John knew that that wasn't how things worked in the real world.

"It was never talked about, it was never brought up," said Anthony. "I think we both learned that you can sometimes agree to disagree, and the only option is to move on. You aren't given another option. We just started out as new friends, so to speak. She was almost twenty-two, and I was pushing fifty. I just didn't want to argue anymore. I left it up to her, and one day, she called me and asked me if I'd like to have dinner. Of course, I said yes, and we had a really nice dinner and talked like old friends who hadn't seen each other in a while. It wasn't about who was right and who was wrong, it was about starting over, and we both understood that without having to say it out loud."

"How did it turn out for you two?" asked John. "Happily ever after?"

Anthony turned his head and coughed up his emotions, then spat it out. "Yeah, I think it was," he said. "All the way up to when she passed, she had become a daddy's girl again. Just like she'd been when she was little."

"Oh, I'm so sorry," said John.

"It happened a long time ago," said Anthony. "She was hit by a car when she was thirty-six, and she didn't make it. She and I had some great adventures together before the Lord took her home, though."

John was very sympathetic, but at the same time was a bit surprised at the turn the story had taken. Anthony could see the look on John's face, and he knew exactly what a disapproving look was when he saw one. "What?" he asked.

"I just don't see you as a Bible thumper," said John. "I see you teaching a class on evolution, not the Old Testament."

"I don't walk around in my majestic robe preaching the word, but I do believe that there is something in the world besides emptiness."

"Why does it have to be empty just because there is no God?" asked John.

"It doesn't have to be," Anthony began, "but I find solace in talking with him when I feel down. I find solace in just knowing that there is someone out there who has my back."

John smiled as he said, "You really believe that crap, don't you? I thought at first you were putting me on, but I can see you really do believe in Him."

"I do. I really do." Anthony smiled a comforting grin. "I think knowing He is there gives me purpose and the knowledge that when he is done with me here, I have something to look forward to afterwards. It's not something I can explain, I just feel it."

"Well, I guess you're a very lucky man," said John. "Not many people get to feel the level of contentment that you're describing to me right now."

"Sounds like a man who doesn't have it." Anthony poured himself another cup of green tea, allowing John a moment to respond if he wished. He would push it no further if he didn't wish to.

REDEMPTION

"I guess you could say that," John said finally. "Contentment has never been a close friend of mine. Now, anger, remorse, and self-pity, those are close friends of mine. You could say we are BFFs, as the kids say."

"You choose your friends, John. The friends you hang out with are of your own making."

"You're right, I won't say you're wrong," said John. He couldn't hang that on anyone but himself. He'd chosen to hang out with these said friends.

"Why do you hang out with them, if you would prefer not to?" asked Anthony. "I mean, why not hang out with contentment and serenity and happiness instead?"

John chuckled a bit. *Is this guy for real*, he thought? "Just like that, huh? Throw away my oldest friends and just go down to the store and get some new friends?" he asked.

"Why not?"

"Well, because it doesn't work like that, my friend. It just doesn't."

"Why not?" Anthony asked again.

"Are you going to say 'why not' to everything I say?"

"Well, are you going to just keep saying the same thing over and over?"

John rubbed his knee with one hand while stretching his back and trying to get the old-man kinks out. "Okay, Mister Contentment. Well, what would you say I should do?"

"It's easy," said Anthony. "Stop being a stubborn turd, and talk with your kids about what you did, what they did, and then forgive each other and move on."

"Is everything that simple in your world, or just the life-changing things?" asked John.

"Everything is as simple or as difficult as you want them to be." But Anthony could tell that he was losing his audience. John was not accepting this newfound philosophy, not even a little bit. "Do you want to forgive and be forgiven?" he pressed on.

"It's been over a decade since Betty passed, and many more years than that since the kids had much to do with me. You don't just fix that like you do a broken light switch, Anthony. Even in your delusional world, you have to understand *that*."

"I do, John, I really do. It took me a long time to find peace with my kids. A long time, John, a really long time. But I called them and I said that I was sorry. I didn't say anything else. I just apologized."

"For what?" asked John. "You were the dad."

"If you feel that way, then why do you want forgiveness?"

"Well, who said I did anything wrong? I raised them, I fed them, I clothed them, and I kept a roof over their heads. I did everything that a good parent is supposed to do for their kids."

"You did the basics, my friend, but did you do the hard stuff?" Anthony sipped at his tea, then asked almost as an afterthought, "Would you like a cup of green tea?"

"No, thank you," said John.

"Have you ever tried it?"

"Yes, and it tastes like you strained that tea through a litter box."

Anthony laughed. "Are you serious? This is some very good tea."

"If you like cat poop, it is."

"Those sound just like the words of an old American who won't try anything new. You old farts won't try anything other than what you knew as a kid. Sad, really."

"First of all, you're an old fart too," said John. "You're just an old fart who likes to drink cat pee. I'm okay with that. As your friend, I'm okay with any of your decisions that don't affect me. Even if I think they are ludicrous, if not downright comical."

"Well, old fart, this cat pee has kept me young, and I'd rather drink cat pee if it also makes me feel like I do," said Anthony. "Wouldn't you get a cupful of good ol' alley cat pee to stop feeling the aches and pains in your back?"

John stretched his back again and tried to get the kinks out a second time. "I guess I would, there. I would drink horse pee if it made my old man aches and pains feel better."

"Now we're getting somewhere," said Anthony with a smile. "I think I can find a cop on a horse around here somewhere."

"Well, you taste it first and tell me if it has any healing properties." John smiled at his friend and smacked his knee. "Now, that is what we call a knee-slapper."

Anthony lost his smile and took a sip of his supposed cat pee. "Let's stop deflecting," he said. "Answer my question."

"Would I drink horse pee?"

"Stop, and answer my question," Anthony insisted. "What's stopping you from getting things right with your kids? Do you think you don't deserve to have them in your life? Do you think you don't deserve to be happy?"

"Well, I guess you figured me out." John took a deep breath and paused for a second. He didn't want to answer until he had the right words. "Well, I guess I don't, really. I was a dad, but never a friend. I was the stereotypical dad who came home and ate, farted a few times and went to bed, and then did the same thing the next day, over and over."

Anthony nodded. "First, I want to say that if my preaching is at all annoying, and you don't want to talk about any of this, you can just tell me you don't want to talk about it, and I will respect that," he began. "But because I went through the same thing some time ago, I know you need to deal with it, and you will regret it if you don't. And I think the kids will, too. That's all I'm saying." Anthony paused there, because he knew he could get on a sermon if he got too revved up.

John wanted to say, "Shut the fuck up," but he didn't. He wanted to say, "Go help someone else, you busy body," but he didn't. He just sat there staring off into space, and he watched as everyday life walked past him. He saw the jogger who always ran past him usually around this time. He saw the kid with the limp being walked somewhere by his mother. He saw the birds on the ground just waiting for that crumb off of someone's sandwich to drop. He just watched, but nothing insightful was really coming to him.

"John?" said Anthony. He could see that the guy was light years away from this bench. He was nowhere near this place.

"Yeah, I hear you," John said finally.

"Are you okay?"

"I'm almost ninety, I live by myself, and my kids have nothing to do with me," said John with a sigh. "If you were a detective, what would you come up with as to whether or not I was okay?" John knew his words sounded snarky, but he didn't care anymore.

"It sounds like everything you just mentioned is just a bunch of stuff that you could deal with just fine if you put in a bit of effort," said Anthony. "Getting out and exercising, calling your kids, and talking with them and your grandkids as a friend instead of a dad or a granddad—all of this could turn your whole life around."

"That easy, huh?"

"Yeah, it really is." Anthony sighed. This guy is never going to get it, is he? "Stop acting like it's too late or trying to place blame. It's something that happened, meaning that you can do something about it if you did anything besides come to this bench and throwing yourself a pity party every day."

"Your world must have a lot of rainbows in it," John said gloomily.

Anthony chuckled. "Some days, it does," he agreed. "Not every day, though, but I try to see more rainbows than thunderstorms. But there can't be rainbows without the rain."

"So, how did you get your kids to come around?"

"Oh, what a story. It was a lot of cursing, a lot of tears, and a lot of forgiveness, I guess." Anthony pulled the painful memories out from the recesses of his brain. "It was bad. It was really bad. I didn't have a whole lot to do with my kids, because I was always thinking of my own pleasure. I wanted to just go skiing, or see the new this or that. I was too focused on myself."

"Why didn't you take them with you?" asked John.

"Because I didn't want to babysit them. I didn't want to be held back from doing the things I wanted to do."

"Sounds like you didn't want kids."

"I really didn't," Anthony admitted. "I was scared that I was going to resent my own children for keeping me from doing the things that I want-ed to do. I wanted to be a free spirit who could pick up and go whenever I wanted. Even though I loved my wife more than anything, and would have done anything for her, being a parent was her thing and not mine. I did it for her, and I think my kids were aware of it, and that hurt us for a long, long time."

"Wow, you were a shittier father than I was," said John, but he smiled to let his new friend know that he was only kidding. "I mean, I knew I was bad, but you were right up there with baking your kids in a pie."

"Yeah, I guess I had a bit of that coming," said Anthony. "But I'm glad to say now that we see each other as often as we can, and that we really enjoy each other's company. My daughter, before she died, I guess said it best when she said, 'I can either stay pissed off at *that* Dad, or get to know *this* Dad.'" Anthony sighed deeply and let it out with obvious pain. "It took a lot longer for me to forgive myself than it did for my kids to. I was a selfish prick, I was an absentee father, I was not the best of people. All of those things are true, but I tried to change my attitude when I turned my life around. I stopped focusing only on me, which was not easy, not even a little bit. It was fucking hard as shit, if you want to know the truth, but I had to. I knew that I had to, and eventually I did."

"I don't think I have that much time left to fix all the crap that needs fixing," said John. "I just don't see it happening, Anthony."

"Let's start at the beginning. Why do you think that you can't fix things?"

"Well, because we're not friends, my kids and I. We're little more than acquaintances these days. I know why I hear from Marcus from time to time. He's paying homage to his dead mother, and for no other reason."

"Did he say that?" asked Anthony.

"No, but I know it's true."

"No, you *think* it's true."

But John knew that he was right, and no old fart on a bench was going to tell him otherwise. "Let's just say I know, and let's please leave it at that."

"So, what would you like to happen before you take that dirt nap?" asked Anthony.

"I would like to look across the room and see that Marcus has forgiven me for how I treated him, and that he's doing it for me and for him, and not out of some obligation that he thinks he has to honor his mother."

"Okay then," said Anthony, "now we're getting somewhere. How?"

"If I knew that, Anthony, I'd have my own show after Oprah."

But Anthony just shook his head firmly. "Come up with something besides excuses. What can you do to start the process?"

"I don't know, you old fart," said John. "If I knew how, I'd do it."

"Stop being a pussy, John," said Anthony. "What can you do to start?"

"If you say that again, Anthony, I will hit you in the head with your own thermos."

"I think you know, John. I think you know, and I think you have a yellow streak running up and down that spine of yours, and maybe that's why it hurts and actually has nothing to do with your age. Where do you start?"

"I guess I know what I have to do," said John. "I have to apologize. I have to say that I'm sorry for not loving my son because of who he chose to love. I have to say I'm sorry for not being there for him when he needed me. I have to say I'm sorry for making him feel like a piece of shit when I should have been making him feel like anything but. I need to say I'm sorry for a thousand other things, too, but that would be a good place to start."

"Okay," said Anthony. "That wasn't as hard as you made it sound. You know what to do, but you just have to fucking do it, now don't you?"

"Yep, I guess I do," John admitted, "and I guess today would be the best day to start. Marcus is supposed to stop by for his bi-weekly check in."

"Sounds like a plan." Anthony had the biggest smile on his face.

"Bump into each other tomorrow, maybe?"

"I think I could be talked into that," said Anthony, still smiling. "I need to know how this little soap opera turns out."

John stood up from the bench with a bit more pep in his step than he'd had in previous days. He was nervous, but also excited.

DO YOU WANT TO GO?

Nikki had always been dependent on a man, but she never thought that it would come to this. Living with her brother allowed her some perks, but not the ones she had become used to, nor the ones she wanted. She didn't care about having all the eggs she could eat or watching as much television as she wanted. The perks she was looking for were the ones that came with jewelry, pretty little sports cars, or her favorite—shopping in foreign shops and boutiques.

She looked at her reflection in the mirror and wanted to punch the glass so hard. She hated finding herself in this piss hole of a town in this piss hole of a shoe house. She loved Johnny, but he was no jetsetter. He was more of the home-body no-body. She spat out the toothpaste, wiped her mouth with the back of her hand, and took one last look. Then she put on her happy face, the "I am so happy to be here" face that she'd learned to master. But now it took more and more effort each morning to put on that face.

She came out of the bathroom with the biggest smile on her face and met her big brother in the kitchen where the eggs, bacon, and toast were waiting for her in her usual spot. She pulled out her chair and winced a bit as the wooden legs scraped across the linoleum. The word "linoleum" had never been in her vocabulary until moving in with Johnny, and she wanted nothing else than to leave that word and this life in a trash can somewhere. "Thanks for the eggs," she said as cheerfully as she could.

Johnny wasn't used to living with anyone, but as far as roommates went, Nikki was okay—not great, but okay. She didn't watch his television very often, and she didn't complain about how the vacuum didn't run constantly. She didn't complain that the laundry wasn't done every Tuesday night after work. She didn't complain about anything, really, none of the things that had wound him up divorced after thirteen years of marriage. She either stayed in her room, or else she was out trying to find her next husband. The problem she kept running into in Johnny's mind was that she was a wrinkled up old prune. She smoked, she drank, and she wasn't what you would call a long-distance runner, or any kind of exercise junkie. She was more of the old, dyed dirty blond hair with streaks of grey, skin like a Komodo dragon, pudgy kind of date. When she could find one, of course.

"Glad you're up," said Johnny, "because I wanted to talk with you about going to see Marcus this weekend."

"What about it?" she asked.

"I just wanted to make sure that you still wanted to go." He almost wished she would say no. He knew in his heart that she wasn't going out of any love for Marcus, or for Dad. He knew that she was on a treasure hunt.

"Yeah, I want to go," said Nikki. "It's been like way too long since I've seen Marcus. What's he up to? I can't wait to talk with him."

Johnny knew bullshit when he heard it. It was as thick as molasses, and almost as appetizing. Nikki could've visited Marcus at any time, and she could've picked up the phone at any time, but until recently, trying to make everyone jealous of her lifestyle was a full-time job. "Yeah, I can't wait to see the little fart myself," he said finally.

"You mean *old* little fart, right?"

"You're older than him," said Johnny. "You do remember that, right?"

"Don't remind me," said Nikki with a heavy sigh. "My arthritis is in high gear today."

"Did you go to the doctor like I told you to? No, of course not," Johnny said, answering his own question. "And why not?" He was getting tired of the "poor me" routine that she'd been working on ever since the day she moved in with him.

"And pay with what, Johnny, my looks?"

"Don't get pissy with me just because you've wrecked the body that you were once so proud of."

"Oh, but at one time it was a beautiful body to look at, wasn't it?" Nikki asked.

"Stop living in the past and start living in today, and take care of yourself," Johnny said.

Johnny was getting tired of her excessive whining. He wanted to knock her upside the head some days, but then on other days he really pitied her and what her life had become. She had no one, even though she did have kids of her own. She had been screwed over by so many guys, and then screwed over twice more. He knew her insecurities were mounting by the day. He felt bad that it was so obvious to him how her life was going to turn out.

He knew that his own life was no bed of roses. His kids barely spoke to him, too, after all, but the difference was that he had a house, and he had a place to park his butt and drown his sorrows on those cold and rainy nights when nothing was going right in the world.

Nikki wanted Johnny to go screw off. He had a lot of room to talk about living in the past. He actually did a splendid job living in the past. Pining over his failed marriage and how his kids were closer to Tina, his ex-wife, than they were with him, all because all of the poison they heard from her over the decades. "I hear you, big brother, I hear you," she said, even though she'd rather have told him to get over himself and leave her alone. She just wanted him to stop. He was such a nag. It was no wonder Tina had had enough. I would have left your nagging, whining ass too, she had thought on more than one occasion.

"I figure we'll go up for the weekend and maybe hang out with Marcus," said Johnny, "and then I was going to swing by Dad's and just say hi." Johnny knew that the subject of their father was a sensitive subject around Nikki. She treated Dad like shit, but Johnny also knew that his dad was no father of the year, either. Johnny knew that this subject could set her off, or she could blow it off as if it hadn't even been brought up. You never knew with Nikki, and Johnny could never get used to her drama.

"That sounds fine," said Nikki. "I want to go, too. I'm tired of the fighting with you and with Dad. I'm tired of hating him, too. Whatever he thinks of me, I don't care. I just want to say hi, and be done with it." She finished up her last bite of breakfast and handed the dish to her brother.

As Johnny set the dish in the sink, he knew that the innocent look on her face was all for show, as was most of her life. Just because he chose to help her, and just because he chose not to pick fights with Nikki, didn't mean that he didn't know all too well who she really was at the core. He knew that she was the most narcissistic, ego-maniacal person that he had ever met. She was always looking for that angle that would somehow enrich her pocketbook. Whether it was a guy, a brother, or a father, John was all too aware of his little sister's bad personality traits. He knew she wasn't as tired of the fighting as she had claimed. She loved the drama. What she was tired of was not feeling like their father's checkbook was going to partly be hers in the future. She knew an old man like their father had squirreled away many a social security check, and she knew that he did nothing and went nowhere except that park where fed the birds. They all knew that the old man probably had a few dollars in the bank. The problem was that no one cared or even wanted it except Nikki, and everyone knew it—even Nikki herself.

Johnny washed his own dish and placed it on top of Nikki's in the sink. "Be ready Saturday morning, because it's going to be a few hours' drive, and I'd like to leave at six."

"Six!? Are you insane?" she almost screamed. "You know I'm not a morning person Johnny."

"Well, I guess you'll have to ask yourself how badly you want to go. If you want to see Marcus, your ass will be over in that seat with a packed bag ready to go. Otherwise, please water my plants while I am gone." It felt good to Johnny to discipline Nikki a bit. He thought he may have to stop feeling sorry for her about her poor circumstances and start putting her in her place a bit more often. It would probably be good for the both of them.

"Fine," Nikki said grudgingly. "I will be there ready to go with a packed bag and a smile on my face. Are you happy?"

"Great, but the smile isn't a necessity." Johnny flashed a devilish grin.

"Fine," said Nikki. "A packed bag and a scowl." She got up from the table and started walking back to her room. She had to get ready and make herself presentable. She had to go fishing today—for men, that is. She left Johnny in the kitchen washing the dishes. She was exhausted just thinking about getting up that early on Saturday morning. The only good thing was that she could sleep while Johnny drove. That made her feel a bit better.

Johnny watched as the spoiled little geriatric left the room. He sometimes wished that he'd never opened the door that day and gotten sucked in by those big crocodile tears pooling up around those crow's feet around her bloodshot eyes. He got a slight smile across his weather-beaten face at the thought of slamming the door on her. Johnny knew who his sister was, and he had never doubted for a single second that he was being used. The only reason he let her plop her things there was pity. She had been thrown out, and everyone knew why. She was cast aside for a younger model, and with her attitude, it was no shock to anyone but her. Everyone also knew that most if not all of her problems were of her own making. Yes, he had to admit that putting up with her was a bit much to deal with at times, but the reality was that no one wanted to help an aging drama queen, and he knew it. She wasn't going to be able to go out and land a sixth or seventh husband as easily as she'd done in the past. Now that she was a pile of wrinkles with a bad attitude, she was just one sad and sorry mess. Johnny knew that she would've been dead in six months if not for him opening his door to her. He wasn't a stupid man, even though many of his friends and even his family would label him as such for putting up with Nikki's theater production all of the time.

He placed the last dish in the cabinet and he too walked out of the kitchen and back to his own room. He had a bag to pack, and he had to think seriously about how he felt about seeing his dad. He hadn't seen him in quite a few years, and now was probably one of the last times—if not the last time—that he would see him alive. His own health wasn't all that great, and a trip so far south wasn't going to be in his driving capabilities too much longer, either.

He had to think about whether there was anything that needed to be said. Was there anything he needed to get off his chest that hadn't already been said? He wasn't sure, but he knew it deserved some thought. Living with Nikki these past few months had made him realize things about how life wasn't always about who was right and who was wrong, and that it was about time for him to deal with some of the choices he had made.

THE AIR IS SO WARM

John Jacobi was sitting in his favorite spot on his favorite bench, wearing his favorite worn-out sweat pants, and watching as the passersby either glanced over and nodded in his direction, or simply did nothing, as if he wasn't even there. He saw plenty of both reactions every morning. He saw the kids who were too shy to acknowledge him, and the kids who wanted to take some seed and feed the birds too along with him. He watched as the old and the young sped past, as the bikers biked and the joggers jogged. He watched the leaves fall from the trees and blow across the cobblestones. He was thinking that today was going to be a really good day. His smile was uncontrollable. And it wasn't long before he saw his friend coming toward the bench from down the way. He couldn't wait to tell Anthony his good news.

As Anthony approached and plopped down on the bench on the opposite side of John, he couldn't help but see that his friend was wearing a rare smile. It was one of those shit-eating grins that you only get when you're bursting with news that you just have to tell someone. "Wow, you're in a good mood today," he said.

"Yeah, I have to admit, I kind of am," said John.

"So, spill it!" Anthony took out his thermos as usual. He didn't break routine just because he could tell that John was feeling all gooey inside. He poured his tea into his tin cup, dropped in a sugar cube, and then sat back to enjoy John's rendition of what had recently happened.

John was a bit nervous now that the spotlight was on him. He wasn't sure whether or not saying anything would jinx it, but he just couldn't help it. He hadn't had this kind of smile on his face in so long that he couldn't even begin to try and remember when. He knew it must have been way before his wife died. And he hadn't known this guy for long, but he knew that if it wasn't Anthony he told his story to, it would have to be one of the birds that he'd been feeding. "I spoke with Marcus yesterday," said John finally. "He and I had a really good talk."

"That's great," said Anthony. "I'm glad to hear it."

"I really listened this time," John continued. "I didn't justify or explain. I just listened, and I think for the first time in God knows how long, I think he looked at me as another human being."

"Awesome," Anthony said. "That is really, really great."

"We talked about everything. His partner Danny, his new job with the kids, his retirement. We just talked. I think we had our first real father and son chat."

"Is that why you're wearing that grin on your face?" asked Anthony.

"The grin is because Marcus invited me to dinner tomorrow night with everyone," John confirmed.

"Everyone?"

"Yeah," said John. "The best news is that Johnny and Nikki are coming down to visit tomorrow, and I haven't seen John in years. Twice as long for Nikki. The last I heard from her was like twenty years ago. She was married to some guy who owned like a hundred car washes or something, and she was living the good life. From what Marcus told me, though, she has moved in with my son, John, because she's hit some hard times. I know my little girl, and I don't believe for a second that she's happy living without her pool boy and her tanning bed."

"Sounds like you think she's a spoiled brat," said Anthony.

"Well, I know Nikki," said John. "She was never one who hustled to make money, she just shook her ass and had the boys do her work for her. Don't get me wrong, she is my daughter and my little girl, but she is no Mother Teresa." John believed in telling it like it was, even if that meant speaking the truth about how he felt about one of his own kids, and his failings in terms of raising her right.

Anthony sipped his tea, which was still hot. He knew that if it didn't burn the roof of your mouth, it was just iced tea. "Sounds like she and you aren't close?" he asked.

"God, she must be sixty-something by now," said John. "Damn, I'm old and that makes her old too. Damn!" John smiled then. "Damn, I am really, I mean *really*, old."

"Were you a detective in a past life?" joked Anthony.

John smiled at the thought of pushing his newfound friend right down onto his sarcastic butt. "That's a hell of an epiphany to have so late in life."

"The wrinkles, the no-hair, the arthritis, the dentures, none of that gave it away before today?"

"Nope, just hit me from out of the blue, jackass," said John with a laugh.

"Hey, I'm not the jackass who just realized that he was old. You could've read your license a long time ago and came to that conclusion." Anthony pulled the bags down from under his own eyes and pointed at them to show John what *old* looked like.

"Well, anyway, you're right," said John. "I'm old as shit, and I guess that makes my kids old too. Big surprise, right?" As Anthony nodded his head in agreement, John continued. "Nikki was always John Junior's favorite. They hung out together and liked the same stuff. They were closer in age, so it just made sense, I guess."

"Why do you sound like you don't approve of her choice?" asked Anthony.

"I don't dislike any of my kids, but I'm beginning to realize that I don't know any of them," said John. "Marcus made me realize yesterday that most of the shit that has gone on in his life I was totally unaware of, and the others as well. I had a rudimentary knowledge of it, I guess, but I've been on this earth for almost ninety years, and my kids have been on this earth for six decades or more, so how come I don't know them, or how come I know little more than their names?"

"I can't answer that one, bud," said Anthony. "I can't explain why."

"Was I that bad of a father?" John looked a bit confused. "How come I have all these kids that I know nothing about?"

"You tell me."

"Because I never cared about them?" John continued. "Was it because I never cared, or was it because they chose Marcus? Was it because I didn't get any appreciation for the sixteen-hour shifts and the sleepless nights? I figured that if they could do without me, I guess I could do without them."

"Are you sure you never cared about them?" asked Anthony. "I mean, are you really sure that that was the real reason?"

"Yeah, I think I really am," admitted John. "I loved them so much, and they disliked me. How can you not end up disliking people who don't like you? Do you know how hard it is to be in a room full of people and know that not one of them really likes you very much?"

"How can you love them so much, and hate them at the same time?"

"I wanted to be their friend, their protector, their dad. Why was that so hard to be?" asked John. "Why couldn't I be that for them?" John took a breath, as he was obviously making himself upset. He sucked all of his pain back inside.

Anthony watched as his new friend had a mini-breakdown right in front of him. But there was absolutely nothing that could be done besides be an ear to an old man who needed to purge. "Do you want to stop?" asked Anthony. "I mean, if you want to stop, that's okay. But from my experience, I think you need to get that sickness out."

John took out his handkerchief and swiped at his eyes. He hadn't realized until today what resentment he'd been bottling up inside. "I think you're right," he said finally. "I think I need to say it all out loud." John paused for a few seconds to formulate just the right words. "God, I hated them so much. I hated them with all my being. I was all alone. I had no one, and they just didn't care. They couldn't have cared less."

Anthony interrupted John. "Are you sure about that?"

"Yes, I'm very sure. All of my kids saw me as just an object that you passed by from time to time. They all grew up and then they ran like roaches when you flip the lights on. They were gone, they were just gone." John sat back as the memories flooded in about the last time he saw this one and that one, and the last time he saw his wife. "How could my wife not have hated me?"

"What do you mean?" asked Anthony.

"I ran them away, because I was not a father. I was an ornament. I was the toy that no one ever played with."

"Is that being fair to yourself?" Anthony wanted to call John a drama queen, but he figured that this was not the time for sarcasm.

John looked upwards towards the sky. "Honey, I'm so sorry," he said. "I can't change the past, but for the first time, I think I see what a jerk I was to Marcus, and to you, and to the rest of our kids. I am so sorry. Only a dick resents little kids. All they wanted was some time with their father. I'm so sorry, Betty." The tears were unstoppable. He just let them flow.

Anthony knew all too well about what John was going through. He'd gone through something very similar when he had his own reckoning. He knew that John was going to feel like shit for a while, but hopefully he'd come out on the other side better, smarter, and more open to fixing things before it was too late. He just watched as his friend came to grips with at least one of his demons.

John looked down and threw a spread of bird seed onto the pavement. He watched as the birds pecked at the seed and didn't raise his head back up until he'd gotten his emotions in check. "Sorry about that, old fool," he said.

"On the contrary," said Anthony. "I think you just had a breakthrough. You got one thing wrong, though."

"What's that?" asked John.

"Why do you think it's too late to fix things? Why do you think you can't have a hundred more conversations with Marcus, just like the one you had yesterday? Why do you think you and the rest of your kids can't get close even after all these years?" He wanted to say so much more, but he chose to stop there.

"I don't have another twenty years to fix this," said John. "I might not have twenty days, at my age."

"Stop deflecting, John. I know it's hard. God, do I know it's hard. But you need to stop saying what you *can't* do and start talking about what you *can* do."

"Like what?"

"Like, more listening, more understanding, more growing," said Anthony. "Your son is gay. He is gay, he is gay, he is gay. Your son is your son, though. That is what should define Marcus, not who he sleeps with. You can start with that."

"I can do that, I think."

"Your other kids can be in your life, or they can choose not to be," Anthony continued, "but you can always pick up the damn phone and say hello. You can do this every damn day until one of them finally answers, and then you actually talk about why you don't see each other and why you don't understand each other, and what—if anything—either of you want to do to fix it."

"You go, Doctor Phil," John joked.

"It's not a laughing matter, John. It took me years to own my crap. Don't take that long. Do it now."

"Okay, okay. God, you're worse than my wife with the nagging."

"I will let that one slide, since I know what a dick you can be," said Anthony.

"If I liked you at all, that would've hurt my feelings."

"And if I had liked you in any way, I would have slapped you way back when you were whining about your troubles. I thought I was going to have to call a *waambulance*."

John had to laugh at that one. "Anthony, all this time I took you for an educated rich snob with a stick up his ass, and you turn out to be a comedian with a stick up his ass. I was totally wrong about you."

"Your apology is accepted," Anthony said, also laughing.

"Seriously, though, I had a great day yesterday with Marcus," John continued, "and I'm so scared that he's going to realize that I'm the same jerk as before, and that his life is better and healthier without me in it. I don't know what to say to Marcus. I treated him like he was not my son for so many years. I resented him so much for the embarrassment I felt. I thought I'd been robbed of having a real son. I treated him as though there was something wrong with him, just because he was not following what I thought he should."

"Did you tell him all that?" asked Anthony.

"No, hell no."

"Why not?"

After a half-minute pause, John said, "I don't know why, really."

Anthony jumped in during John's quick pause. "Is that really how you feel, or are you just saying it to try and make yourself feel better?"

"I do feel that way," said John. "I'm not going to pretend to understand how a man can find another man attractive, and I never will, I suppose, but I'm not going to pretend to know everything about it, either."

"So ask him, maybe?" Anthony suggested.

"Ask him what? What's it like? I don't want to know."

John could see that Anthony had something to say, so he let him interject. "Ask him about his life, which includes his partner," Anthony began. "Ask him about when he knew, and how he knew, and apologize for making him feel like a freak and an outsider, and making him feel all alone. You're not going to be able to get this rock off your chest until you come clean with the hard questions and answer for them."

"I guess I've got a lot of thinking to do," said John. "What am I going to say? How am I going to explain?"

Anthony cut John off once more. "Why on earth are you making this so damn difficult? Why can't you just get them all in a room, or one at a time or whatever, and just say I'm sorry?"

"I guess that's a start."

"It has to start somewhere," Anthony continued, "and be aware that you may be ready and they may not, or maybe one out of the three is ready, or maybe none. But they may be open enough to hear you, and you have to start somewhere."

"Yeah, I guess." John didn't particularly like getting a lecture from a man he had just met, but on the other hand, he had to admit that Anthony was right, and besides, there wasn't a line of people all waiting to be his friend.

"You're scared," said Anthony. "I get it. Oh, I definitely get it, but time is running out for you and your kids. Tomorrow is never promised, and no one's saying that you're going first, even though I'm sure your old cantankerous old ass will. Do you want anyone to show up, or not?" Anthony stood up and gathered his belongings. "I'm hungry, he said. "Do you wanna go get something to eat at Trish's? I think a hot dog would hit the spot right about now."

"How did you know I was thinking about grabbing a dog on my way home?" asked John.

"It just seemed like the right brain food right now." Anthony watched as his friend got to his feet, and then they proceeded side by side to head off in the direction of Trish's.

IT'S TOO LATE

Marcus wasn't used to getting the cold shoulder from Danny, but on occasion, it came out in blazing force. "Are we going to talk about this or what?" Marcus asked.

Danny threw the dish towel down onto the counter and spun around to meet Marcus's stare. "What is there to talk about, Marcus? You had your first decent conversation with your father in sixty years, and now he deserves a second chance? You think he's changed somehow? You got all this from a one-hour conversation with that old man?"

"I guess I did?" Marcus met Danny on the other side of the kitchen island. "Danny, look at me, please look at me," he said. "I want to talk about this, but to do that, you have to be okay with it, and you have to lose the anger and the hate."

"I'm never going to be even a little bit okay with that old fucker being here. He finally said he was sorry, so you're jumping on the 'let's make up, daddy' bandwagon?"

"That's not fair, and you know it," said Marcus.

"Marcus, that man has treated you like a leper for as long as I can remember," Danny began, "and that's not counting the stories I heard from you or your siblings about what a real dick he was to you when you were a kid. And now, after one outstanding conversation with him, you want him to come to dinner at our house with John and Nikki? What's next, you want him to move into the guest room?"

"What's so wrong with that?" asked Marcus.

"Do you hear yourself right now?" Danny asked. "Do you? Because I feel like I just stepped into the twilight zone. Sixty years of hate and bigotry isn't washed away just because he said he was sorry. It just doesn't work like that."

"I know that what I'm asking isn't easy, but I'm asking you to do it with me, and for me. I'm asking you to be my rock. Can you do that for me? No one else. Can you—and only you—do this for me?"

Danny watched as Marcus begged and pleaded, and he knew right then and there that Marcus needed this. Danny may never understand or even want to, but Marcus wanted this right now more than anything. Something had happened, and whether or not Danny believed that it was genuine, it didn't matter. Whether it be for closure, or for a new beginning, or just to be the better person, Marcus needed this, and it wasn't up to Danny to grasp why . "Okay," Danny finally relented. "Okay, but I swear, the first bigoted thing that old jackass says will be his last, agreed? I get to throw him out on his old, wrinkly ass."

"Okay, but you have to promise me one thing," said Marcus. "And that's that you won't be all pouty and judgy."

"You know damn well that I'm not gonna promise anything like that," said Danny. "I'm going to burn a hole in that man's forehead with my eyes if I can, and—"

Danny was cut off sharply. "Stop!" Marcus pleaded. "Just stop. "

"What's up your rear?" asked Danny.

"You are. I ask you to do this for me, but you don't want to do this for me," said Marcus. "You want to do this so that you can make the night a living nightmare for everyone. If you can't do this for me, I understand, but if you say okay, that means okay."

"Okay, okay," said Danny. "Who took your drama queen out of its box?" Danny let out a heavy sigh. "Okay. I said okay."

Marcus wasn't sure whether to believe Danny or not, but he decided to take him at his word. He did, however, have to ask himself why the hell this seemed so important to him. Why did he care about this old bigoted fool, as Danny had described him? What was going on?

"Good," he said finally.

Danny brushed the hair away from Marcus's face and kissed him square in the center of his forehead. "Okay, Marcus," he said. "Okay. I don't understand it, I don't believe in it, and I don't even think the man will appreciate it, but I will be the perfect host, just because you asked me to."

"Good. Thank you."

Marcus was too upset about this, and he kind of knew why, but he wasn't going to say that he understood it fully. He knew that it had something to do with working with those kids all day. He'd heard some gruesome stories, and even though everyone had their sad stories, he couldn't help but think about the advice that he had given to a lot of them. "If you don't forgive so and so, he will own you," he had said. It ate at him all day, and he didn't understand it until his father and he started talking, or better yet, until he talked and his father listened. He wasn't used to that dynamic with his dad. He had always been the listener.

Marcus sat down on a chair at the kitchen table. He tried to think back to the conversation. There had been something different about his father. He'd a look in his eyes that was soft and remorseful. He couldn't explain it, really. He saw pain and loneliness in those eyes, and they were not unlike the eyes of the kids he had talked with all day. He didn't know how to explain it to Danny, but he knew that it was going to help himself more than it was going to help the old man. But so what if it did? He wondered what Johnny and Nikki would have to say about his surprise. Would they be cool, or would they lose their shit? He wasn't sure, but he did know that at his age, he wasn't going to make it a long discussion or debate. It was his house, and this was who was coming to dinner. They could come and have an awesome dinner, or they could go to the McDonald's right around the corner. It was their choice.

Danny had always been able to tell when Marcus went into think mode, as he called it. There was no real talking with Marcus at this point. It was the end of the discussion as far as Marcus was concerned. Danny stepped in with a piece of coconut cake that he placed it in front of Marcus. "Here you go, babe," he said.

Marcus snapped out of his thoughts. "Thanks, Danny," he said. "I guess I *am* hungry, now that I think about it."

"Do you want a sandwich or something? I have roast beef in the fridge."

"That sounds good, thanks."

Danny went over to the other side of the kitchen to get the necessary ingredients to make Marcus a sandwich. He felt sorry for him. Not only did he have to live with the things that had happened to him, but in some weird way he had to find peace with being okay with the man that had done those things to him.

Marcus continued with his thoughts. It was like a mathematical formula that he was trying to figure out in his head. It had to have an answer. He didn't want to tell Danny just yet, but he felt that the answer was to hate *that* father, and maybe get to know this one. Was he a different guy altogether? He doubted it. But what if he was? He never dreamed that in a million years that he would ever have heard the words "I'm sorry" from that old man's lips, but he did, and he'd meant it. Marcus could tell. What to do next, he wondered? Do they start a new friendship? Does he just chalk it up to an old man worrying about the next step and needing forgiveness? Will he ever be able to truly forgive him? He really wasn't sure about anything.

Danny could see the smoke coming out of Marcus's ears, he was thinking so hard. He tried to snap him out of it. He placed the sandwich next to the piece of cake. "What you thinking about?" he asked. "You want to talk about it?"

Marcus pulled the plate toward him and took two big bites from the sandwich. *Did he want to talk about it?* After a few bites and a hard swallow, he managed to say, "Well, do you want to know, or do you just want me to feel better?"

"Both, I think."

"I sat there all day telling these kids how to get over their shit, but I don't think I'm taking my own advice," he began. "I feel like a phony. I think I need to shit or get off the pot, which means I have to do some things that I and you may not be ready for, but I think they need to be done nonetheless."

"Like what, for instance?" asked Danny.

"Like figuring out whether I want this guy in my life and whether I can really be his friend," said Marcus. "Or am I just going to continue to go through the motions just to make me feel better? I'm not sure if I can, but I know I have to."

"What the heck did he say to you?"

"It was his demeanor, really, not just what he said. It was the way he just said 'I'm sorry.' It was genuine, and remorseful, and full of shame. I don't know how to explain it. I just felt it."

"Wow, that must have been some whopper of an apology." This was one of the few times in his life that Danny was at a loss for words. He cidn't know what to say.

"It was as if it wasn't really him, you know?" Marcus continued. "It was as if he was possessed by an actual caring human being." He paused briefly, and then continued, "I just can't explain it fully. It is more gut and instinct than rational thinking."

"Well, I may not like the old fucker, and I may want to beat his ass for everything he has said and done to you, but I trust your instincts, and if this is something you feel is necessary, then I'm right there beside you," said Danny. "What can I do?"

"I'm not really sure yet. I guess you should just treat him as if you'd never met him, if that's possible? Maybe have more pity for him than hate, maybe?"

"Well, I guess I can try," Danny said with a sigh. "I really, really want to punch him in his face, though. Can I punch him and then have pity on him after?"

"Um, I don't think that's how it works," said Marcus. "I think we can only have pity on you if his face looks like hamburger. We want to have pity on him because he wished he could redo things, but can't. Do you understand?"

"Yeah, I think I do. I think I get what you are saying." Danny wanted to understand, but truthfully, he just wanted to punch the old man in the throat.

Marcus could tell that Danny's halfhearted attempt at humor was really his way of saying that he was sorry he couldn't help him with what he was going through. "Just be the lovely host you always are, and I think that everything will work out just fine."

"Okay, I think I can be fabulous," Danny said. "You know I can be fabulous!"

"No one can be more fabulous," Marcus agreed. He slid the plate over and began to devour the small piece of cake. The coconut fell to the tabletop.

Marcus watched as Danny left the room to give him some privacy. He really had a good guy in Danny, he thought. It had been over twenty years, and he was a very lucky man. He wasn't exactly sure what tomorrow's dinner would bring, or the day after that, or the day after that, but he knew for sure that whatever happened, he was not going to be hiding in a corner about it anymore. It was time to get everything out in the open. It was time to talk about it. It was time to get all this shit out and have his brother and sister deal with their baggage, and for him to deal with his. And then maybe, just maybe, they could all try to get past all the shit that kept them dealing with these ghosts that seemed to haunt them all. He was tired of it, and if he had any say, it was going to stop after tomorrow.

ON THE ROAD...

Johnny looked over at the passenger seat and wanted so much to see the sister that he loved so much, but truthfully, all he saw sitting next to him was an old hag who thought life owed her something. Nikki was no longer the twenty-year-old with perky tits who could get guys running to the ATM to get her some money. Now she was an old, lonely, desperate woman sleeping in his passenger seat instead of sucking the life out of her own kids. All he saw was someone who he felt sorry for and pitied more than anything. He wanted so badly to tell her to get the fuck out, to go get a life and stop ruining his, but all he could do was feel sorry for her.

Johnny watched as sign after sign whizzed past as he drove down the interstate towards his little brother's house. He wasn't exactly sure of how he felt about good old Dad coming to dinner, but it wasn't his house, nor his rules. He couldn't remember the last time that he and his father had sat down at the same table together. He was pushing seventy, and his memory wasn't that bad yet, but it took some effort to think back that far. He wanted to be positive, and he wanted it to be something he looked forward to, but the reality was that a lot of shit had been said in anger over the past few decades between him and his father.

Johnny thought back to the last time, as a much younger man, when he and his father had gotten into a shouting match because he didn't appreciate all of the stuff that his father had done. Like how it was some big deal to the old man that he felt appreciated. They got into such a shouting match that Johnny just didn't feel like the old man even cared about him, only himself. He kept saying that all the kids had shunned him. It was odd thinking about that now, but he figured that his father was probably right. They all did shun him—not only because of how he treated Marcus, but the way he treated all of his kids. We were there to help him, to take care of him, he thought. And John had never really put that together until much later in life.

Johnny wasn't mad at his father anymore, though. He didn't hate him like before, because truthfully, he didn't really even know him. He saw him every few decades or so for an hour, and you can't get to know anyone in that brief amount of time. He knew that he wasn't one hundred percent innocent. He knew that he'd said some really hateful things to his father over the years, mostly due to feeling like he had to protect the rest of the kids. It was no wonder that he'd become a police officer. He'd had this protection thing going on his whole life, and not being a cop didn't deter that habitual personality trait.

He looked over at his sister drooling on her chin. "Not the most pretty thing," he said in a whisper.

"Huh, did you say something?" Nikki straightened herself up and wiped the slobber from her chin.

"No, just talking to myself," said Johnny. "No one else will talk with me."

Nikki snickered at his comment. "Why didn't you wake me up?"

"And miss your snoring serenade? Never."

"I don't snore, you jerk," she said, punctuated with a slap on his shoulder.

"Yeah, and a bear doesn't poop in the woods, either."

"You really are a jerk," Nikki said again.

"Stop the presses."

"You're a jackass and a jerk. So, where are we?"

"I'm sorry I had to get the princess up so early," he said, "but we're making good time. We should be there in about seven hours, I guess, and we can check into our hotel right near Marcus's neighborhood."

"Why aren't we staying with him again?" asked Nikki.

Johnny knew that this was the stingy, selfish, and rude-as-hell sister talking at the moment. "Well, because they have just one guest room, and their apartment is on the small side, that's why." He could hear himself losing his patience.

"Okay, fine, I just asked."

"And I just answered." John changed the subject. "So, what do you think about Marcus's news about Dad?"

Nikki wasn't sure what the right answer was that Johnny wanted to hear, but she tried to be bubbly and positive and go against her instincts. "I think it's great," she said.

"Why?" Johnny asked, surprised.

"I don't know," she said. "Because he's our Dad."

"So…"

"Well, we could get to know him, you know?"

"Why?" asked Johnny. "I mean, why does a woman who has seen him maybe three times in fifty years want to see him now and get to know him?"

"Don't get mad at me," she said, flustered.

"I'm not mad at you, Nikki, I'm just trying to understand."

"What else can we do? Its Marcus's house, not mine. I can't tell him who to invite or not invite."

"So, you don't want Dad there?" Johnny asked.

"I didn't say that. I said that I didn't care one way or the other."

"That's not what you said, but I think that's closer to the truth. "

"Why are you doing this?" Nikki asked defensively.

"What, Nikki? What am I doing? I'm just asking you how you really feel in your tiny little heart about having dinner with Dad after all these years."

"I don't give a fuck, okay? I don't give a fuck about that old man, and I don't give a shit whether he's there or not. I don't care if he chokes and dies right on the table, and I damn sure don't care if he is all alone and just wants to make it up to me right before he kicks the bucket. I don't care."

"But, do you care?" Johnny turned and presented a broad smile.

"You are such an ass," said Nikki. "That man has given me so many nightmares. He was such a mean person. Not just to me, but to everyone, especially his kids. I felt so sorry for Mom for so long."

John listened as she droned on about how her life was so hard and how no one helped her, even though she would be homeless and starving if it weren't for the guy sitting literally right next to her. *She's a real piece*

73

of work, he thought to himself. But he just drove as she droned on. She touched on the time when she wasn't allowed to go out with Tommy, even though everyone knew, including her that he only wanted a piece of ass, and that that was about all she was really good for.

"Don't you have anything to say?" Nikki could tell that her brother was just trying to tune her out.

"What do you want to talk about?" he asked.

"Dad," she said. "What else?"

"Like, what about Dad?" Johnny was trying to pay attention to the road.

"What do you think about him being there?" she asked.

"I'm not going there to see him. I'm going there to see Marcus and Danny. As far as I'm concerned, it's just one of their friends joining us for dinner."

"Do you think they really are friends?" asked Nikki.

"Who cares?"

"Don't you?"

"Why?" asked Johnny, his eyes on the road.

"Because of what he did to Marcus," said Nikki. "That's why."

"What he did to Marcus, or what he did to you? Or, more aptly, what he *wouldn't* do for you?"

"What does that mean?" she asked sharply.

It was about time that they got this out in the open, and Johnny figured that now was as good a time as any. "Nikki, you were a spoiled brat who thought you could, or should, get anything you wanted just because you were pretty," he began. "But you were a bitch to a lot of people, and Dad did not reward that. So you thought, or had people think, that he didn't love you, just because you didn't get a new car, or a new this or that, and you know it."

Nikki had a look of awe on her face. "That's bullshit and you know it. You got a car, and you got a motorcycle. But when it was my turn, we didn't have it."

"Nikki, what I remember is dad matching the money I had saved from a thousand menial jobs and helped me go out and get a decent car," he said.

"He would have done the same with you if you had showed one ounce of ambition rather than using people to get what you wanted." Johnny continued to stare at the road, and he added, "You know damn well that it's true, so don't act like the wounded bird."

Nikki managed to say, "He treated us all like shit, especially Peter and Marcus."

"Dad was an asshole," Johnny agreed, "and that's not a question to anyone. The question is how much of one was he? In his mind, he thought that making sure you had a roof to call home and food in your belly was being a good dad. No one ever said he was father of the year, but he treated Mom like a queen. It was us that he wasn't fond of, and that was because we didn't grasp the good that he thought he was doing."

"Sounds like you're on the 'welcome back, dad' train, too."

"I don't know," Johnny admitted. "I've hated that fucker for so long, but now after my own kids just call when they need something, I think I have a different side of the coin to look at. I don't hate him anymore. I haven't in a long time. I try to, but the truth is, I'm too old to worry about that shit anymore. I did shit, he did shit, and all it got both of us was an apartment full of T.V. dinners and a bunch of old wounds that I can't even remember how I got."

"I remember how he used to hit Marcus," said Nikki, "hoping that the gay could be smacked out of him. I know you remember, Johnny, because you were always the one stepping in and trying to get dad to find something else to smack around. And that was usually you."

"I remember," Johnny said softly. "I haven't forgotten anything, little sister. "

"Seems that you have."

"No, I just don't want to feel that sickness anymore. I'm sad for you that you still do."

"That prick doesn't deserve our forgiveness, and I will never offer it to him."

"Even if that means not getting in the will?" Johnny said.

Nikki turned to face him head on. "What is that supposed to mean?"

"Don't play dumb, sis, it's not your strong suit." Johnny was about to leave her on the side of the road. He was just so sick of her games.

"Whatever he leaves us will be split four ways, I would guess, so I don't care."

"What if he leaves all his money to the cat foundation, or the Veterans association, or something like that?" Johnny asked. "Would you be okay with that?"

"Yep," said Nikki.

"Liar."

"What do you want me to say, Johnny, that I don't think that bastard owes us?"

"Us, or you?"

"He owes all of us," said Nikki. "You know it, and so do I."

"Do I?"

"Stop being a dick, Johnny." Nikki was getting tired of all of the accusations, even if she knew in her heart exactly how right he was. She knew that she wanted him to pay for all the crap that she'd gotten when she was a kid. No matter how spoiled she was, he should've been there for her, and she knew that he hadn't been.

"Okay, but let's be clear," said Johnny. "If you choose to hold onto all that crap, go ahead, but please don't think for me. I will hug him or punch him according to what I decide, and no one else."

"Okay, God, so just hug him already and get it over with," said Nikki.

"I just might."

Johnny knew that that probably wouldn't happen anytime soon, if ever, but he was sure after talking with Marcus that it was time to put all of this crap behind them. No one was saying that he should be their best friend, but to be this nemesis hanging over their heads like a dark cloud wasn't healthy for anyone, and they all knew it.

GROUP

Marcus sat quietly as he usually did in his metal fold-up chair amongst a half dozen troubled kids or so, and a couple volunteers, in a wide circle. He didn't complain that the chair felt like a rock pressing against his spine, because he was doing it to help the kids. He just sat there and listened. It was time for group—or, more fittingly, group counseling, if truth be told. He sat a few chairs down from Tom, who tried to be in the group but outside the group at the same time. He was there more as a calming presence than as a participant, and he did a damn fine job of just being a fly on the wall.

Tom and the other counselors took a lot of pride in who they let into group. Not all the kids who came were dysfunctional or maladjusted. Some kids truly just wanted to hang out with their buddies and play games and then go back home to a very loving mother and father. They only invited the ones who had obvious scars, whether physical or emotional. Some of them were so withdrawn that it took weeks or even months for them to open up enough to even say hi and have a conversation in group, and others seemed on the outside to be fun-loving kids, while on the inside, they hated their lives.

Tom took a lot of time, patience, and effort to make sure that the kids felt safe in group. He had seen some amazing things happen, and unfortunately some not so amazing things. He tried to head them off before they became the gang bangers or sociopaths that life was pushing them towards. He was very proud of the success stories, even if they all weren't there yet. He was very proud of every kid who had the guts to tell their story, and he appreciated and respected every counselor who tried to help. He loved sitting back and watching those moments when a kid got to realize that it's not them that had the issue, or that it's not them who needs to change.

Not all of the kids participated in group, but the ones who did really could choke you up. Sometimes Marcus had a hard time keeping his tears at bay. It was especially hard to hear one of the kids open up for the very first time. The raw emotions were usually composed of unleashed hate and anger and frustration coming out in almost violent outbursts, but on some rare occasions, that was all that was needed. Some of the kids just needed to share how they felt, and with help from the rest of the kids, they were able to realize they weren't alone, and that they could get past whatever troubles they were having. Sometimes Marcus was really glad that he had let Tom talk him into this.

Marcus watched as the group leader, A.J., worked his magic with the kids. He was a former child psychologist who, in Marcus's opinion, had left a lucrative high-paying job because he just wasn't reaching the right kind of patients. He was very unconventional in a lot of ways, but he seemed to be able to talk those kids into opening up, even when they were hellbent on not doing so. Marcus watched in awe as A.J. brought the truth out of the kids. They were never really running up to the front of the line to tell their deepest, scariest, and locked-up-tight secrets, but A.J. had a real knack for talking with the boys. Marcus was amazed by how A.J. made them feel like they were in a safe place and that it was okay to tell everyone what an ass hat their dad was, or how their mother smoked enough cocaine to choke a horse. Sometimes it was the grandfather or a handsy uncle, but no matter who it was, they had usually screwed some kid's life up royally.

A.J. started talking with one of the newer kids, Eric. He wasn't un-aware of the tough times the kid had been through. Usually, before the kids were invited to talk in group, they had already spilled their guts to Tom or A.J. or one of the other kids in the group. "Eric, do you want to talk to the group about why you are here today?" said A.J. "You don't have to say anything you don't want to say. We're all here for a reason, so no one is judging you."

REDEMPTION

Eric kept his head bent low and cast his eyes from face to face, looking for signs of disapproval. "No thanks, Mister A.J.," he said, "maybe next time."

A.J. knew this boy kept coming for a reason, though. He had enough experience to know when someone wanted to tell their story. "Are you sure?" he prodded. "Why don't we start with something simple, like: do you like coming here?" A.J. crossed his legs to show his bare feet sticking out of a pair of flip flops. Some might call him eccentric or even odd for how he spoke and acted, but Marcus always thought him a very progressive and down-to-earth therapist. He was not as old as Tom or Marcus, but he was aware of the crap that life sometimes throws people.

"I came here to play pool, and to hang out with my friend Billy," said Eric.

"Billy Lorte is your friend?" A.J. saw Billy nod his head in agreement from his own chair. He knew from Billy that Eric was messed up due to his father. Some of the kids like Billy made A.J. and Tom aware of the other kids who needed some help. Billy was one of those kids six months ago, but he was doing so much better with guidance and encouragement, and Billy took great pride in paying it forward.

"Yeah." Eric kept his emotions out of this conversation. He just wanted this guy to choose someone else to talk with. He hadn't come there for therapy. He'd come to shoot pool and get away from his father.

"So, did Billy let you know that this is a safe place to talk?" A.J. knew that Eric's dad seemed to be a functional alcoholic. "You can talk about anything you want."

"I know," said Eric. "Billy told me that everyone here is cool. He told me that there were a lot of good pool players here who could teach me how to do some crazy shit on the pool table."

"So, first, we don't cuss here," said A.J. gently, "and secondly, is there anything else that you want to talk about, school or home, or if anything is bothering you that you might feel better just getting off your chest?"

"I do have a question," Eric began. "You said everyone here knows how I feel? I mean, everyone here knows what it's like to think your father is a piece of shit? Everyone here knows what it's like to wonder why shit—I mean, stuff—is so screwed up all the time? I doubt it."

"Yeah, most of the kids who are invited to group have things that they need to get off their chest, that's all," said A.J. "No big secret to why we're all here. Just a bunch of guys who can relate to one another."

"So why are you here, then?" asked Eric. "How can you relate to what I'm going through, or how I feel?"

A.J. knew that Eric was deflecting instead of just dealing with his problems head on, but that was okay. Not everyone was ready the first or second time, or even the seventeenth time. Some of the kids took months to open up. Some came once or twice and then never came again. Since Eric had only been coming around for a few weeks, A.J. knew that he wasn't asking him so much how he related, as much as he was asking him how he'd dealt with his own problems. "I can definitely relate, as can Mister Tom and Mister Marcus," said A.J. "We didn't just end up here doing this at this particular time in our lives because we thought it beat watching television."

Eric looked over at Marcus minding his own business and said, rudely, "So what is your deal? Why are you always sitting here but you never say anything? How come we don't hear your stories?" Eric pointed to each of the adults in turn.

A.J. knew just as well as Marcus that this kid just wanted to hear other people talk, and not do the talking himself, but he also seemed to be on the verge of exploding with his own story. A lot of kids wanted to see others bear their soul and become vulnerable before they found the courage to do so themselves. He'd seen one boy point out another, but this was the first time he had seen a counselor get pointed out. "Eric, we are here to talk about your issues," A.J. began, "and if you don't want to do that, it's just fine, but we're not here to ask the counselors about their lives, okay?"

Tom leaned in and added, "You'll just have to trust us, Eric, that we know where you're coming from and that we can help if you let us." Tom didn't get involved often, but he knew that if this was to set a precedent, then any of the adults would be under scrutiny before the kids would talk, and that wasn't why they were there.

Marcus raised his hand to ask Tom if it was okay if he answered Eric's question. He was a bit shocked at what Eric had said, but it did make him realize that he was there to heal just as much as these boys were. It was wrong of him—and every other volunteer—to assume that the kids were the only ones that needed to get something off their chest, and truthfully, he didn't mind. Tom gave him the sign that this was his decision, and Marcus looked back at the boy after getting approval. "Eric, you're right to ask why someone like me, or A.J., or even Tom or any of the others has the right or even the experience to tell you how to feel, or even how to fix it, if you don't know squat about us except our names."

Eric blurted out, "Exactly, that was what I said."

"No, actually, you didn't," Marcus continued. "You tried to put someone else in the hot seat so that you wouldn't have to talk about your own pain, and I get that, but don't ever think that you've had it rougher than anyone else. Don't ever think someone owes you anything, okay? Let me give you a life lesson that you can take to the bank. Every living person on this planet looks in the mirror and sees some sort of deformity, or imperfection, or character flaw. It's up to us to learn to live with it. You don't get what you wish for, kids. You get what you work for."

Eric just leaned in just a bit closer, as did the other boys, and watched as Marcus went from a wallflower to someone who had something to say. "Okay, I was just saying that if you know me so well, and you have the answers," Eric said, "then can you tell me how to live with an asshole like my father? I would like to know how you dealt with it."

"Fair point, and fair question," said Marcus. He looked at Tom to make sure where he was going was okay with him. Tom gave a simple nod and leaned back in his chair. "Eric, everyone sitting here has a twisted up life that they're living through at the moment, or trying not to let bad memories control their lives."

"So, why are you such an expert?" Eric was kind of curious, but was still speaking with a sarcastic tone. He was sure that none of the counselors ever talked about themselves, and why should they? They were here to judge, not be judged. He was sure that if truth be told, these kids barely knew anything about them besides their name.

Marcus eyed up his interrogator. He was a fifteen- or sixteen-year-old kid with a huge attitude, that was clearly obvious. Everything from his tattered shoes and tattered jeans and his worn T-shirt told Marcus that this kid was hanging on by a thread. He didn't know this kid's particular story, but he'd heard enough stories from these boys to know that only the faces change.

Marcus leaned forward and interlocked his hands in his lap. He cleared his throat. "Well, I'm over sixty now, and I'm just beginning to take the steps to get my life in order after what my father and I went through. Let me get this straight to you, boys. I don't hate him, I haven't hated him in a very long time. I pity him now, because he is every bit as alone and isolated as I was as a kid."

Marcus stopped and had to take a deep breath before he started down this rabbit hole. He looked around the room at each of the kids, and even the counselors looked as though they were intently listening to his story. It was strange for all of them to hear a calm and articulated story, as opposed to the hate-spewing stories that were usually told there.

One of the other boys chimed in from across the room, "So, what did he do?"

Marcus smiled and looked down at his hands. "Well, my father and I did not agree on a lot of things, but mostly it was my way of living that got the old man so riled up that he couldn't see straight. I was young when I found out that I was just different from the other guys. I didn't know what it was at first, but over time, I realized that I just liked guys and not girls." Marcus stopped there.

Eric jumped in, "You like guys? Is that why you took this job, so you could be around boys?"

Before anyone could utter another word, Tom jumped in. "Eric, and this goes for the rest of you too, I know Marcus well, and I approached him. I know his backstory and I knew he would help you kids." Tom was politely told to stop by Marcus.

"Thanks, Tom, but they have a right to know. Eric, Dante, and the rest of you boys can ask me anything you want. You can ask for advice, or not, and I get that, and it's okay, really. I've been married to a great guy for over twenty years named Danny, and he, not any of you, does it for me, let's just get that out there. If knowing what you know now makes you uncomfortable, I respect that." Marcus cleared his throat once again. "Let me tell you something I know for absolute certain. It's just something you know inside, and no one should be ashamed of that, nor made to feel ashamed."

Marcus was interrupted by one of the kids. "So, what did your father do?"

"You all still want to hear? I don't want you to feel uncomfortable in any way."

The same boy blurted, "I don't give a fuck who you are sleeping with."

Marcus smiled. "And the rest of you?" Marcus received an overabundance of nods and a few shouts of "finish the story!" Marcus leaned back and stretched. He was pleased, because the conversation could have gone sideways.

Marcus renewed his original position. "Well, my father was one of the guys who just couldn't have a queer son. What would the neighbors think? How would he explain it to his buddies at the lodge? So, the only good Christian thing that could be done would be to beat that nonsense out of him."

"He beat you?" the boys asked.

"Well, only enough to get the gay out of me," said Marcus. "And I'm glad to say that it didn't work. I took a lot of punches, and a lot of verbal and mental abuse besides the physical abuse, and took it all. Then I ran like the wind out to California as soon as I was old enough to go to college. By the way, in today's world, I would not recommend that course of action for any of you, unless you feel you have no other choice. It's a hundred times harder to live on your own than it was back in my time. What I would advise, though, is to listen to the wiser older gentleman telling you his story, and learn from it. I would say that each and every one of you have some real shit at home to deal with. I know some of you, and I know the pain you are dealing with. The mother trying to stab you, or the father trying to beat you, or even both who don't or can't make you feel like you're loved or that you belong."

Everyone stared at Marcus as he continued, "Have you kids ever had that one pet that just would not love you back like you loved it? For me, it was my pet turtle, Crush. We didn't ever have any dogs or cats, so we had to be creative if we wanted a pet. Crush was a cool little turtle that I found as a baby out by the creek near our house. Well, anyway, I used to play with that turtle and catch it crickets and feed it only the best lettuce and the best beets, and anything else I could swipe from the kitchen while my mother wasn't looking. I used to take it outside so that it could get exercise, and I really thought a lot about that damn turtle. One day, though, I turned my back on him while we were out stretching our legs. I let him get too close to the creek, and in a flash, he was gone. For the longest time, I couldn't understand why he left. I loved him and fed him and thought the world of him. Why would he not do the same? It was many years later that I realized that he was just being who he was. I guess what I'm saying is that whether it be your mom or your dad or someone else, sometimes you have to accept the fact that you're never going to get that love back, no matter how much you do everything right. That person may not be able to return it. Do you understand, kids?"

"Is that how you felt when you were a kid?" introverted Mikey chimed in.

"Oh yeah, Mikey, I felt it in spades," Marcus confirmed. "When I got a bit older, I understood a lot more, but before that, I had a truck load of daddy issues. My father made me feel like there was something so wrong with me and that no one was ever going to be able to love me. The truth is, it took a long time for that to fade, but it did, eventually. The sad part and the most important part is that these feelings are not going to be fixed just here. It's going to take a lot of work, a lot of forgiving on your part, and mostly, a lot of understanding. Misery loves company. You kids aren't miserable because of the cigarette burns, or the beatings, or even the yelling. You're damn pissed off about the isolation and loneliness and the soul-crushing solitude that they make you feel on a daily basis, not under-standing how you could love someone so deeply who hurts you so much. You want to hate them so badly, but for some reason, you just can't. How can you love a person who so clearly doesn't return that love? I get it, and so does everyone here." Marcus took a deep breath and enjoyed how good that made him feel.

Eric just matter-of-factly said, "I guess you never know!" He hadn't expected to hear such a sad story from someone who seemed to have it all together.

Marcus added, "Don't ever assume you know what's going on behind a person's eyes. Get to know them, get to know their story." Marcus leaned back and exhaled and regained his stoic composure. "Now, is there anything you want to talk about, Eric?"

"I can't top that."

"Don't try to. Tell us why you came here, besides shooting pool and playing shuffleboard. Do you have a story? Do you have one you'd like to share?"

"My father is a prick," said Eric, "what else is there to say?"

A.J. spoke up. He had to regain control of the session, or it would be Marcus that these kids turned to in the future. He wasn't jealous of Marcus, but he felt as though Marcus's story, although heartfelt, was not how he would have handled the situation, and he knew with all his years as a counselor, he knew how to handle these kids better than Marcus did. "There has to be a reason why he's a prick?" said A.J.

Eric looked from Marcus over to A.J. with an almost shocked look on his face. "He's just a prick."

"Is he a prick to anyone else?" A.J. continued.

"I don't know, I haven't checked anyone else for cigarette burns and bruises."

"So, he beats you? He put cigarettes out on you?"

"Only when he can't find the ashtray," said Eric. "I only get hit when I'm late from school. He has to go out, and he can't leave until I get home."

"Why not?"

"I guess because he is a responsible parent?" Eric said with obvious sarcasm.

A.J. knew he had to proceed slowly. "Explain, please."

Eric looked out at the sea of faces and stopped when he got to Marcus. "When I get home, I make sure that my mom doesn't have any male visitors while he's out."

"Your dad is worried about that?" A.J. could see that Eric's whole attitude had become calmer after locking eyes with Marcus. He hated to admit it, but it seemed that in one session, Marcus had done what it had taken him months to do. It seemed as though Tom was right about Marcus. This guy was a complete natural.

"My dad is worried about everything when it comes to my mother." Eric rolled up his sleeve and showed an old scar. "See this? That's because I told him to stop hitting her. One of these days, I am going to fuck his shit up, and he ain't gonna have no one to blame but his own self. He's so worried about mom. He puts rocks on her tires so he knows if she went anywhere while he was out." Eric's intentions were not to ramble, but to give short, non-emotional nothings until A.J. moved on to someone else.

Marcus was definitely impressed. It was like A.J. instinctively knew the kids who needed to blow off some steam and get something off their chest.

A.J. calmly said, "So you stick around for your mom?"

"Who else is going to make sure he doesn't kill her one night when she won't open up her legs for his drunk ass? Who is going to keep him from—" Eric's anger and rage turned inward and his emotions betrayed him. The young kid he really was came shining through in the tears that glistened beneath his eyes and fell to the floor.

Marcus jumped in. "It's not your fault, and there's nothing wrong with you."

Eric continued through the tears, "Yeah, I know. Someone needs to break both of his hands so that he can't hit me, or can't hit my mother, and can't get so blind drunk that he doesn't remember anything the next morning. That's what needs to be done."

A.J. interjected, "Mister Marcus is right. This is not on you in any way."

"Well, its somebody's fucking fault." Eric wiped the tears from his cheeks and composed himself. He saw understanding in the eyes around him, but he saw pity, too.

"Unless your father gets help, the fault lies at his feet," said A.J. "You can help him, but you can't fix him, no matter how much you love him or wish to protect him, or wish he was different." A.J. was almost near tears himself. This boy's story was bringing back a lot of old memories that he thought he'd dealt with, but obviously needed to be reexamined. He squeezed the elbow that had been broken from when he'd gotten in the way of his own drunk father, knowing that squeezing it too hard brought back the pain as well as the memories of that night.

Marcus sat back in his chair and let the group leader do the leading. He didn't want to tell A.J. how to run his group, and he didn't entertain the idea that he was anywhere near A.J.'s league when it came to dealing with these kids.

Marcus understood now why Tom was always there, but never got involved. He was there to observe, but he was also there to give the kids strength. Marcus had been doing a lot of thinking about his own father and where their new relationship—if that's what you could call it—was about to take them. He wasn't sure in his heart whether he could ever be friends with him again, but the one thing he'd thought of most in the past hour was that the fear he was feeling was not ever going to go away. The fear of his father rejecting him again was just the tip of the iceberg, and he knew it. He could never explain to these kids how a dad could not love his son. How a parent could look at his own flesh and blood with disgust and revulsion. How can he or anyone else move past that kind of pain? He was going to have to learn to deal with the tears and the hate and the years of not having his father in his life if they were to make amends. He knew, or was at least ninety-nine percent sure, that his father was sorry. He could see it in his eyes. But there was that one percent that wondered whether he was just afraid to be alone at the end. It was a real question to ask, and at this time, Marcus didn't have the answer.

He wondered, "How can I give these kids life advice when I'm still struggling with my own?"

WHAT DO I WEAR?

Anthony was sitting on the bench waiting with tea in hand when his friend John came strolling by with his bag of bird seed and his coffee from the corner shop. As John sat down, Anthony said, "A bit late this morning, huh?"

John chuckled. "Yeah, these old bones creak more some mornings than others."

"Mine don't creak and crack, mine Crackle and Pop," Anthony joked.

"They don't snap?"

"No snapping, please. That means rehab, and I'd rather not think of that again."

"Yeah, I've been in one or two myself," said John. "All they do is treat you like a rug that just needs to be taken out and shook once or twice a week. It was horrible." John gave a shiver as if remembering the unpleasant experience.

"An old rug that no one wants to keep around, and is just one step away from trash day," Anthony agreed.

"Old rugs and old men usually smell funny too." John remembered the nurse who had come in from time to time, not to do anything or help, but just to check him off her list. The rehab center was a very dismal place. He remembered the depression and loneliness he'd felt there, never getting a visitor and not having anything to look forward to besides death.

"What are you thinking about?" Anthony asked.

"Oh, just a few old memories from a few years ago. I think every one of those damn so-called rehab centers should be burnt square to the ground."

"Bad experience, huh?" Anthony said.

"All I personally saw was laziness, ineptitude, corruption, and unpleasant people who were supposedly there to help people get better. What a fucking joke."

"So, how about we turn the lights on and get out of that dark place you're in at the moment?" Anthony suggested.

"Click," said John.

"Lights on?"

"The lights are now on."

"Good." Anthony continued after a pause, "So, what's up for the weekend?"

"I'm going to have dinner with my family tonight. I'm so damn nervous, I may shit my drawers any second," said John.

"Did you bring an extra pair?" Anthony asked.

"No, I'll just have to duck walk home, I guess." John smiled at the thought.

"Let's not duck walk today, please. Especially when you're so close to my nostrils."

"I'll do my best not to offend your delicate little nostrils."

"That would be very much appreciated." Anthony joined in with John as they laughed at the thought. "So, why are you so damn nervous, besides the obvious terrible father thing?"

"Wow!" John exclaimed. "You're not mincing words, are you?"

"What?" Anthony said with a shrug. "You might as well face it, because you know that's what is terrifying you."

"I have so much to say that I'm sorry about, but I have as much chance as being forgiven as I do of making it to heaven."

"Why do you say that?"

"Let's be real here, Anthony. I beat my kid hoping that he would puke up his gayness. That doesn't sound like a good daddy to me."

"But it did back then, obviously."

"At the time, I thought I was saving him from a life of gay bashings and ridicule and isolation. I thought being gay was just something someone decided to do."

"And now what do you think?" asked Anthony.

"Now, I couldn't care less," said John. "I don't care about any of it anymore. I'm just sorry, I'm so sorry that I lost a son. I'm sorry that I lost all my kids."

"What else?" Anthony prodded.

"Well," John said, and then he paused for a minute to really understand the question. He wasn't really sure how to articulate how he felt. He wasn't good with the emotional stuff. The older he got, the less communicative he became about anything below the surface. "Well, I guess I would like to know how to fix it between me and my kids, but I think just so much has been said and shouted and screamed over the years that I don't think it's possible."

"Stop being an ass," said Anthony. "You may not ever have a good relationship with any of your kids, but tonight is not about that. It's about way more."

"It is? Like what?" asked John.

"It's about being honest, you old jackass. It's about coming clean regardless of the outcome. Let's face it—you may never get forgiveness or redemption, but if just one of them gives you a second chance and accepts your apology, then it was worth it. If one of them allows you into their heart, isn't it worth the fear you feel right now?"

"Preach it, brother."

"I'm serious, John. If you truly want to say that you're sorry, you have to be serious. No one is going to take a cavalier confession seriously."

"I know, I know," John admitted.

"What do you want to happen at this dinner? Do you just want to fill your belly and go home? Or do you want to do something or say something that may fix this rift you keep talking about? I know it's not easy, but if you expect them to just come to you and open up right away, then you might as well not even go tonight."

"I want to have my kids not hate me," said John. "I want to not feel the way I feel. If I'm wrong, or even if I'm totally in the right, is immaterial at this point. They hate me for whatever reason. Whether it be how I did this or that to them, or didn't do. It used to be all that I could hear, but now it just seems like it's all just white noise. What can I do to make it right? That's what I want to know."

"Okay," said Anthony. "Well, you better know what you want to accomplish tonight before you go over there and eat two biscuits and become a wallflower because you're too chicken shit to face what needs to be done and what needs to be said."

"So, what do I say?" asked John. "I mean, since you seem to have been through this and have all the answers, what do I say?"

"Let's start with where I made my mistakes," Anthony began. "What do you want to say to Marcus? What would you say if just the two of you were locked in a room together with nothing to do but talk about your feelings?"

"I guess I would say that I'm sorry. I mean, what else can I do but say I'm sorry? I can't change the past."

"After you said you were sorry, and that you wished you could change the past but you can't, then what?"

"What do you want me to say, Anthony?" John asked, exasperated.

"I don't personally give a rat's ass what you say to Marcus, or Nikki, or any of the others. What do you want to say to them? What do you want them to understand?"

"I guess I would want them to know I'm sorry." John wanted to answer the question like Anthony wanted, but he just didn't know what to say.

"Is that all you got?" asked Anthony. "I'm sorry, I'm sorry, I'm sorry? You might as well stay home and phone in your apology." Anthony knew that John would have to be pushed or he was going to wimp out. He knew exactly what it felt like.

"What the fuck do you want from me?" John snapped.

"Do you want me to shut up so we can talk about bird seed and the old lady walking down the cobblestone? She looks like she probably saw the last dinosaur."

John wanted so badly to say, "Shut the fuck up, shut the fuck up and leave me alone," but unfortunately he knew that for one, this wasn't what he really needed, and also it was meant as a friendly gesture. He didn't know how or why, but he did know that this guy may be the difference between a great night with his kids and a nightmarishly bad evening. "No, I know you're just trying to help."

"Then, what do you want to say to those kids, John?" Anthony asked.

"What can I say? I was a terrible father? I'm sorry I fucked you all up? I wish I'd been a bit smarter in my understanding of gay people?"

"That's a pretty good start."

"I want to tell my kids, especially Marcus, that if they let me, I want to help them, help them with advice or anything else," said John. "I would want to help them and their kids, and fuck, just *see* their kids. Some I haven't seen in years."

"Better," Anthony said.

"I can't make up for all that was did and all that was said," John said, "but I can try to just be a phone call that they want to make every so often."

"Better still."

"I want to get to know Danny, Marcus's husband. I want to say I'm sorry for all the shit I've said over the years. I want him to know that it's just not my kids who I need to apologize to."

"I think you're getting the hang of this," Anthony said with a big smile.

"There is so much that needs to be said," John said again with a sigh, "but I don't think I will be able to say it all."

"You're not trying to be their best friend tonight. You're just trying to show them that you've changed and that you're asking for a second chance to be in their lives, even if it's just as a friend who they chat with from time to time. Oh, and don't ramble on and on. Just sit back and do some listening, for the most part."

"Yeah, all that." John was getting excited.

Anthony paused. He had to get John's mind from racing until he had a stroke or something. "So, what are you going to wear?" he asked.

"What?" John was snapped out of his deluge of memories and plans for tonight.

"What?" Anthony began again, "do," and he stopped once more, "you," again with a pause, "plan on wearing?"

"Clothes, I guess. I don't plan on showing up naked."

"Please don't do that. You've already traumatized these people enough." John needed to be snapped back into reality for a second. Anthony gave John a second to absorb. "You need to wear something that shows you made an effort, that this means something to you. Something between a tux and a pair of pajamas, maybe."

"Okay, got it. Anything else?" asked John.

"Yeah," Anthony said. "Don't drive, and don't have them pick you up. Catch a cab, and show up at his place with flowers and looking sharp. Reality is not everything," he added. "*Perception* is everything. And you need them to perceive that this is the most important night of your life."

"What else?" John asked.

"I can't do everything for you, John," said Anthony. "You're going to have to figure out some of this stuff on your own." Anthony couldn't hold in his laughter. "I'm just screwing with you," he said.

"I thought so, but I wasn't a hundred percent sure." John wanted to kick the old man in his knee, but he figured he might injure himself in the process, and the old man was right about one thing: tonight was the most important night of his life. "Thanks, Anthony," he said.

"My pleasure, sir," said Anthony, "and your ass better be here all the earlier tomorrow with a big smile on your face so you can tell me all about it."

"You'll be the first to know, my friend."

WHAT DO YOU WANT ME TO COOK TONIGHT?

Danny walked into the living room and saw what looked like his husband doing the vacuuming. Marcus never vacuumed. He never did much cleaning at all. He would pay for a housekeeper to come in, but he wasn't much on housekeeping. He was Danny's big strong man. He relied on Marcus way more than Marcus would ever realize. "What are you doing?" he asked immediately.

Marcus was startled back into reality. "I'm cleaning," he said.

"Yeah, I can see that, but why? The house was already clean." To Danny, the house always needed cleaning, but it was his job to look like it never needed it. "Come on into the kitchen," he added.

"Be right there."

Danny stepped over the vacuum cord and entered the kitchen. He saw that Marcus had already cleaned in there, too. Every surface was gleaming. The shine was hurting his eyes. "Wow," he muttered to himself, impressed.

Marcus rolled up the cord to the vacuum and then placed it back in the closet near the door. The apartment wasn't big, but it was quaint. It was home. People always remarked on how warm it was when they came over for parties. Marcus knew that Danny had made it the envy that it was, not him.

After closing the door to the closet, he joined Danny in the kitchen. "What's up?"

"First of all, wow, and secondly, what the H?"

"What do you mean?" Marcus asked with a grin.

"Don't play stupid soldier on me, mister," said Danny. "It's not the best look for you. You know damn well what I mean. You've played super maid while I was at the grocery store. So, what gives? Who are you doing this for?"

"Would it be a crime if it was for my father?"

"No, but it would be shocking," said Danny. "It would be weird. It might even be creepy, but it would not be a crime. You're right about that."

Marcus gave Danny a queer look and then added, "I just want it to look nice, is all."

"I hear you. I really do. I am just wondering—" Danny was cut off abruptly.

"You were just wondering what the hell my problem is," said Marcus. "How could I clean for a man I supposedly hate so much? You're right about all that stuff, but the one thing you're not aware of is how I feel about it. I feel like no matter what I do, or what I say, it's going to be the same. I've been caring around this hate for so long. I want it to be over with, done and buried. I wish you could understand."

"Uh, as much as I really loved that one-man rendition of 'Poor Marcus,' I was about to say that I'm just wondering what you want me to make for dinner."

"Okay, sorry, what are the choices? You know what I like to eat, so what do you want to cook?" Marcus had a look on his face that he knew always made Danny forgive him no matter what he said.

"I was thinking about the ultimate all-time favorite," said Danny. "Chicken pot pie with a salad and some rice, or some sort of macaroni salad or something. Or maybe go a bit less inventive."

"Like what?" asked Marcus.

"I was thinking that maybe we could show off a bit and do the pot roast. It's hard, but it's so worth it. Keep it on slow burn for four hours or so, and it transforms the meat into breakaway pieces. I went out and got a whole beef shank, so I can cook it with white wine, beef bouillon, and layered with vegetables. It will have crunchy roasted radishes, herbs, and potatoes, and a just a touch of love mixed in."

"Well, what are you waiting for?" said Marcus. "It sounds perfect. I want everyone here to wish they had someone like you making sure they were treated well and fed like a king every day of their lives. Can you do that for me?"

"Every day and any day," said Danny.

"Can I help?"

"You can keep me company."

That didn't sound like as much fun as doing the actual cooking, but Marcus was okay with parking his rear in the chair and indulging in his new favorite pastime—telling stories about the kids while Danny turned the kitchen into an aromatic paradise. "So, what has been going on with you?" he asked.

Danny got a slight chuckle.

"What?"

"Are you nervous about tonight?" asked Danny. "Marcus, it's everyone else who should be nervous."

"I know, but I can't shake it," said Marcus. "I've been talking with these kids the past few days, and their stories are haunting me. Some of them are so eerily familiar and bring back so many memories that it makes my skin crawl."

"Do you want to talk about it?" Danny pulled the groceries out of the paper bag one by one and put aside everything that he was going to need to make the most delicious dinner that any of these yahoos had ever tasted. The only bad thing was that no one besides Marcus even came close to deserving the meal he was about to prepare.

"Yeah, I think I do." Marcus stretched his legs out beneath the kitchen table. "This one kid, David, he's really messed up. A blind man could see it. Everything this kid touches seems to turn to shit, and aside from coming in and trying to get his life together, everything else seems to be crap. His home life sucks, his grades suck, and his anger towards everyone and everything is going to have him locked up or dead on a coroner's slab one day, I can feel it."

Danny disposed of all the grocery bags and put away the things he wouldn't need for tonight's dinner while still making Marcus feel that his story was being heard. He lined up all of the vegetables and cans and spices and the meat. He placed the potatoes, the radishes and the carrots in front of him. He would need to dice and chop them up first. "What do you think you can do for this David?" he asked.

"I don't know," Marcus admitted. "What I do know is that the stories he tells sound like my stories. How his dad is not a real dad, but more like a jailer. How his dad comes in and some days sees him, and other days walks past him like he was just part of the furniture. I remember saying the very same things. I mean, it was like I was hearing a very old echo bounce back at me." Marcus rubbed his arms like he'd just got a chill.

"Can you do anything for this kid besides be an ear?" asked Danny.

"I don't know, but I can't get this kid and others just like him out of my head," said Marcus. "I thought I was going to go show some smart ass punks how to put a spin on a pool cue, or at best be a shoulder to cry on, but this isn't what I expected at all."

"Do you want out?"

"I think just the opposite. I think I have to help them to help myself, you know?"

"I think I do." Danny could see that Marcus was acting different. He seemed as though he'd found something to give his life purpose again. NASA had done it for a while, but ever since his retirement, it was obvious that he'd been floundering, looking for that purpose, a reason to get up and go outside.

"These kids are so screwed up," Marcus said, "and I'm not so delusional that I think I'm going to go in there and fix all their issues. Just the opposite, really. There may not be a fix. There may only be learning to cope with the reality that it happened and to live anyway. That part I think I can help them with. To do that, though, I think I have to look my father square in the eye and be okay with the past, and be okay with him."

"Well, do you think you can?" Danny asked. "I mean, to say you forgive is one thing, but can you really truly just forget everything that was done and everything that was said?" Danny wasn't sure if he could.

"I'm not sure," Marcus admitted. "I'm really not sure. The other day, I saw a side of my father that I don't think I've ever seen in my life. I mean, it's one of those things where you had to be there. You had to see his face and his whole manner, I guess."

"You were there, so I trust you."

"I can't even begin to explain it, and I can barely understand it myself."

"I think you're so tired of carrying this burden that you have just been on auto-pilot, doing it now just for me and for the family, and not so much for yourself anymore," said Danny. "It's quite simple, really. It's time. That's really all you need to say, to understand everything you've just said."

"Wow, you've been watching *Dr. Phil* again, haven't you?" asked Marcus.

Danny shrugged his shoulders as if to say that he was proud of himself for being so profound and articulate.

"Yeah, you might be right," Marcus said. "I've been holding onto this crap for so long. I think I was expecting to be pissed, instead of actually *being* pissed. I don't hate Dad. I don't know when I stopped, but I don't hate him anymore."

"I'm proud of you for not hating your own father," Danny said, rolling his eyes.

"Screw you."

"Too old, I think?"

"I definitely am."

"Seriously, Marcus, I'm proud of you, but not for what I said. I'm proud of you because you just dropped a fifty-pound rock that you've been carrying around, and the best thing is that you're *okay* with leaving it behind."

"Thanks," said Marcus. "Now that I've discovered what I was needing to do, what next? Do I call him every day and ask how his walk down to the park was?"

"Does he still walk down to that park?" asked Danny.

"Almost every day, he says. He has a few friends that he talks with, evidently. I guess they talk about the old days when the earth was still flat." The two of them busted out laughing.

Danny was finished making his secret brew, and was ready to throw everything in the pot and let it simmer for the rest of the day until their guests arrived. "Let's go in the living room and watch some television until your brother and sister get here," he suggested. "Do you have to go get your father?"

"Nope. He said he would be here at six. That's all he said."

"Okay then," said Danny. "I think we should sit back and relax until dinner. Anything you want to watch?"

"You know it doesn't matter to me," said Marcus. "Whatever you want."

CAN YOU PASS THE BREAD?

Nikki and Johnny were at the front door looking up at the intercom box. They were both ready to get this over with. It seemed as though they'd done nothing but snip at each other the whole drive. Johnny knew that something had to change with the way they were living together. These passive aggressive arguments were getting old for the both of them. He was going to have to make some rules, and if she didn't want to abide by those rules, he'd have no choice but to end their current living situation. Too much had gone on the past few days to dismiss Nikki's behavior as that of a recently divorced woman who just needed to work things out. His sister was fully taking advantage of his kindness. He wasn't used to living with anyone, and he truthfully yearned for the days when he woke up and heard nothing but his own thoughts.

Nikki could also see that the relationship between the two of them had soured. She knew that Johnny's problem was that he was a sour old man, and he was taking it out on her. She was also confident that if she lived with him much longer, her hands would find themselves around his throat one of these days. She wasn't sure what her next move would be, but she knew for sure that her brother didn't want her there anymore, and that his depression and negativity about everything was one hundred percent to blame.

A loud squawk came out through the intercom. It was Marcus's voice telling them to come up, and then there was a beep, and the door was open to the public. Johnny grabbed the handle and opened it so that his sister could pass. And as the two of them made their way from the elevator to the apartment, nothing was said, but in the silence, there was so much being said. It was obvious that they'd come to a part in their lives that blood wasn't going to fix what was ailing the two of them. Only time and space could do the trick.

Johnny knocked, and as soon as his knuckles hit the wood, the door flew open. Danny greeted the pair and opened his stance to let them pass.

The first thing that hit Johnny was the smell of something delicious awaiting them. Living the bachelor life, he didn't ever see nor smell this kind of meal. His delicacies were pot pies and microwaved bagels in the morning. It had been quite a while since he'd been in this apartment, and all he could say was that it was full of love. It had been a few years, but that feeling of love was still thick in the air.

Nikki too was now looking forward to whatever meal could smell that divine. She walked past Danny to see Marcus moving towards them, and only a second later she found herself in a bearhug. It wasn't until she was placed back on firm ground that she got her wits about her. "Hey, little brother," she said. It wasn't the Gettysburg Address, but it was better than just standing there like an idiot with her mouth hanging open.

Marcus moved his attention to his oldest sibling, "No bearhug, I promise," he said to Johnny. "It's really great to see you two. How was the drive?" Marcus shook his big brother's hand and motioned for everyone to come and sit in the living room.

Johnny moved over to the loveseat and plopped down. It was a very warm setting. It was a home, that was obvious. Unlike his own house, he was sad to admit. The fireplace was on low, even though it was at least seventy-five degrees outside, but it didn't matter. It made the mood, and he very much enjoyed it.

Danny asked, "Can I get anyone anything to drink?"

Marcus yelled, "Water with lemon please."

"Me too," yelled Nikki, "that sounds great."

"I guess I will round it off to unanimous," Johnny bellowed as well.

"Coming right up," Danny called from around the corner in the kitchen.

Johnny began, "The drive was nice. A lot of trees to see. Some are starting to turn just a bit, so I guess summer is almost over for the year." Johnny didn't want to rehash the truth, which was that it was mostly a silent trip and awkward as hell.

Marcus smiled and said, "Well, it's so nice seeing you two. It's been way too long."

"I love your apartment, Marcus" said Nikki. "It's so cozy. I just love all your decorations." Nikki wasn't always free with compliments, but on this occasion, she was actually sincere.

"Thank you so much," said Marcus. "It was all Danny. I just sat back and watched the magic happen." This, too, was sincere.

Danny reemerged with a tray of glasses and a pitcher of water with lemon slices floating at the top. He set the tray down and began to pour. Johnny took his glass, as did Nikki, and lastly Marcus. Danny poured himself a glass and plopped down on the recliner. "So, what did I miss? Anything juicy?"

Marcus leaned back after taking a sip of his water and placing it back onto the coaster on the coffee table. "Their trip was fine," he said. "Lots of trees, and summer is almost over. Is that about it?"

"No, don't tell me it's true," said Danny. "Not the end of summer, it can't be."

"Yep, afraid so," Marcus confirmed. "I heard it straight from Johnny's lips. It's unrefutably true, I hear." Marcus produced a big smile as he saw the confusion blooming on his guests' faces.

Danny came to the guests' rescue as any good host would. "Stop it, Marcus. These people don't feel like hearing your foolishness."

"Did they just meet me or something?" Marcus wasn't ready to give up on the fun.

Johnny chimed in, "Don't stop on our account. I was expecting a show and a meal. " He started laughing, as did the other men. Nikki, on the other hand, was still a bit baffled. Johnny wanted—and he assumed the others wanted as well—to tell her that if she had read a book once in a while in school instead of passing her ass around under the bleachers like a joint, she may have gotten the joke as well.

Nikki continued to look dumbfounded, but she just took a sip of her water and figured that it was a guy thing and just left it at that.

Marcus said abruptly, "Okay, okay, Danny. I will behave."

"No, you won't," said Danny, "because I think even at your age that you're incapable of being a normal human being sometimes."

"And?" Marcus said flatly.

"And, I love it," Danny admitted.

"That's what I thought you'd say."

Johnny said, "Aren't we missing someone?"

Marcus snapped back to reality, "Oh, our dear father will be here at six," he said. So I guess that means he should be arriving any time now."

Johnny couldn't contain it any longer. He had to say what was on his mind before their father showed up. If he even showed up. He may chicken out and blame a bone spur, or bad back, or something, so as to not have to be grilled by the family. "What's the deal?" said Johnny. "I mean, not being a jerk, but what really is the deal?"

Marcus looked at Johnny and then at Nikki, and then spun to his left and looked at Danny before replying. "I guess it's pretty simple, really, when you boil it down. I'm so sick and tired of hating him. I'm sick of not just hating him, but thinking that I have to. Thinking I have to because everyone else is. How you and you and you feel are up to you, and I would never try to sway how you feel about him, but me, personally, I'm sick and fucking tired of hating him for the rest of you."

"Have you made up and are friends now?" Johnny said with obvious sarcasm.

"Not really, Johnny," said Marcus. "But he seems to be a totally different person, and I'd like to get to know him. Nothing else. I may even hate this bastard, too."

"What if all I see is the same guy?" Johnny asked.

"Then you go right ahead and hate him. Hate him until your dying day, if that is truly what you want. I can respect that. I have to."

"I've been doing a lot of thinking, and I mean a *lot* of thinking, about this on the way up here," Johnny said. "I don't know what I will say, or what I will do, and I don't want to disrespect you or Danny in any way, so I just want it said now before he gets here." Johnny felt like he was in an intervention or something. But then he just leaned back. He was done sharing.

Danny spoke up. "I know I'm not of your blood, and I know I didn't grow up in your house of horrors as a kid, but I do have one or two things to say. First of all, I'm very proud of Marcus letting this weight go. It has to be hell dragging this burden around day after day, and it's about time you all stop letting this hatred keep you from moving on and affecting your lives. Secondly, I just wanted to say that if you feel you need to blurt out how you hate him, then go ahead, because Marcus' relationship, even though I don't fully understand it, is his to define, and I back him one hundred percent."

Marcus lifted his index finger to wipe away the tear that had pooled at the corner of his eye. "Why the hell did you have to go and make me cry, you old fool?"

Johnny spoke up. "Nikki, do you have an opinion on this topic?"

"Well, I guess I'm up for anything, if you guys are," said Nikki.

"Where have I heard that before?" Johnny couldn't resist.

"Stop being such a dick, Johnny."

"I don't know what on earth you mean."

"As I was saying," Nikki began again, "if you guys want to forget the past and just get to know this guy, well, I guess I can try. It's not going to be easy, but I will try."

Johnny—and he assumed the rest did too—knew that that was some of the worst acting in the world. *Just come out and tell us that you will befriend the old man and deplete his checking account like you seemed to have done to mine,* he wanted to say. *'Tell them how you couldn't care less if the old man died at the dinner table as long as you're in the will.'* Johnny wasn't buying this whole dutiful soldier routine. He knew too well what a gold-digging bitch Nikki was at her core.

Marcus saw the look on Johnny's face, and he couldn't say that he disagreed with the thoughts he suspected were drifting through his brother's head, but at the same time he didn't want any of this petty teenage bullshit tonight. He wanted everything to go smoothly. He didn't care about Johnny's bullshit, nor did he care about Nikki's obvious lack of morals. "Okay, you two," he said. "Cut it out."

"I'm just saying—" Nikki began.

Marcus blurted out, "Nikki, you are not *just saying*, you are just *implying*. I'm sure you'll bounce back." Marcus wanted to take a poker to her skull, but he took a deep breath and let the anger out as best as he could.

Just then, the buzzer rang on the intercom system. Danny got up from his chair and left the bickering kids behind. He pressed his thumb on the button and said, "Yes?"

"It's me, John," came the voice through the speaker. "Marcus's father."

"Come on up, John." Danny looked back at the siblings squabbling and knew right away this was going to be a disaster. If it didn't turn out to be a huge disaster, he thought in an instant that he would start believing in God.

He looked back to see Marcus getting up from his chair to meet Danny at the front door. Marcus met Danny just as he was opening the door. His father was standing at the front door with a bunch of flowers in his hands. "Come on in, Dad," he said.

John walked through the threshold and into the brightly lit apartment. He saw that it was very nice. He looked around and wanted to say something like, "This isn't anything like what I would expect a gay's apartment would look like." It wasn't lit up with brightly colored doo dads and gaudy furniture as he had envisioned before walking in. It was conservative, yet very homey. "What the heck smells so good?" he said.

Danny took the flowers from his father-in-law and just matter-of-factly answered with no emotion, "Pot roast. I hope you enjoy it. Thank you for the flowers."

"Whatever it is, it smells scrumptious." John was motioned over to join the rest of his kids in the living room, and it was by far the most awkward thirty feet he'd ever walked in his life. It was obvious that every step was being scrutinized. He put on a brave smile and waved from across the room.

Danny wasn't really sure how to feel or act, and he knew what he had told Marcus, but the overwhelming need to kick John in the shins was almost overpowering. He darted off to the kitchen to cool off.

John walked into the pleasantly spacious living room and saw his son and daughter sitting down on the couch. No one got up to hug him or even to shake his hand. He sat down in the chair previously occupied by Danny and sat to listen, not talk, as Anthony had advised. Another piece of advice from Anthony that he took to heart was that he was dressed in a nice shirt and a nice pair of pants. Not something he'd wear to a wedding, but definitely the best thing he owned in his closet.

Marcus handed his father a glass of lemon water and then sat down himself back where he had been previously. "So, Dad, how was the drive?"

"I didn't drive," said John. "I caught a cab so that I would be here on time." John thought that that too would show that he was taking this evening very seriously.

Marcus thought that the flowers, the fact that his father was dressed in something besides a sweat suit, and that he'd been driven there by a cab all meant that his father was trying to make the best of impressions. He took that as a high compliment. "Well, I'm just glad you are here," he said.

Johnny wasn't sure what to say, if anything. He had thought that it was going to be no big thing, but it turned out to be a very big thing. He wanted to say so many things that he could barely keep them all inside. He got up from his chair suddenly and proceeded to say, "Marcus, can I use your balcony to grab a smoke?"

Marcus didn't think Johnny smoked, but he also knew that smoking was not really on Johnny's agenda. He just needed some air. "Absolutely, smoke it up," he said. He watched as Johnny made his way to the balcony and closed the door behind him. He hoped that that wasn't the end of Johnny's visit. Marcus had a fleeting thought that made him grin. *Thank God we're too high up for Johnny to jump down, leave Nikki here, and run back to Baltimore.*

John watched as his son disappeared onto the balcony. He was ready for this. He was ready to be blamed, punched, spat at, and anything else. He was just so happy to be there and to see his kids again. He couldn't really explain it, but he knew that this was the make or break moment for him and his kids. "You have a great home, Marcus," he said. "I mean, really. Very beautiful."

"Thanks, Dad. It was all Danny, believe me." Marcus sat back as if the whole night would be anything but common.

John looked over and saw his daughter sitting there like a bump on a log. She didn't engage, nor did she show any signs of life at all. "How are you, Nikki?" he asked.

Nikki was startled out of her daydreams. "Uh, I'm okay, Dad, and you?" She didn't know what to say. She wished she could smoke so that she could join Johnny out on the balcony. She wondered, too, when Johnny had started smoking. He kept it very well-hidden, she thought.

John could feel the tension in the room. It was as thick as tar, and he was trapped in a situation where his gut told him to screw this and leave, but he'd promised himself that he wouldn't go down that road. He had to make it better, not worse.

Marcus, too, noticed the awkwardness permeating in the air. "I hope you like pot roast, Dad," he said.

"It smells delicious," John confirmed. "I'm sure it will taste as good as it smells."

"Let me see if Danny needs anything," said Marcus, leaving the father and daughter alone to hopefully say something real to each other. He stood up and, like a flash, found himself in the kitchen. It wasn't like Danny to hide in the kitchen. Marcus had to make sure that everything was okay.

BALCONY VIEW

Johnny watched the old man for a few seconds from the balcony through the crack in the curtains. In some regards, he was shocked that this old man could still have such a powerful influence over him. He thought that all the pain and hate and anger and rage towards everything he'd done and everything he'd said was buried, but just seeing him—and feeling the knot in his stomach—told him that it wasn't as buried as he'd wanted to believe.

Johnny spun around and tried to focus on something else, anything else. The view from up there was actually pretty nice. The lights sparkled, and the cars, although noisy, were a light show all their own. He watched a lady with a shopping bag walk up the block. She was carrying what looked like groceries, but from this far away, he couldn't be sure. She looked up at him and they exchanged waves. He wondered if this place was different from his hometown, where carrying groceries was an invitation for someone to snatch and run. He hoped this wasn't that kind of neighborhood.

Johnny took his eyes off the streets and sat down on one of two green chairs. The plants hanging off the wrought iron railing really made the balcony seem pleasant. Even the balcony had a homey and welcoming touch. It seemed that everything in this whole house, besides his father and sister, were warm and welcoming. He sat with his leg crossed over the other and wondered what the real issue was. Was it Dad who had him so wound up, or was it his sister, or was it something else? He wasn't sure. He definitely had a pang in his stomach as though his appendix had ruptured when he saw his father, but it wasn't like before. He just saw an old man. The last time they'd seen each other, Dad had been in his late sixties. Now he was in his eighties, which meant that it had been a whole lot of years since he'd seen his dad.

He had been expecting to have that fire that he needed in order to justify hating someone as much as he'd hated his father. At first, he felt that fire, but it wasn't blazing as before. It wasn't as engulfing as he remembered it. Was it that he, too, was older, and he too had issues with his own children that had never been resolved, and now he had finally flipped that coin over to see what was on the other side?

Johnny thought of his own kids. David and Erica were both grown and very successful young adults, but he too rarely heard from his children. Like father, like son, he figured glumly. The last time he'd heard from David was probably almost a year ago, and just to say "Merry Christmas." He couldn't remember hearing from David aside from then, and Erica even longer. He was so much more like his own father than he ever wanted to admit. His father ostracized himself with his kids through bigotry and homophobia and plain ignorance, whereas Johnny knew he would be forgiven because he was in the right and he had been out there saving lives as a cop. It hadn't dawned on him fully until recently that missed birthdays were missed birthdays, and not being there was his fault, based on choices he had made. No one forced him to work doubles and triples because some jumper could only be saved by him. He smiled at the thought of him calling Tina and apologizing, but too much had happened between them for that to happen.

He laid his head on the railing and looked back out over the landscape and realized that he needed to stop waiting for David and Erica to come to their senses. They needed their father, and even though he wasn't preaching intolerance and indifference, he wasn't teaching them anything at all, and he realized that this may be even worse.

He peeked back through the curtain and saw his father sitting there listening to his sister. He seemed to be having trouble remembering what it was that he hated so much about his dad. Was it how he'd treated him, or was it how he treated Marcus? What was that defining moment when he decided to hate this guy's guts? He thought and thought, and then he fell upon the one moment that brought that to clarity.

He and his father had gotten into a huge argument. It was more aptly called a screaming match. He remembered how his father had to be right about everything not being his fault. He knew what was best for Marcus, and everyone else, and if you didn't take his advice, then there was nothing he could help you with. It was always, "You should do this," or "You need to do that." Never "what do you need from me?" or "how can I help?" He remembered how his wife had almost gotten hit when she jumped in between the two of them trying to make peace. That one moment of rage and hatred for his father had fueled many a decade of hate.

Johnny saw the guy in there now in Marcus's living room, and it didn't seem to be who he remembered from before. This guy was reserved and conservative. A tired old man. He kind of felt sorry for him. He could only imagine what it must be like to be in a room full of people who didn't like you. It took guts, and for that he had to give the guy some grudging respect.

Johnny continued to peek through the curtain and stare as his father tried to make conversation with his daughter, and he could see that it wasn't going well. You could see in his face and in hers that there was not much to say. As Marcus got up and went to the kitchen, though, he could see a transformation in his sister. She became talkative. She became the one initiating the conversation. It was obvious to Johnny that his little sister didn't wish to have any witnesses to her schmoozing. Her ass-kissing was legendary when it came to getting something she wanted.

Johnny wanted to bust in and yell, "Don't fall for it, Dad," but wouldn't that mean that he had his father's back? He had to think about that for a minute. Why would he care if Dad got taken to the ringers? Maybe he would take her off his hands, even? She could take the old man for every cent he had, and why would Johnny even care?

No matter what Jonny thought of his father or his sister, though, he wasn't going to see someone take advantage of an older person who just wanted to make amends, a thought which surprised him. He sat there and watched, hoping Marcus would come back and rescue the old fart, but after a few seconds—after a lot of seconds—it was obvious that no one was going to come rescue him.

Johnny stood up and, against his better judgement, opened the balcony door to go inside to save his father. He knew in his heart that he loved her, but at the same time, in that same heart, he knew that she was a gold-digging bitch from hell. There wasn't a ditch low enough that she wouldn't jump into if it meant that money was coming her way.

He stepped cautiously inside and proceeded to walk over to where he had just been sitting before. He didn't say anything, he just sat, but there was no mistaking the cross look that he'd gotten from his sister for messing up the plan she was trying to put in motion, the one that ended with dear old dad forking over some of those Social Security checks.

"Welcome back," said his father. He wasn't dumb to what his precious little girl was doing, but the reality was that he would sign over his entire bank account right there and then just for a chance at a civil conversation with them all.

Johnny nodded as if to acknowledge the remark, but gave nothing in return. He wasn't there to be friends, he was just there to make sure Nikki didn't take advantage of an old man.

Nikki spoke up. "So, Dad, as we were saying before, what are you do-ing nowadays?" She tried her best to ignore her brother and his obvious plan to stop her from getting what she believed she deserved.

John watched as the obvious disdain—or maybe even disgust—was so evident on his son's face regarding his sister. His boy did not like his sister very much, he thought. He considered for a split second what a jerk he was for thinking that at least those looks weren't pointed at him. "I do okay, I guess," he said. "I get up, I get dressed, I do my exercises, I get cleaned up, and then usually I find myself watching life zoom by at the park from my bench. There are a lot of very interesting, if not peculiar, people frequent-ing that park."

"That sounds nice, I guess," said Nikki. "I'm sure it's a lot of fun. Do you want to do anything besides go to the park and watch life zoom by?" Nikki was trying very hard to talk to him, but they had absolutely nothing in common and nothing good to say about each other.

"Like what?" John asked.

"Oh, I don't know," said Nikki, "I mean, there are so many places to go, and places to shop for things, and maybe update your wardrobe?"

"Is there something wrong with what I'm wearing?"

"Oh, no," Nikki said with a whimsical little laugh. She realized that she had to backpedal. She had to regroup.

Johnny spoke up, against his better judgement. "You look fine, Pop. You look fine, and don't let Nikki tell you otherwise." He was so sick of her little mind games.

"Thanks, son, I appreciate that," said John. Maybe this night was going to be fine after all. The one that he would never be able to turn would be Junior, he thought. Just too many things that had been said that would never be able to be unsaid.

"I just meant if you wanted to, you could update your wardrobe," Nikki said. "That's all I meant." She shot Johnny a glare.

John wasn't about to say what was on his mind, because that would have been the easiest way to fall back into his old ways, and he wanted something positive to say to Anthony tomorrow. Not that the night went to shit after he told his daughter what a real piece of shit she was. "I think I like my casual wear," he continued. "It may have a rip or a tear or a hole somewhere, but it's very comfortable."

Johnny chuckled at the obvious attempt to tell Nikki to blow off. Meanwhile, Nikki had daggers in her eyes. It had become obvious the last two days that she was going to have to do something about her living arrangement. Johnny had become cruel and heartless, and she wasn't sure how she could live with a man who had those qualities. It hurt her to say, but her big brother, who she had looked up to for so long, was a colossal jerk, and it wasn't healthy for her to live with him any longer. "Yeah, Dad, I think you should wear what you find comfortable too," she said.

"Thanks, honey." He turned to look at Junior once more. "So, how have you been, son?"

Johnny didn't want to fight. It had been so many years, and so much had changed in him. He figured his father had changed as well. It just wasn't worth the digs back and forth. "I'm okay," he said with a shrug. "I retired a few years ago, finally, and I'm just piddling here and there with volunteer work. I help a few food banks from time to time, and I give the old folks a ride to doctor's appointments and stuff like that."

"Thanks," said John. "I guess the next time I have a doctor's appointment, I should call you." He smiled, hoping not to be told to go fuck himself. But to his surprise, he got a smile back from his oldest son.

"Yeah, I guess I could take you to your doctor's appointment," said Johnny, "but I can't promise who would take you home." It was meant in jest, and Johnny was sure that his father knew as much.

"I guess I deserved that one, and a few dozen just like it," John said, smiling a smile of appreciation. He was so thankful that the knives had not been brought out. He looked at both of his kids and maybe didn't see love there, at least not yet, but he also didn't see the blazing hate that he'd kind of been expecting.

All in all, it was a good start.

WHAT'S WRONG?

Danny watched as Marcus came into the kitchen with a panicked look on his face, but he ignored it. He wanted to be happy and to do this for Marcus, but he was still trying to figure out how. "Before you start in on me, I'm trying," he said.

"I just wanted to know what was wrong, is all." Marcus was under the impression that Danny was on his side.

"What's wrong is that man out there makes me want to break the law," said Danny. "He makes me want to go up for a few years for geriatric assault and battery. That's what's wrong, Marcus."

Marcus took a deep breath before responding. He knew that this wasn't something he could yell his way through and get the outcome he would hope for. "I understand, but I thought we talked about it, and I thought you were okay."

"I guess I lied through my pearly white teeth," said Danny. "My goosebumps got goosebumps when he came in. I didn't want it to happen, but it happened anyway. I'm sorry."

"It's okay, Danny, really," said Marcus. "I should've taken your feelings into consideration as well, and I guess I didn't do a very good job of that."

Danny wanted to yell, but he managed to hold himself back. He just tried to block out all the hate and focus on why this old guy got under his skin so much, besides the obvious. He advised young kids all the time to be themselves and to love who they want and to not let people like this fucker here dictate how they feel about themselves. So why is he letting this guy do this to him?

"It's fine, Marcus," Danny said finally. "I'm going through something stupid, and I need to get over myself. And I need to do it sooner than later."

"I know you have some bad blood with my father," Marcus began, "but I want all of us to just get over it—and ourselves. It's time to move on and stop living in the sixties. I'm so tired of rehashing the terrible things that my father did. I'm so tired of thinking that something is going to change if I just remember it differently this time. I don't want you, or me, or Johnny, or even Nikki to sit here in my house and let this old bastard see that he still owns us."

"I get you, Marcus, I really do."

"Do you, Danny? Do you really?" asked Marcus. "My father is, or was, a grumpy old man my whole life. He never once said, 'Great job, or 'Wow, you really did that?' I know these things. I won't ever unknow them. I can't sit there anymore and trade war stories with my siblings about who he hurt more. I don't want that for myself anymore. I don't want that for you. I love you, and I know carrying that baggage is going to get heavier and heavier the older we get. I want us to drop it and let it rest."

Danny was listening to the lecture on how to be a better person and forgive, but while he really wanted to come through for Marcus, he had his own horror stories about parents and kids and so-called friends. It wasn't only Marcus's father who he detested, but it was every old man snickering, or every kid whispering, that made him have a type of PTSD when he was around someone like John Jacobi. Danny wanted to articulate to Marcus that it was not John Jacobi that he hated, but it was what he represented. What he stood for.

Danny wanted more than anything to leave that big rock outside and never pick it up again, but the truth was, he didn't know how. He wasn't at the point where Marcus was, where the rock was already dropped and discarded. He still had that rock, and for all intents and purposes, he wasn't sure whether or not he was strong enough to get rid of his the way Marcus had done. He envied Marcus for being able to do it so easily, or at least make it look easy. Maybe he should spend a few days trying to help a bunch of wayward kids who were just trying to figure out who they were. Maybe he would find the inner peace that Marcus seemed to have discovered.

"I will try, Marcus," he said. "I swear I will. I want to let this crap go, too. I want to take my own advice."

"And you can," said Marcus, "but just like quitting drinking or smoking or drugs, you have to *want* to quit. You have to ask yourself if you can go out there and talk with a person who you think is the embodiment of everything bigoted and vile that makes you want to hurl your lunch."

"Please don't make me hurl my lunch, I had some really tasty beef stew today." Danny produced a grin. "I hear you, I hear you. I wish I could say that I could go out and give that old bastard a hug and just feel all warm inside, but I would completely be lying if I told you I could do that."

"How about not being able to do it today, but staying open to the fact that it is possible at some point?" asked Marcus. "Maybe at some point you may be able to shake his hand without wanting to slit his throat."

"I could probably promise that, I guess," Danny agreed.

"Good," said Marcus. "Then we're making progress."

"I just hate what he's done to you," said Danny. "But I also know that if it hadn't happened to you, then you may not be the man I love so much today."

"That's the spirit," said Marcus. "Now will you come out and be the charming host that everyone says you are? Will you knock his socks off with your wittiness and magnetism?"

"How about if I just knock his block off?" said Danny. Then he raised his hand. "I'm just kidding, I swear." He threw down the towel that he had been wringing his hands on for the past two minutes, and he joined Marcus on the other side of the kitchen island. "Let's go knock some socks off, shall we?"

Marcus and Danny left the kitchen arm in arm.

IS IT WORTH IT?

Marcus was shocked to see his family not screaming at each other when he walked back into the living room. He was more amazed to see Johnny back from his so-called cigarette break. He hadn't expected to see him before dinner was ready. He looked over at Danny, both dumbfounded that there wasn't at least one dead body.

"Look at you all," said Marcus cautiously.

John turned to see his son and his partner walk over to where the conversation was getting a bit heated. "Hey, Johnny was just telling us about his life," said John.

Marcus sat down, as did Danny, on the corners of the couch. "So, what's the word, Johnny? I haven't heard much about you lately."

Johnny looked up to meet his brother's gaze. "I'm just surviving, I guess," he began. "I do my volunteer stuff still, and I help the kids out when I can with stuff around the neighborhood. My kids are out conquering the world, and I don't hear from them much, but I know they're doing great things."

"How old are my grandkids these days?" John spoke up.

Johnny couldn't stop himself from saying, "Please don't call them that. My kids are doing just fine, and, never mind." Johnny couldn't help it, even though he swore he wouldn't take the bait.

"I'm sorry, I didn't mean to offend," said John.

"Leave Dad alone, Johnny, you know he didn't mean anything by it," Nikki chimed in.

"Shut up, Nikki," Johnny snarled. "The only thing you care about is getting into Dad's bank account, so save it. He isn't that dumb."

"Both of you, shut up," Marcus interjected. "Are you six or sixty?" Marcus had been expecting this, but he was kind of expecting Dad to be the one yelling.

John said, "I'm sorry I upset you, John."

"Dad, it's not you. I know it's not you. Like father like son is all." Johnny had to be honest—he was a lot like the old man in a lot of ways, and the longer he lived, the more he saw it.

"What do you mean?" John was all ears.

"I'm just like you, Dad," Johnny admitted. "I have kids who barely know my name, and I have grandkids who I wouldn't know if I saw them on the street. That's what I mean, is all."

"Why? You're a great guy. You are not me, son. You're nothing like me."

"How would you know, Dad? How on earth would you know what kind of person I am?"

Marcus was about to say something when his father waved him off. "I'm sorry that you feel that way," said John, "but I know a whole lot about you. I know you're always the one stepping up, and sometimes that's not to your best interests. I know that your whole life has been about helping others, and it was your family who paid the price for that kind of dedication. For that, I am sorry.

"Stop saying that!" said Johnny.

"Okay, but you think I don't know you, when in reality I know a lot about you," said John. "I have clippings of my son the hero cop. I reread that article a dozen times when you helped those kids off that broken fire escape. I saw you as if I were there."

"How do you know about that?" said Johnny. "Did you tell him?" He looked over at Marcus.

"Not me," said Marcus defensively. "I don't talk about anyone with Dad except the two of us. If you want him to know something about you, then it's your job to let him know."

"I didn't hear anything from anyone," said John. "I had the *Baltimore Sun* delivered to my house for a long time. I just wanted to know what you were seeing every day, and once in a while, I would see your picture or see your name, and I was so proud."

"How come you never told me? How come you never once said that to me?" Johnny was raising his voice to the level of almost yelling.

"I made a lot of mistakes, but it seemed as though after Peter died, it was like you all felt the freedom of not having to talk with me," said John. "It was just so much easier to not see the man that reminded you of your dead brother. I think for a while I had convinced myself that maybe you all were better off without me in your life."

Marcus was curious about something. He asked, "Why would you think Peter dying would have anything to do with you? He died of a car crash."

"I saw you all at the funeral," John began. "You didn't want me to come near you. I knew I was a bad father, I owned it and I lived with it, but I was trying to help you with the fact you all had just lost your mother and then had to lose a brother, too. I tried to be there for you, but the truth was that I didn't want that pain on top of my own. I was withdrawn, I was sullen, and I didn't fight for you. After Peter, I guess I somehow just convinced myself you all were better off without me." John sniffed back the tears welling up in his eyes. His voice became a bit coarser. "I missed your mother so much, and I still do," he continued, "but like I always did, I thought about my pain and no one else's, and I was just as happy for you and I to just stop talking, stop even, because I too didn't need the reminder of your mother and Peter. I stopped considering us a family. Instead of reaching out, I persuaded myself to think it was all for the best."

Johnny spoke up, shocked. "So, what changed? After all these years, what on earth could you want to be different" Johnny was actually pretty flattered that his father knew about some of his cop days, but he was furious that he never heard one word of praise about it. The one thing he had begged and pleaded for, the one thing he yearned for from his father. He didn't know whether to blow his lid or be thrilled that his dad did know, and thought that he was special. He had always hoped for his dad to know he was special, and that maybe he would reach out and fight for him.

"I could tell you guys that I'm old and want to get right with God, or that I just miss you all, and want to be a family again," said John. "I could tell you all that, but it would be just a bunch of hollow words that mean absolutely nothing to any of us."

Nikki was afraid to be shot down by Johnny for being a gold digger, but in this case, she was genuinely curious. "Why?" she asked.

"Well, my dear daughter, because it would be false," said John. "It would be incorrect and insincere. I wallowed in the muck of my own making, and blamed God for losing my son and my wife. I blamed you all for not helping me through the toughest time in my life. No, I hated you all for not being there to help me, like I helped you when I—" John held his hand up and choked back the words.

Marcus stifled his comment, as did everyone else.

"I hated you all, but I hated you not for what you did to me, but the constant reminder that you all represented," John managed. "You were a constant reminder that Peter died, and that your mother died. I know, I deserved to wallow in that pain. I was a lousy human being, and I hated everyone who reminded me of that fact." John stopped for a second and then continued, "You know, I think that is the first time I've been able to articulate it that well."

Marcus finally spoke up angrily. "So you think your pain was worse than ours, and that you deserved to be pitied more? You deserved to cast us aside because it helped you not have to face your own demons? Do you even understand, or fathom how many years you wasted of my life?"

Danny saw that Marcus was on the verge of screaming through his tears. He stopped Marcus before he got any more upset. "Marcus, please. He's not saying he's proud of it. He's trying to be as open and honest as he can be, so that maybe, just maybe, you can find a piece of ground that you all can stand on." Danny was flabbergasted that he was coming to this man's rescue.

Marcus stood up and walked to the back of the couch to take a few deep breaths.

John turned to Danny then and said, "Thank you, Danny."

"Don't thank me at all, John," Danny replied. "This is one hundred percent for Marcus and no one else."

"Fair enough." John turned back to his own children. "I'm not going to sit here and justify or beg forgiveness. I'm telling you the truth and hoping that maybe by some miracle we can find a path that leads us out of this." John was trying to remember the advice Anthony had given him about being as honest as he could be, but the reality was that the unedited truth made him out to be a real dick.

Marcus returned to the corner of the couch. "Okay, Dad, I have a question for you. I need you to show that same honesty in the answer you're about to give."

"Okay," John agreed.

"You're sitting here talking about change, and how you're really trying to make amends, but I have a question that I'm just dying to hear the answer to. Have you accepted the fact that I'm gay? I mean, have you accepted it to the point where you would tell your buddies at the park that they're all wrong and they just don't understand?"

John was expecting this question. He blurted out, "I have to be."

"What the hell does that mean?" said Marcus.

"It means that I personally don't understand it, but that wasn't your question, was it? Your question was whether or not I accept it. The answer is that you are my son, so I have to be okay with it."

"I remember a father who whooped my ass because he caught me and Steven Thompson up in my room." He took a deep breath and continued, "So, what changed?"

"I did, I guess." John would be happy to oblige if it meant an outcome where his children stopped hating him and could move on. "I could sit here and tell you all night long how I'm just a changed man and nothing like I used to be. But that wouldn't be the truth. I'm still an old man who thinks a certain way, and being gay isn't something I understand. But hell, I don't understand my phone either, but that doesn't mean I want to throw it away."

"What part don't you understand?" Marcus continued. "The part that I needed to hear this fifty years ago, or the fact that you've had fifty years to get to this so-called epiphany? How can I believe any of this newfound wisdom is real? I just don't know whether or not you're just a lonely old man looking for someone to be in your life."

Danny, Johnny, and Nikki sat there and watched as the only thing that could have happened tonight played out before them. They all knew what this night was really about. It wasn't about Johnny or Nikki, or even Danny—it was about Marcus and his father either making up, or killing each other, and all three figured it was a toss-up as to which way the wind was blowing.

"Marcus, it's like this, and I can only say it once," said John. "I thought at the time that I was doing you a favor, but I was wrong. I'm not going to show up on your door step every day like a broken record to tell you how sorry I am. I'll say it now for all to hear, whether it be here or at the park or at the grocery store. I was wrong. I was wrong, I was wrong." John paused for a few seconds and then continued, "No, no more lies. The truth was, I told myself and your mother too that I was doing it for your own good, but the truth is I didn't want my friends to know that my kid was gay. I'm being as honest as I know how to be here, Marcus. I don't understand it, but what I don't understand mostly now is how I could have cared so much about what Fred at the hardware store thought, and care so little about what my own son thought."

Through obviously held-back emotions, Marcus said, "Dad, I will tell you I think this is the very first honest conversation you and I have ever had in my life. But let me be just as honest with you. All the shame you made me feel, all the friends you made me lose, all the feelings you made me bottle up inside just so as not to get you upset. I hated you—shit, I hated Mom, too, for letting you do the shit you did to me. I hated everyone who was associated with you. I didn't tell you this before because I didn't want to talk about it, I didn't even want to think about it, but despite everything you did to me—the beatings, the verbal abuse, the isolation—even with all that, I didn't need you to grow up to be a great man. Actually, I did it in spite of you."

Danny and the others just watched quietly. They knew that even with all the crummy things John Jacobi had done to all of them, it didn't hold a candle to what he had done to Marcus. They all watched somewhat amazed that their father didn't offer any excuses as he let Marcus purge, and none of them fully understood it, but it was happening in front of them. All three assumed that John had had this coming for a while, and they also knew that no one knew it more than John did.

Danny wanted to come to Marcus's aid, but knew that this had to play out no matter which way it went. He would help hide the body if need be, or—and he couldn't believe he was saying this, but he would help him find peace with this old man if that was what he truly wanted. Then he also remembered that there was a dinner that was ready in the kitchen. He stood up and very quietly remarked, "I'm going to set the table, I'll holler when everything is ready." No one even acknowledged his statement. Johnny and Nikki just watched their father, waiting on his reply to Marcus.

Danny stepped away as fast as he could. He was done with this drama.

John pushed his two hands down on the arms of his chair. He didn't know how to respond. He realized he was just going to have to be honest. "I'm sorry," he said again.

"Stop saying you're sorry, we covered that already," said Marcus. "But why are you here, Dad? Why are you sitting here after all these years? No one says that they thought we'd be better off without him and then express just the opposite out of the blue. Let me get this straight—you think we're better off without you, but you want to have a relationship with us now, even though you barely know us due to your own ignorance and selfishness? And now you've seen the error of your ways? Is that what this is?"

"You have every right to judge me. I deserve it." But John was cut off by Marcus, who shot back, "Damn right you do."

After a deep breath, John said, "As I was about to say, no! Far from it. It's total selfishness on my part. I thought that if you could do without me, then hell, I could do without you. It was that simple. After your mother died, I just didn't care about anything anymore. I had a ton of excuses for why I got to hide away, and then after Peter died, it was like I deserved everything that was happening to me. I hated myself for screwing up so much with all of you. I didn't get to fix things before Peter died. I never got to tell him I was proud of him, and that I wish I could have been there with him, so he wouldn't have had to die in a hospital all alone."

"So that's why you want to be in our lives?" Marcus said. "Something that happened decades ago?"

"No," John began, "and this is where the selfish part comes in. I had a fall about six weeks ago. I fell in the parking lot of my building, and I couldn't get up. It was mid-day, and no one was around. I didn't have the strength even to get to my feet. It was like my legs refused to work. I laid there for almost an hour until a neighbor finally came out and helped me up."

John let out a heavy sigh as if remembering the hurt somehow. "None of that is important, though," he continued. "What *is* important is that in that sixty minutes of counting rocks and wishing I had my phone on me, I knew that if I died right then and there on that asphalt that the only person at my funeral would be the preacher. It scared the hell out of me. I can't even explain it. I mean, it scared me to the point of begging a God that I don't even believe in to help me fix things before I met my maker. And if I have two days or twenty years, I don't want to feel like I did on that ground. The emptiness and loneliness was suffocating. The hollow feeling that everything in this world was looking down on me as if I were the smallest thing on the planet and did not deserve to be in it. In that moment, it was hard to understand anything about why I should even be here. All I can say for sure is that the choking feeling I felt when I realized that I didn't deserve help from a single person opened my eyes up, and I had to do something, anything, to maybe never feel that feeling again. Does that make any sense?" John sat back and used his shirt sleeve to push away the tears streaming down the side of his cheek.

Marcus had no ready reply. He wanted to roar and purge, but the truth was that he just sat there and stared at his father, and then at his brother and sister. He was unsure of what, if anything, to say following that confession. It was totally selfish, but at the same time, it was also the most heart-wrenching thing he thought he may have ever heard.

Everyone was suddenly snapped out of their thoughts by Danny's voice from the kitchen yelling, "Dinner is ready! Get your butts out here."

WELL?

John had gotten to the park a half hour earlier than he usually did. He had so much to think about, so much racing through his head. Last night had taken a toll on him, but at the same time, he was glad that he'd endured it.

John threw a handful of seed out to the birds, and he watched as they came forth to accept his gift. He watched as they pecked and pecked, taking up the seed piece by piece, and he assumed that they were very appreciative of the gesture. There were so many different colors and attitudes to watch. One was the aggressive alpha, obviously, and one was the outcast that never got a bite unless it was thrown right in front of his beak. John felt a bit sorry for that one. Not all pigeons were alike, he assumed. They had a pecking order just like any other animal.

He watched the joggers run by him dressed in their brightly colored jogging suits. He watched until they rounded the corner and could no longer be seen at all. Life was teeming this morning, he noticed. It was a beautiful Sunday. The air was just a bit brisk, and the sun was just trying to get started in warming the day up. It brought out everyone to enjoy the scenery, the sun, and the interaction with other human beings.

He wasn't sure whether or not Anthony would come today, but either way was okay with him. After all, he had a lot to think about. Last night's events were still playing over and over in his head. His memory was cut short by the sight of a familiar face—the young boy with the limp. He and his mother were obviously taking in the beautiful day with a walk through the park. John did something that he hadn't done before. He said, "Hello."

The boy didn't reply, but the mother did. "Hello," she said. "Say hello to the nice man, Sammie." The boy still didn't say anything, just hid behind his mother's thigh. "I'm sorry," she said to John. "He is kind of shy."

"That is quite okay. Maybe someday he will help me feed the birds."

The boy peeked out from behind his mother and gave John a big broad smile. He still didn't speak, but he was obviously interested in feeding the birds.

The mother gave John a big smile. "Maybe someday. You have a good day, sir."

"You too. My name is John, and you and Sammie have a great day as well."

"Thank you, John." The woman and the young boy proceeded to walk down the cobblestone path and out of sight.

"You spoke to someone," said a voice. "That's great." Anthony began to set his utensils down on the bench and make his usual cup of tea.

"Yeah, I guess I did. Where did you come from?" John spun around, looking back and forth.

"I was over there waiting for you to finish with your conversation. It was like a real hallmark moment."

"I guess it was," John admitted.

"It's a big deal," Anthony continued. "You actually initiated a conversation instead of acting like a child who expects people to come to you. I was very proud." Anthony brushed off a leaf from his seat and plopped himself down to enjoy his tea. "Well?"

"Well, what?" John felt as though a bit of ribbing was in order.

"What happened last night?" Anthony asked. "I figured if you weren't here today that they cut your body up into little pieces and threw you into a bog somewhere. I'm sort of glad that did not happen, though, because who else would feed these poor starving birds every day?"

"Yeah, some of these guys really need me," John said. "Like this little guy here. He's the runt of the pack." They both let out a laugh, since the bird he pointed to was a fat, almost turkey-sized pigeon.

"Don't make me ask again, please," said Anthony.

"Ask what?"

"Never mind. I have some shopping to do today, anyway."

"Don't get your shorts in a bunch, old man."

"They are always in a bunch. So, go on." Anthony took a sip of his tea. He was hoping for a good story, a story that made the trek out on a Sunday worthwhile.

John threw a handful of seed down, and while keeping his head focused on the birds feeding, he began, "There was a whole lot of yelling and shouting."

"Really?"

"No, not really, there was some," said John, "but all in all, I'm still alive, and I wasn't fed to the sharks."

"Your gums are flapping, but you aren't saying much. How was the dinner?" Anthony looked a bit perturbed.

"Well, there was a bit of crying, a lot of cussing, and a whole lot of purging, if I had to define the evening," said John. "Mostly it was Marcus doing most of the talking, but I took your advice and was as raw and honest as I could be. It made me dig deep into what really were the problems that I had with my kids. I set aside all the stock answers like it was their fault for not reaching out, I was trying to help the boy, I needed them, too. All that shit went right out the window, and I told the unabridged truth."

"Wow," said Anthony, impressed.

"Wow is right," said John. "Wow is an understatement. I told Marcus I didn't understand a lot of things about him, but that I wanted to. I told him I was sorry, and even though I don't understand his choices, I was glad he was happy, and that I don't want anything from him other than a friend, if he would allow it."

"I bet that went over really well with his partner."

"Danny was an alright guy. He was a good, nice guy. I expected him to stab me when I walked in, though. I've said some really shitty things to him and Marcus over the years. I can't take those things back."

"Would you?" Anthony asked. "I mean, if you could go back, would you?"

"I would hope so."

"Don't give me some stock answer. Would you?"

"Knowing what I know now, then yes."

"What do you know now?" Anthony pressed.

"I know that my son is happy," said John. "He has a partner who loves him and treats him like a king. It was obvious all night."

"But they're gay." Anthony said this more as a jeer than a comment.

"Yeah, and theirs is probably happier than most marriages."

"What does that do for your view on the gays?" Anthony flashed air quotes to the last part of the sentence.

John threw another handful of seed out to the birds. He thought about it for a second, and then said, "I don't really know. I don't think I'll ever understand a man liking a man, but I guess it has to be okay."

"Did you just grow as a person, John Jacobi?"

"Yeah, I guess I did." John seemed to be just as shocked as Anthony was.

"That's a good start, then," said Anthony.

"Yeah," John admitted. "I told them about the fall that I told you about, and how it affected me, and why it did so. I told them about how I was mad and pissed and that I blamed them for not being there for me when my wife died."

"You said what?" Anthony asked. "That was their mother. Why on earth would you think it was the other way around? You should have been there for *them*."

"Yeah, but I wasn't. I wasn't there for anyone, because I hated everyone. I even hated God."

"Why God? What did he do?"

"Don't be daft, Anthony. If there was a God, he could have saved her. He could have helped her."

"I won't bore you by saying that you just don't understand his ways, or that you have to have faith, because you don't have it, and I doubt if you ever did," said Anthony. "God is not a genie that pops out and grants wishes, John. So why on earth would God come to your rescue when you probably never even picked up a Bible?"

"I tell you like I told you before," John began. "If he does exist, he has a funny way of showing his love to the nicest, kindest person on this planet.

If he did exist, why would he allow people who have faith, I mean real faith, to die horrible deaths? People dying of painful cancer or some flesh-eating bacteria or shit like, people who die knowing that their faith is absolute, and scumbags like murderers and stuff live to be ninety? It doesn't make any logical sense. My wife didn't deserve what she got. I deserved to die, not her."

"Why you?" Anthony asked.

"Because I was a piece of shit to my kids, my wife, and anyone else who had more than one conversation with me."

"Why?"

"What the hell do you mean, why?" asked John. "I just was."

"But *why*?"

"What do you want me to say, Anthony?"

"I want you to be honest with me and yourself. Why?"

John had to think about whether there was something he was missing. "I don't know," he admitted. "I hated my life. I tried so hard to love God, be a good Christian, and go to church with the wife and kids." He stopped cold, as though he had just invented the wheel in his head. It was an *ah-hah* moment. "I hated him for giving me this kid who was different. Everyone in my family hated me because I treated poor Marcus badly." John abruptly stopped. "Let's change the subject," he suggested.

"Okay," said Anthony. "What do you want to talk about, then?"

"I know just the thing," said John. "You've been spouting off about God every chance you get, and I just want to tell you that you really don't look the part."

"How so?"

"You look like you should be in a college lecture hall telling kids all about how God could not possibly exist. So, I'm curious about your faith."

"Well, it's not a short story," said Anthony, "but I will try and give you the abbreviated version. I just want you to know that you don't have to believe just because I do. I think you want to believe, or convince yourself that you believe, because I think deep down, you do. I've always been like that, too, when I was young. I'm not trying to convince you of anything.

I'm not here as a preacher or a prophet. I'm just telling you that you don't have the market cornered on self-hate, and this is how I got through it."

"Okay, I'm with you so far," said John. "But what made you a full-blown believer?"

"Do you want to try and poke holes in my faith?"

"Absolutely not. I'm just kind of envious of someone who is able to fall asleep with that kind of peace. Someone who can walk with their head held high, knowing that they're the luckiest person in the world to have someone always having your back. I'm very jealous and resentful, if truth be told. I don't know whether I've ever fallen asleep with that kind of peace."

"It is so comforting," Anthony confirmed. "Whether there is a God or not becomes irrelevant. If you perceive it to be true, then it is. Have you ever loaned anyone money and sat up at night worrying about when and if you were going to get your money back? Probably not, because without the money in your hand, you could see it coming back to you without any proof, just faith."

"I guess," said John. "So what happened to your 'I don't care if there is or isn't' attitude?" John sat back to hear this tale. He rested his arm on the back of the bench and gave Anthony his full attention.

"I guess it all happened in pieces," Anthony began. "I guess the first time I can ever really remember saying 'what if?' was when I was coming home one day from work, a bit earlier than usual because I had to take one of my kids to the doctor or dentist or something. I wanted to get home and to beat the traffic, so when I was going down Patuxent Road, I was going a lot faster than I should have been. Anyway, the road was very hilly, and some of those hills were a bit steep. I was doing sixty in a thirty, and I came over this hill, and bam—practically inches in front of me, a school bus with kids getting off, and there was nowhere for me to go. I screamed, and then—the end."

"The end, what?" asked John.

"I'm just kidding," said Anthony. "I slammed on my brakes, but the bus was gone, the kids were gone. I was fine, my car was fine."

John was not impressed. "That doesn't sound divine," he said, "that sounds like a hallucination."

"I'm not finished with the story," Anthony said.

"Oh, okay, sorry."

"Well, anyway, I was so shaken up that I went down to a crawl," he continued. "I was shaking, I was so upset. When I went over a few hills later, that same bus was there, the same kids running around. Everything was just as it had been a few moments ago. This time though, I wasn't doing a hundred miles an hour. I can't explain it. I know that it happened. I know in my gut, if I was still flying, I would have been creamed and maybe took a kid with me. I know to most it was just a hallucination, but to me, it was one hundred percent real, and unless you can give me a logical answer, I have to draw my own conclusions."

"What about a vision, or premonition?" John suggested.

"Never had one before or since like that."

"Wow. That is kind of freaky. So that is what made you believe?"

"Not really," Anthony said with a shrug. "Like I said, it was a cumulative effect."

"More school buses?"

"Of a sort, I guess. I was playing out on this old farm house that I was renting from this old couple. It was a good long while ago. Anyway, I was playing hide and seek with my two grandkids. I came outside, and I was yelling about how I was going to find them and they couldn't escape me, and all that good stuff. After a few minutes, I couldn't find them, but a sweat had washed over me. I could've been a malaria patient for how I was reacting. I couldn't explain it. I thought maybe I was having a heart attack or something, but I knew something was really wrong. But before I could take care of myself, I had to find the kids. I yelled out to them, told them I wasn't kidding and that we had to go inside. But I got nothing, no noise, nothing. I started to get upset. I was sweating like a pig, and I couldn't shake the eerie feeling that was suffocating me, as if I couldn't breathe. I ran and yelled, yelled and ran. The farmhouse was a few acres of land, and some of it was wooded, so I ran to the edge of the woods, hoping to find them hiding behind a tree. By the time I got to the edge, I was so out of breath. I felt so nauseated. I would swear that in my heart, I knew this was where I was going to meet my maker, so to speak. I came across the edge of the woods and leaned my hand on this old ancient refrigerator to catch my breath. I was panting and puffing and sweating, and without even knowing why, I opened the door to that damn refrigerator, I just opened it not even thinking about what might be there. I could have been leaning on an oak tree or a fire truck, for that matter. I just opened it, and my two precious grandbabies were in there. They were a light shade of blue."

"God," said John. "Holy shit."

"Holy shit is right," said Anthony. "I pulled them out and started rubbing them and then, after what seemed like an eternity, their color came back. My granddaughter opened her eyes and asked if she was in trouble. I sat there and cried for ten minutes straight John. My grandson came around a few seconds after her, and he just said 'I'm sorry Pop Pop, please don't cry.'"

"Fuck!" John exclaimed.

"So, explain how that happened?" Anthony implored.

"I can't," John admitted. "I've never heard anything like that before." John was speechless. He had goosebumps going up his arms.

"I have other stories like that, but not as to the core as these two were. I found myself not caring about what job I had, or how much money I had accumulated in the bank. I found myself instead helping others, and volunteering to help out wherever I could. I found myself helping kids or helping the young and old alike."

"Like me, I guess?" asked John with a smile.

"You think it's a coincidence that I got up that one morning out of all mornings and decided to change my routine and have some tea at this part of the park?"

"I don't know. I guess you just felt like getting out of the house for a while, maybe, and changing up the scenery?"

"That is one possibility, true," Anthony admitted. "It could also be that I was meant to stop by and have a cup of tea with you."

"So, you think I'm some sort of divine holy community service or something? Just poor old John who needs a helping hand?"

"Get over yourself, old man."

"Why not?" asked John.

"I can't make you believe no more than you can make me stop. I know one thing very well, and that's that the real darkness is believing in nothing, nothing but hate, hatred of one's self. No one is going to forgive you, John, if you can't even forgive yourself. It's just a plain fact, God or no God."

"So how would one go about doing that?"

"How was the dinner, John?"

"What the hell does that have to do with it?"

"How was the dinner, John?" Anthony asked again.

"It was great. I can't believe that it went that well. By the time the cake came out, I'd been asked a thousand and one hard-ass questions, but I think it was therapeutic for us all. I cried, Marcus cried, and I could've sworn I saw a tear in John Junior's eye at one point."

"You still have a problem, though. You don't deserve it, right?"

"Exactly."

"Why not?" asked Anthony.

"Haven't you been listening old man? I just don't."

"Why?"

"You're lucky I am not a fighter anymore," John said.

"You may have to start again with them," Anthony began. "You may have to fight with everything you've got just to stop the urge to ruin a good thing that might happen for you, just because you're an ass." Anthony came out with a big smile. He wasn't joking, but it was funny nonetheless.

"How?" asked John.

"It's easy, really. You have to accept the things that you did. You did them. You screwed up and you did them, period. Now you say that you'll do what you can with the time you have left. You don't have to help someone change a tire or lift a slab of concrete, but you have to be open to helping someone instead of just walking past them and presuming that it's their problem, and not yours."

"Is that what you do?"

"I don't do anything, really," said Anthony. "I'm just open to helping someone who needs a hand, that's it. Nothing really hard or difficult."

"That's it, huh?" asked John skeptically.

"Yep, that's it."

"Should I reach out to my kids?"

"Do you want to?" Anthony asked.

"I kind of do."

"Then do it." Anthony felt good. He felt really good, as a matter of fact. He was walking John down a path that might just bring him the peace he had never known before. To Anthony, it was great for him to just be a part of it.

"When I get home, I'm going to ask my kids if they will let me take them all out to dinner," said John. "A nice restaurant."

"Or, or you could ask if you can stop by and bullshit with them and get to know them even better?" Anthony suggested.

"I like that idea too, even better," John agreed. "I could get Johnny and Nikki to come over too, and just talk about stuff."

"Now you're talking like a man who can see something besides his own misery. Now you're sounding like a man who wants to do something with his remaining days besides feel sorry for himself."

John stood up slowly, he wasn't sure how to thank Anthony, since they had only known each other for a short period of time. But he felt that he had to do something. He stood and stretched the kinks out of his antique body. Then he walked over to Anthony's side and said nothing, just reached out and shook the man's hand.

"You're quite welcome, my friend," said Anthony in response.

"I have a few calls to make," John said, "so I'm going to go home and make then, and then maybe take a nap."

"See you here tomorrow?" Anthony asked.

"If God is willing."

Anthony watched as the old man walked along the cobblestone path. He could swear that John had a small pep to his step that he hadn't ever noticed before.

WHAT DID HE WANT?

Marcus finished a call on his cell phone and placed it gently onto the kitchen table after entering the room and seeing Danny next to the stove. He had a perplexed look on his face, to say the least.

"Who was it?" asked Danny.

With a surprised and somewhat quizzical squint, Marcus replied, "It was Dad."

"What did he want?" Danny was as surprised as anyone would be. After last night's awkward, silent, then screaming, then silent some more dinner party last night, he thought that it would be weeks, if not longer, before anyone heard from old John.

"He wanted to know if we were busy today," said Marcus.

"For what?"

"He just wanted to know whether maybe he could come over."

"For what?" Danny asked again.

"He asked if he could come over and just bullshit," Marcus said, incredulous.

"What?"

"Yeah, that's what he just said. 'Can I come over and bullshit with you and Danny,' period."

"God, I hate repeating myself, but for what?" Danny now had the same look on his face that Marcus had.

"He said he really enjoyed last night," Marcus began, "but he would like to get to know us more, with whatever time he had left."

"Creepy much?" Danny said. "Is he dying?"

"I don't think so. He never gave any indication that he was sick. The last time he said anything about a doctor was when that the doctor said he was in good shape. I think he just wants to make up for shit." Marcus held up his hand. "If you say 'for what?' again, I will throat chop you."

Danny closed his lips for a second. "Okay, but why on earth would your father want to come out and hang out with a couple of old queers who he has nothing in common with?"

"I don't know," Marcus admitted. "I really don't know. He seems to be under the impression that last night was a huge success, and he wants to ride that wave, I guess."

"Was he at a different dinner party than we were?" Danny asked.

"I don't know. I don't know what to make of any of this, really. I think it's great that he's trying, but I don't know for sure. Why would he just call out of the blue after being royally chewed out? It's strange."

"No, it's fucking weird." Danny stopped before going any further. "So, what did you tell him?"

"I told him the truth. I said that we weren't really doing anything, that we just got finished with breakfast, and if he wanted to come over, that he was welcome."

As much as Danny wanted to fly off the handle, he pointedly did not. He just said quietly, "Okay, well, what time is he coming over?"

"The way he sounded on the phone, I'm surprised the doorbell hasn't rang yet," said Marcus. "I could swear I heard his door shut before he hung up."

"What do we say when he gets here?"

"Why do we have to say anything?" asked Marcus. "We don't owe him any kind of apology for last night. He doesn't owe me anything. If he wants to come over and get to know us, then I'm okay with that, but you have to be okay with it, too."

"I am," Danny said slowly.

"Are you?"

"Yeah, I said my piece at dinner last night. I told him what I thought of him, and I told him what I thought of his ignorant philosophies."

"You sure did. I thought you were going to deck him with that huge spoon you were using to dish out that stew."

"I know, I almost did," Danny said. "I wanted to smack him with it and then shove it down his damn throat. If I heard him say one more time how he just so innocently didn't understand gay people, I think I was going to barf all over him."

"Well, he is eighty-seven years old."

"I don't care if he's a hundred and eighty-seven," said Danny. "How could you not just let two consenting adults live their lives, gay or other-wise, without your *I know what you should do* attitude. I know he's your father, Marcus, but that is one redneck, knuckle-dragging Neanderthal. Why can't all these old fuckers just die already?"

"I'm not going to argue with you there," said Marcus. "Not that I want him to die, but I definitely want that mindset to die away." Marcus wasn't feeling the whole *I'm just an innocent bystander* routine any more than Danny was.

Danny set his plates down in the kitchen and said to Marcus, without turning, "I guess we're going to have to educate that old fucker, whether he likes it or not, and I have a few friends who like older men that owe me a favor."

"Oh God, please leave Jerome and Dexter out of this."

"I was just kidding," said Danny. "Well, not really, maybe." He cracked a smile.

Marcus picked up his cell phone and just stared at it for a few seconds, as if his father's face had appeared on it. "I don't get it, Danny, I just don't get it," he said. "The things he said last night were so off, but at the same time, it was as though he knew a lot more about all of us than I would ever had imagined. It was like we've had some secret homophobic stalker or something. He knew things about me and about Johnny that we didn't even know about each other."

"Well, why are you having him over if he creeps you out?" Danny asked. "Why not just tell him to piss off?"

"I don't know, really," said Marcus. "Part of me says that I'm happy that he's trying, while the other half asks if it's already too late."

"Why is it too late?"

"Isn't it?"

"Is he still breathing?" Danny took a deep breath to emphasize his comment.

"I want to forget, I really do," Marcus began, "but sometimes I look at him and I just—" He stopped there. He couldn't articulate his next thought.

"What is it?" Danny prodded.

"I don't know," Marcus admitted. "I just don't know. Am I supposed to harbor this anger towards him my whole life? Is it even worth a minute of my time? Of *our* time? I just keep going back to the question of what he really wants, and why now? It does kind of creep me out, but in another way, it's allowing me peace in a way that I think I've been searching for, and for quite a long time. I don't know if you can understand it, but I just feel better letting the shit go, you know?"

"I think I do understand," said Danny, "and whether you become friends or not really isn't the point. The point is to rid yourself of that baggage that I've watched you carry for over two decades."

"You're a good man, Danny."

"I know."

"The proper reply was 'thank you.'"

"I know." Danny laughed as Marcus put up his fist. "It's quite simple, really, Marcus. In a split-second decision, without thinking, can you see yourself sitting in the same room with this guy, laughing at something?"

Marcus had to think. He wasn't sure how to answer the very simple question.

"Don't think," Danny said, "just answer."

"Yes," Marcus said.

"Why yes?"

"I'm not sure."

"You better get sure," said Danny, rolling his eyes, "because the doorbell just rang."

"Let him in, please."

"Are you sure? We can still turn the porch light out and pretend no one's home."

"Wow, are you mean!"

As Danny walked toward the front door to buzz his father in law inside, he said without turning around, "Last chance."

Marcus appreciated the humor, but he just replied, "Let him in, please." Marcus was nervous, and he couldn't tell why. Why did he care so much? Many things were racing through his head, but the big question was that: *Why did he care so much?*

After a minute or so after buzzing John into the building, Danny opened the front door to find his father-in-law only a few steps away. "Come on in, John," he said. He wasn't mean, nor was he glad. He just tried to keep his emotions out of it completely.

"Thank you, Danny," said John as he stepped inside. "This place looks even better with the sunlight coming through the windows."

Danny knew that flattering him about his apartment was about the easiest way to get on Danny's good side. "Thanks, John. Please come in and sit down. I'll get us all some drinks."

"Thanks, Danny," said Marcus, motioning for his father to sit in the living room where they'd been together just the night before.

John sat in the same chair as he had done the previous night, and he waited for Marcus to sit down across from him. "I guess you're wondering what brought me back so quickly?" he asked.

"I guess that would be a fair assumption," said Marcus. "Especially since last night didn't go as smoothly as I'd hoped it would."

"On the contrary, I thought it went amazingly."

"I guess you saw something I didn't?" said Marcus.

"I saw everything you saw," John confirmed. "I saw the hate, I saw the contempt. I even saw the revulsion in a few eyes."

"I'm confused, then."

"You sat and talked with me," said John. "You gave me the time of day, so to speak. That's all I saw."

Danny came in shortly afterward with a pitcher of orange juice, a bowl of ice, and a few glasses. "I hope I didn't miss anything juicy," he said.

Marcus spoke up. "My dad said that he thought last night went amazingly. He said the fact that we didn't kill him where he stood is a testament to how swimmingly the amazing night was." Marcus air quoted the last 'amazing.'

Danny was obviously a bit surprised by the look on his face, more like stupefied. "Really," he managed to say.

John said, "Yes, really."

Marcus had to say something. "Please explain."

John had to catch his breath. He was just so thrilled and happy that Marcus and Danny had let him back in. He took it all as a very good sign. "Where do I start?" he said. "I guess the beginning would be the right place."

"That would be preferable," said Marcus, "if it makes this vague thing that's going on a bit more clear."

Marcus sat back, as did Danny. Both were very curious to hear John's tale.

John took a deep breath, and then exhaled slowly. He wanted to be as honest as he knew how to be. It was the only way this was going to work. "I want to start off with saying I'm sorry to you Marcus, and I'm sorry to you too, Danny. I've said some shitty things to you both over the years. That being said, I wanted to explain all of this."

"Please do," said Danny. "I'm all ears." Danny wasn't trying to be sarcastic. He really was curious as to what this old fart could say to make any difference with regards to how he felt about him. *It would literally take an act of God*, Danny thought to himself.

"I hated my life after Betty died," John began, "but I think I hated my life before she died, too. I didn't understand why this had to happen to me. I didn't understand a whole lot of things, I think. I can sit here all day and just recite the 'I'm sorry' alphabet, but I know that I'm not going to do that. What I *am* going to do, however, is ask if we can start fresh. I'm not asking you to forget. I'm not asking you to just wipe everything away as if it didn't happen. But I'm asking both of you if I could in some way get to know you. Not just Marcus, but both of you. I want this very much."

Marcus blurted out, "But why? I mean, I'm not trying to be a colossal dick, but I just have to ask why. Do you have just one more month to live or something?"

"God, I hope not," said John. "I have a lot to do."

"Why now?" Danny chimed in. "You're saying you went from thinking queers were disgusting and untouchable to wanting to give us big hugs. There has to be a reason."

"I agree with Danny, Dad," said Marcus. "There has to be a reason."

John looked at Marcus and then at Danny, and then down at his glass of orange juice. "I guess it started a few years ago. I started going down to the park every morning, because my doctor said my back was bothering me because I had 'couchpotatoeitis.' It's a rare disease that only the lazy old farts like me get when they sit and sit and sit and never do anything but watch television. Well, anyway, I started going down to the park, and after a few weeks, my back started feeling a lot better. I even started feeling better in general, about everything. I fed the birds every morning. I fed them and watched the kids get taken to school every morning. I guess I just started thinking."

"About what?" Marcus was puzzled. What did all of this have to do with him?

"About feeling so utterly alone," John continued. "I had dozens of people walk past me, and some acknowledged me, but most did not. It made me feel like the last man on the planet. The suffocating, lonely feeling I felt made me do a lot of thinking. I thought about your mother a lot—a whole lot. Then I started thinking about you kids, and the question I kept coming back to was this: Was this how you felt? I thought about it a lot. I thought about my role in it, and how I had been just like those joggers who ran past me every morning."

John wanted to try and explain the regret that kept popping up in his mind. "I sat on that bench a lot, and I guess I just watched life go by. I saw kids with their parents, and people in general doing things besides sitting there throwing birdseed down to a bunch of pigeons and calling it life. I think I was existing, not living, and it wasn't until I listened to my friend Anthony that I realized I had to do something about it."

Marcus asked, "Is Anthony one of your friends in your building?"

"No, he's another old fart who comes down to the park a lot of mornings and drinks his tea, and just soaks in the atmosphere. Like myself, he gets claustrophobic sitting in that little box of an apartment. When you get old, the fastest way to air out is to walk around."

Danny had to smile at that one. He understood where his partner got his weird sense of humor from.

"At first, I thought he was this stuck-up snob who cared more about proper English and etiquette than anything else," said John, "but the more we sat there and bullshitted, the more he grew on me. He told me something one time that stuck with me, and even though I don't believe in God like he does—and oh boy, does he—I know he's a decent guy. He asked me why I kept coming down there when I could just as easily go see my son. I told him that you may not want to see me, but he was right. What did I have to lose? The worst was that you can say for me to go fuck off, and I figured I could live with that. Sometimes I really want to punch Anthony square in his jaw, but he's right. I'm tired of being a pissed off, self-pitying jackass who thinks it's everyone else's fault. It's mine, and I have to own it before I can fix it."

Danny said, "Wow, I'm speechless. I swore it would take an act of God to get me to buy your bullshit. Now that I know there is a God, I hope he's okay with the gays."

John laughed and joined in with Danny as he laughed as well. Marcus just looked bewildered. But then just watching them made him start to laugh, too. Not at what was said, exactly, but how these two were carrying on. It was like watching a mongoose and a cobra have a cup of coffee together.

After the laughter subsided and everyone took a drink of their juice, John said, "I guess you have a few thousand questions, but the reality is that you're either going to be okay with my explanation, or not. And the great thing about it is that either way, I will be okay. I know if I'm bringing you pain by being in the same room, then I should not be in the room. If I'm bringing harm and confusion to you in any way, I should remove myself from that. On the other hand, though, if you accept my apology, and you accept my explanation, then the three of us need to figure out what's next."

Danny looked over at Marcus. Then he said, "What do you see as your best case scenario, John?"

"It's easy, really. I want to get to know both of you, and when I step out of line, you can tell me so. If I say something that isn't nice, you tell me. I want you to stop treating me like an eighty-seven-year-old who needs to be coddled, and just tell me when I'm being an ass."

"Wow, Dad," said Marcus finally. "I don't know what to say."

"Me either, really, John," Danny agreed. He hadn't seen things going this way.

"What can I say?" said John. "I can't say 'let's forget about the past.' I can't say that I wasn't a shitty father, a shitty human being. What I can say, though, is that I would like to try starting today. I'd like to try not being all those things. I don't even expect you to give me an answer today. I just wanted you to know why."

"Did you stop at the ATM on the way over?" Danny asked.

"Danny, stop being a jerk." Marcus knew Danny was trying to break the awkwardness, but in his opinion, it wasn't working.

"No, Marcus, he's fine," said John. "He's not a jerk, and no, I did not stop at the ATM, because I actually came over to ask you for money. Surprise!"

Marcus, Danny, and John stared at each other for a split second and then all started laughing at the obvious attempt to break the awkward tension.

Danny said, between bouts of laughter, "See, Marcus, now *that* was a joke. Do you see the difference between his joke and yours?"

"What I see is an old fart named Danny sleeping on the couch tonight."

"Better," Danny admitted, "but not quite there." They all laughed out loud once more.

John composed himself and began to speak. "Look, Marcus, I said before that I'm not asking for anything from you or Danny, or any of the others. I'm asking for all of you to think about it and let me know what you think. If you want to hate me, then hate me. I get it. Danny, the same goes for you as well. I don't want you to do anything that you don't want to do or say. The same goes for John and Nikki. If you would do me one favor, please ask John and Nikki if they are willing to have this conversation as well. Maybe not today or tomorrow, or even next year, but if they ever want to talk about things, I would love to do so."

Danny leaned back, because he saw that Marcus had something to say. He took a sip of his drink, and he truthfully could not tell what Marcus was about to do.

John, too, saw the look on Marcus's face. "What is it?" he asked.

Marcus didn't know where to start. "Dad, I've been so mad at you for so long," he finally began, "and I don't even remember a day when I *wasn't* mad at you. No, scratch that, a day when I didn't hate you. I hated the way you made me feel about myself, and I hated the way you made me feel different, like I was broken and there was no way to fix me. It took decades to even come close to thinking that I deserved to be happy. This man here helped me through all that crap you had me drowning in, and he alone made me feel like I had worth. I don't know how to forgive that kind of pain. I want to. I want to so badly, but I don't know if I can. I know it's not what you wanted to hear, but I'm being as honest as you were. I can't say whether it could even go past a few laughs. You'll never know what it's like when you see the look in people's eyes when they look at you and you can tell that all they see is a gay man, a queer, a freak. Not Marcus Jacobi, but Marcus the fag, Marcus the queer. And truthfully, Dad, you never taught me how to handle those looks. You never gave me anything, really. I don't know if there are words to say or actions that can be taken to fix this. I don't know if I'm even strong enough to look at you without seeing that stuff first." Marcus stood up abruptly and said, "Excuse me." He ducked into the hall powder room.

Danny and John were left looking at each other. Danny wasn't sure he could add anything to what Marcus had said. "I'm sad to say," he began, "but a lot of what he just said is true for me as well. You have said some shit to me that would make me smack you upside the head if you weren't that man's father. I would like to think I could get past all that, but I'm like Marcus. I just don't know how."

John slowly got to his feet. He wasn't surprised, but he was happy that he'd found the courage to try. He didn't expect a red carpet or a welcome sign. He wanted to do this so that he could feel as though he wasn't that sniveling coward who would rather watch a grand kids' soccer game from way in the distance rather than do what he'd done here today. He was proud of himself. He felt good. Truthfully, it had been a long time since he'd felt that way about anything he'd done. "I'm really sorry I upset Marcus like that," he said finally. "That was not my intention."

"I know, John. I think I understand exactly why you came."

"I think I should go," said John, "and let you and Marcus enjoy the rest of your Sunday. There won't be too many gorgeous ones like this left."

Danny walked the old man to the front door and opened it. He felt oddly sorry that John was leaving. It wasn't something he could explain, nor even something he understood himself.

"Talk to you later, John," he said.

YOU SEEM HAPPY

Anthony was already on the bench when John walked up. Like always, he was sipping his tea and enjoying the ambiance, or so it seemed. John, as always, sat gingerly, and slowly on his side of the bench. "Wow, you seem to be is a good mood," said Anthony. "I take it you took my advice and stormed over there and made them open the door." Anthony grinned at the thought of this frail old man kicking a door in.

"No, I didn't bust the door in," said John, "but I'm glad I went over. I couldn't believe that not once, but *twice* we all busted out laughing together. I had such a good time."

"Wow, that sounds pretty good," said Anthony.

"Marcus told me that he hated the way I made him feel about himself, the way I made him feel different, like he was broken."

"Damn." Anthony shook his head. "So then why are you so damn chipper?"

"I don't know whether I can explain it or not," John began, "but even though he said he wasn't sure he could ever see anything besides pain when he looked at me, I felt good about myself. I owed him that purge. I have to be okay with the repercussions, even if that leads to me never seeing my son. It's weird, but just letting him unleash on me the way he did made me feel so much lighter. I feel like I needed to do that and hear that to move on, and he needed to say that to move on. Does this make any sense?"

Anthony nodded. "That's the best thing you could've done. You may never be best friends, and that's okay, but you won't be anything at all until both of you purge all of that negative shit out of your systems."

"Marcus did some purging, alright," John said, "and if it helped even a little bit, then I'm happy—no, I'm *delighted* to have helped him."

"What about the gay stuff?" Anthony asked. "How do you feel about it?"

"I don't know," John admitted. "But I don't see a gay son anymore when I look at Marcus. I just see my son. I see someone who I never got to know. I can't really explain all the changes, but I think it was this park. This park to me has given me a lot to think about. I created all that shit, and now it's up to me to undo it, or at least to try."

"I went through it with my kids, as you know," said Anthony. "We're good now, but it took a long time for me to call them without feeling that awkward silence. It killed me that I had to think of something fast so that the awkwardness wouldn't get too uncomfortable and they would find a reason to get off the phone. I know all too well what you're trying to describe."

"I just wish I'd of thought of this years ago," said John, "instead of crying in my beer because no one loved me. I think I was getting sick and tired of hearing my own tears hit the floor."

"So, what's next?"

"What do you mean?"

"What's next? Do I have to spell this out for you, too?"

"I guess so, because I'm stumped."

"Damn, you *are* thick," said Anthony. "So, if they don't contact you, then that's it? That's all?"

"Stop playing this 'riddle me this' crap and just tell me," said John.

"You have grandkids, jackass. Do you know anything about them? Do you *want* to know anything about them?"

"I never thought much about that, really. I never really thought I would get past the kids telling me to go fuck myself."

"Okay, but now that it seems you have," Anthony continued, "what next?"

"I will hit you if you keep saying that to me."

"Then answer the damn question. What do you want to do next?"

"I guess I would like to write each of my kids and each of my grandkids a letter, doing my own type of purge," said John, "and ask John Junior and Nikki if it's okay to get their address, I guess." John was still a bit hazy.

"Well, now that was easier than you thought, wasn't it?" said Anthony.

"I made it past the first hurdle with Marcus, but I haven't gotten very far with John, I'm afraid. He was pretty standoffish at dinner the other night."

"So, find out. Ask him. Stop waiting on shit to just happen. If you decide to take that path, you'll hate yourself, believe me."

"Experience in the matter?" asked John.

"Mucho experience," Anthony agreed. "Mucho grande."

"Now you're Spanish?"

"Da." Anthony smiled.

John smiled back. "I know Johnny is down here for a few days. I'll reach out to Marcus tonight and ask him to ask John to give me a call, or if I can call him."

"See, now that path was hard to get through, but it wasn't *that* hard. Right? I said, right?"

"Yeah, right." John was deep in thought. What if Johnny said no? Or what if he said that it was okay to talk to him, but not to his kids?

Anthony could tell that John was somewhere else in his mind. "Can I stop you right now? Don't live in the what-ifs, please, it will only drive you crazy."

"More experience in the matter, I take it?" said John.

"Da," Anthony agreed.

"Yeah, I have to get out of my head. I'll do everything I can to make things better, but living in that what-if world will definitely do no one any good."

"Good. So, what's next?"

"I swear to God—"

"I'm just kidding," said Anthony, laughing. "God, you're like a ball of rubber bands ready to snap, but don't snap over here, please."

John threw the last bit of seed he'd brought on the ground for the birds. "I'm going to write a few letters tonight," he said, "and I can't do them sitting here. Thanks for the advice, and thanks for listening to an old man whine about his troubles."

Anthony watched as John got himself and his belongings together. It was not a quick process by any means, but it was a fun one to watch. "You're welcome, my friend. I hope it all works out for you."

"Tomorrow?" John asked.

"Sure, why not," Anthony agreed.

John turned when he was only a few feet away from their meeting spot. "See you tomorrow," he said.

"Dasvidanya."

"Really?"

"Nyet?"

"Goodbye," John said with a chuckle as he walked away.

YOU NEED YOUR OWN PATH

Nikki and Johnny had been battling between passive aggressive and silent treatment techniques. Neither was happy with the other, but they both knew that at some point, it was going to need to come out. The jabs, the anger, the looks that could kill. It wasn't long when a knock came on Nikki's hotel door. She was surprised, because she wasn't expecting anyone. She went to the door and opened it, but the face on the other side was not a face she was hoping to see. It was a face that said bad news was coming.

"Come in," she said reluctantly.

Johnny walked past his sister but remained standing near the door. "We need to talk," he said.

"Okay." Nikki knew the beginning of a breakup when she heard one.

"I've been doing a lot of thinking the past few days," Johnny began, "and I have to get it off my chest." He was rushing his words to get it over with.

"Okay. What do you want?" But Nikki knew.

"I keep thinking a lot about what Dad said the other day. About how he stayed away from us because he thought it was healthier for us. I thought at the time what horseshit that was. He was a coward, and he was hiding behind that crap. The more I thought about it, though, the more I realized how I was doing the same thing with my kids, even though I thought I was justified. I don't hear from my kids more than twice a year, and I keep blaming them. Now I need to break this cycle once and for all. If Dad can let us unleash on him like we did, then I have to do the same."

"Okay, but what about me?" asked Nikki.

John wanted to scream at her and tell her to stop being such a fucking narcissistic drama queen, but he didn't. He just simply said, "You need to find a place to live, and soon. I'll help with what I can, but my plans are taking a different path than yours, and you need to find your own." John was tired of screwing around with this leech. He hated feeling that way, but it was the only true way to describe his sister.

"How the hell am I going to do that, Johnny?" Nikki asked, raising her voice. "How am I supposed to just up and find a place to live?"

"I've been thinking about that a bit, too," said Johnny. "What if I got hit by a bus tomorrow and got my brains splattered all over the road? What would you do then? Whatever that is, I need you to act out that scenario."

"God, Johnny—"

"What, Nikki, what would you do?"

"I don't know," she said finally, her shoulders slumping.

"You need to find out, and you need to do it quickly," said Johnny. "My journey is a solo one, sis. I need to be closer to them if we're ever going to make this work. I'm going to sell my house and move to Chicago, where Tina and David and Erica are. I'm going to do what Dad did while they're in their thirties and forties instead of waiting until they're retired. I hope you can understand."

"You're a good Dad."

"Don't do that, Nikki. Don't do that thing you do to gain allies. I'm not your enemy, but don't do that."

"Okay, fine." Nikki was starting to sweat. What was she going to do now? She knew she had no chance in hell of moving in with Danny and Marcus. It was obvious what Danny thought of her.

"We'll stay here a few more days," said Johnny. "You have some thinking to do. Do you want to stay here in South Carolina? Do you want to go back to Maryland? Wherever you decide to go, I'll help you get a security deposit paid and first month's rent, but after that, you're on your own. I hope you can understand that I need to do this for me and my kids. It's not about me, and it's not about you."

Nikki didn't understand, nor did she care to. She wanted to punch her brother in the face for doing this to her. She wanted to get him to change his mind and go back to the way things were. "How about you move to

Chicago, and I'll house sit until the place is sold," she suggested. "That way, you can start on your path a little bit earlier."

Johnny wasn't going to let her get him upset, but at the same time, her audacity was off the charts sometimes. "No, I think it's best that you get your own place as soon as possible. We both have a lot of stuff to do to get on to our next adventure."

"What adventure?" Nikki asked. "The one where my brother makes me homeless?"

"Don't do that either, Nikki. I'm not one of your husbands."

"What the hell does that mean?"

"Don't be a stupid bitch on top of a greedy one, okay?" He almost couldn't believe that the words came out of his mouth. He sighed. "I'm sorry," he said. "You're my sister and always will be, but you're not my responsibility. Being everyone's savior got me into this mess with Tina and my kids. Now it's time I break that cycle and let you fend for yourself."

"Okay, Johnny." She wasn't happy in the least, but it was evident that Johnny wasn't going to budge.

"On another subject, Marcus called me earlier," said Johnny. "He said Dad came over Sunday morning, and they had a talk. Just the three of them."

"What for?" Nikki asked.

"Marcus said that he wasn't like our dad at all. This guy was open to things, and Marcus said the whole thing was completely weird."

"Wow."

"Yeah," said Johnny. "He asked Marcus to have us to come back to their house and have Dad over again, and he asked how we felt about it. He called back again today, and Dad asked if he was allowed to write his grandkids a letter. I almost shit myself when he said that."

"What did you say?" asked Nikki.

"I told him it was fine, and to give them their address. I told him he doesn't need my permission to write to his grandchildren. They're grown adults."

"Still kind of weird, though."

"Way weird," Johnny agreed. "It was one of the things that got me thinking about everything, about what my son would say if I asked him whether I could write his four year old a letter. Honestly, sis, I hope I never have to have that conversation with either of my kids. It scares the hell out of me."

"So, what do you want to do?"

John wasn't going to be sucked into an argument where Nikki could play the helpless victim. "I'm going to go over to Marcus's house tomorrow night for drinks. I think Dad is going to be there. If you don't want to come, no one is going to think any less of you."

"Can I go with you?" Nikki asked.

"Of course," said Johnny, "you're more than welcome. I need to tell Marcus and Danny what I told you. I think for me and my kids, and even my relationship with Tina, I think I need to do this, and do it before winter comes. Chicago is a cold bitch come January. I've reached out to my kids. I'm not expecting any great homecoming, but I'm going to move closer to them regardless."

"I understand," Nikki began, "and I'll do my best to get a place as quickly as I can. I appreciate your help and everything you've done for me." It was some of her best acting, she thought, because what she really wanted to do was scratch Johnny's eyes out for what he was doing to her. He was leaving her in a bind, betraying her, and she knew he didn't even care. He didn't love her, because if he did, he wouldn't be doing this to her. It was just that simple.

"I'm glad to hear you say that," said Johnny. He didn't believe a word of it, but it was going to have to do. "Once you find a place, let me know how much the rent is, and when you can get your stuff out of the house."

"Okay, but today, let's do something just the two of us," Nikki suggested. "How about we go get a burger from that burger joint down the street? After that, tomorrow, we will go see Marcus and Dad, and see what he wants." As she said it, she thought that maybe her father would give her an early inheritance. She decided that this area looked like a good place to live. There was no way she was going to find a rich husband in this town, but she may be able to find a guilt-ridden father willing to buy her forgiveness.

"Okay, my treat," said Johnny.

"Of course, silly." Nikki grabbed her bag and followed her brother out the door. How much could she get him to help her with, she wondered. She knew that if he sold that rancher in Maryland that he would have plenty of money to help her out. Selling the house just became a much better idea, in Nikki's estimation.

IN THE PAST FEW WEEKS

Marcus had found his mind wandering more and more the past week or two. He'd never dreamed in a million years that his life would have taken the turn that it had. He found himself calling his father just to say hi, and that in itself was incredibly strange. And he didn't know why, but it made him feel better. He wasn't sure what was going to happen with this new undertaking, but it was something he felt needed doing.

He had been talking with his dad, and at times he felt like that little kid talking about the things in life that a father talked to a son about. Since he didn't have any kids of his own, it was odd talking to his father about certain things. His father had no issue talking to him about his ailments, or his doctors' appointments, and for some odd reason, it gave him a feeling of trust. It gave him a feeling of being at ease, a feeling he was so desperately trying to reach with some of the more distant kids at the club.

Most of the kids who Marcus dealt with were transition house kids who'd just gotten out of rehab or were trying desperately to not feel so alone in this world. He tried to make them feel like they had at least one friend who was there for them.

Marcus's father made him feel that way in an awkward, 'I don't know what to say' kind of way. He told story after story about when his mother was alive, anything to keep the conversation going. In a way, Marcus truly enjoyed the stories. He heard things about his father and mother that he couldn't believe. He wished he could write down some of the stories and maybe make up a collection, because some of them were very funny and entertaining. He enjoyed the ones about when his father was a kid and making a dime a day, and how he had to walk uphill both ways carrying a bag of rocks while having an itch he couldn't scratch. All those stories about how tough he'd had it made Marcus laugh. Not because of his father's ordeal, but the animated way in which he told the story. He didn't remember his father being such a good story teller, but maybe that skill was acquired later in life.

There was the flip side to that, though, because there were times when he just wanted to scream into the phone about what a lousy piece of shit his father was and how he wanted to hate him so much. In his mind, he wandered off as his father recalled yet another memory from when he was a kid, during which he couldn't help but imagine his father being hit by a truck, with Marcus behind the wheel. As time went on, this was becoming less and less frequent, but Marcus knew that those thoughts may never leave completely, all because he chose to be gay.

Now it was time to be the good son. He was on his way over to his father's house now to help him with the groceries that he'd just bought for him. He couldn't believe that he was now getting his father stuff from the store. But his father had fallen and twisted his knee, and he called to ask if Marcus would do him a favor, which almost floored Marcus right on the spot. He wasn't sure whether to be flattered that his old man thought that they'd reached that level of friendship, or find it a bit too fast and off-putting. He was somewhere in the middle, still, but for some odd reason, he agreed to go get him a few cans of beef stew, a few bananas, and a loaf of bread. It didn't seem like a whole lot, but as Marcus caught the two bags sitting in the passenger seat, he knew they were more than just a small favor.

This was a turning point, he knew, and Marcus wanted so badly to feel like it was a good thing. So then why did he feel a knot in his stomach? Was hating him so familiar that he didn't want to lose something he'd almost always had? It was almost like losing an old friend in some ways. Did he not believe that his father deserved forgiveness? What was it that kept him from giving in completely?

Marcus stared at the groceries, but still nothing came to him. He had hoped that the message that would give him all the answers was written on the bag, but unfortunately nothing was untying that knot in his stomach.

REDEMPTION

Was he letting Danny down if he decided to not hate his father anymore? He and Danny had talked about it at length, and he'd come to the conclusion that Danny felt that John was the kind of family member that you weren't going to change no matter what. He was the uncle who said racist things. He was the one you were never going to get to admit he was wrong. Marcus was okay with that, because Danny had stuck up for John recently, and Marcus almost fell to the floor when it happened.

No matter how much he wondered, or how much he pondered, Marcus never really felt that there was ever going to be an answer that sat well in his gut. He was going to be nice to his father. He was going to call him every week or so. But the level of attachment and bonding that they would have would always feel superficial to Marcus. He hoped he was wrong, but it was the only variable that seemed to fit the puzzle.

Marcus pulled up to the parking garage in front of his father's fifty-five or older community. It wasn't a bad housing development, but it was not cheery or even inviting. It was like a can of sardines, and all of the sardines, including his father, were just sitting in rows waiting to be thrown away. He felt kind of bad for all the tenants who didn't have the mobility that his father did. He could get up and walk a fair bit before having to stop. According to him, he only stopped a time or two before getting to the park, which was almost a half mile or so from his development.

As Marcus pulled into the space nearest his father's door, he grabbed the two bags of groceries and quickly exited the car. He had to get home fairly soon, or else he was going to get an earful from Danny about being late for dinner. He wouldn't be that upset, but he would rag Marcus all night until he said he was sorry, and he didn't feel like hearing that tonight. He just wanted to go inside, plop the groceries down, and get home.

When he knocked on the door, he heard his father yell, "Come in." Marcus slowly opened the door and peeked in. "Where are you?" he asked.

"I'm in the bedroom. Just leave the groceries on the counter, and I'll put them away later."

Marcus did as he was told. He took out each can of soup and stacked them neatly. "I got everything you asked for. I'm going to leave the bread and all in the bag."

"That sounds great," John said.

Marcus peeked his head in his father's room to say goodbye, but then he exclaimed, "Holy fuck, Dad!"

"What?" asked John. "It's not as bad as it looks."

"The hell it ain't, Dad. You look like you just got out of surgery."

"It's not that bad," John said again.

"What the hell did you do?"

"I told you, I fell."

"Under a moving bus?" Marcus asked, incredulous.

"No, I fell in the kitchen," said John.

"Then why do you have a knee brace on with a heating pad wrapped around it, and a walker sitting next to the bed?"

"The doctor said I sprained a ligament, or some shit. All I know is that it hurts like a fucking toothache."

"What doctor? You didn't say anything about a damn doctor. You just said you twisted your knee."

"I didn't tell you about the time I bit my fingernail down to the quick, either," said John, "but you know what, it happened, and it hurt like a son of a bitch, too."

"Dad, what the hell happened?" Marcus said. "Seriously."

"I fell doing dishes," said John. "I bent down to pick up a dish towel that I'd dropped, and I bent my knee the wrong way and fell. The end."

"No, what else happened?" Marcus insisted.

"Okay fine, here goes." John looked down at his obviously mangled leg and rubbed the brace right above the knee. "I did fall. But the part I left out is that I spent four hours on the floor in pain. Each time I tried to lift myself up, it put pressure on the knee, so I went back down to stop the pain."

"How the hell did you end up getting up?" Marcus asked.

"I heard the toilet flush next door and I started yelling and banging on the wall," John said. "I finally got someone's attention, I guess, because Sarah, my neighbor, peeked in and saw me laying there on my back with the dish towel over my eyes. She didn't want to hurt me, so she called the rescue squad. They finally got me to my feet and took me to the hospital.

The guy said some things, but I couldn't understand everything he said. I think he was from Pakistan, or one of those countries."

"Dad, stay on topic," said Marcus, annoyed by the comment.

"I'm just saying I didn't understand everything he told me," John said, "but I did understand that I had a severely sprained ligament and I needed to go to a rehab center for a few weeks."

"So, why aren't you there?"

"Have you ever been in one of those places? Worse than death, as far as I'm concerned. I think I would rather shoot myself in the head with an elephant gun first. Besides, I will get better eventually, and the hospital has the physical therapist coming twice a week. An old man like me doesn't bounce back like a spring chicken."

"Are you able to get up?" Marcus asked.

"Sure."

"Indulge me, please."

John rocked himself back and forth until he could get his elbow underneath him. He grabbed the knee brace with the other hand and swung his entire leg over the empty air, and then lowered it slowly, very slowly, to the carpet. "See, no problem."

"You were so slow, you'll piss yourself by the time you get yourself up and into the bathroom."

"Who says I haven't?" John said. "I'm old. Old people piss a lot. I mean, *a lot.*"

"Dad!"

"Dad what?" John said, waving Marcus away. "When I get better, I'll buy a new bed. I have a few dollars sitting in the bank yearning to be released back into the wild."

"Do you need something to drink?"

"No, I'm good, I have my bottle of water here."

Marcus noticed the bottle of water on the nightstand. "Can you get up?" he asked.

"Yeah, I use my walker," John said, "and I just put the bare minimum of weight on my leg, and I get around pretty good. I go out and fix myself some soup, or microwave a burrito. I'll be okay in a week or two. I'll be glad when I'm back to normal, though. This leg sometimes hits me with a pain that make my eyes go shut and my nose hairs curl up."

Marcus couldn't believe what he was seeing. Is this what the tenants here were like every day? He felt bad for them. His father may not have had much before, but he had his health. He could walk and he could go places, but now he was just another old man stuck in his house and laying in his own piss. It broke Marcus's heart.

He walked over to where his television was sitting and pulled out the two drawers underneath. Then he grabbed a pair of socks and a few pair of boxers, and he started to make a pile of clothes on top of the dresser. He grabbed a few pair of sweat pants and a few T-shirts.

"What are you doing?" asked John.

"You are staying with me and Danny until you can walk normal," Marcus insisted.

"That's very nice of you, but I will be okay, honest," said John.

"But you will be better than okay, and you'll get that way at our house."

"It's okay, Marcus, you don't owe me anything. You don't have to feel guilty." The gesture had meant the world to John, even if in reality he knew it wasn't going to happen. Danny would never let it.

"Did I ask you?" said Marcus. "No, I'm telling you. Get your old wrinkled ass up and get your meds together, and start making your way to the front door. Put anything you want or might need for the next two weeks where I can get to them, so that we don't have to come back here until you can take care of yourself again."

"But I have to get my mail," said John.

"I'll stop by every few days and get your mail. Any other reason you need to stay here?"

John was stunned. He hadn't expected this, nor did he really want it. He didn't want to be a burden or make anyone feel awkward, even his own son. "Marcus, I think you're thinking with your heart and not your head. I will be fine."

Marcus groaned. "Get your shit together before you leave here with me dragging that damn knee brace behind me. I'm going to be late for dinner, and I better have a damn good reason for being late, and taking you home may be the one excuse that gets me to not hear Danny's lip, okay?"

John reached for the walker and pulled himself upright. The whole past five minutes had been completely surreal to him, like something from a dream.

Marcus grabbed the clothes and carried them to the small end-table near his father's front door. He turned and spotted the plastic bag that he'd brought in from the grocery store. He began to stuff the smaller items of clothing into the bag. "Do you need any help moving around?" he asked.

John hobbled out of the bedroom with his walker and with a few things tucked into the basket. "I'm fine," he said. He hobbled over to the refrigerator and pulled out the medication that he would need for the next week or so. He put that in his basket as well. "I think that's everything I need."

"Okay," said Marcus. "Grab that plastic bag on the counter and put everything you want to take with you inside it, and let's get going. Don't forget your keys, in case I need to come back for something."

"Okay." John inched his way toward the front door. He still couldn't believe that this was really happening.

Marcus also couldn't believe it. His mind was racing about what was he doing and what Danny was going to say. How was he ever going to make this up to Danny?

"I'm going to pull the car up close to your front door. I'll run back and help you get to the car. You'll definitely need some help getting down those three steps to the sidewalk." Marcus ran out the door and was gone in a flash.

John couldn't put into words how he felt about what was transpiring. He was playing out so many scenarios in his head, trying not to get ahead of himself. He didn't know what was going to happen, but he was elated, to say the least. He didn't want to be alone in this apartment anymore, and even though his friendship with Marcus and Danny was still in its infancy, he was willing to take the chance of screwing everything up rather than stay in this apartment by himself one more minute.

By the time John got to the front door and grabbed his keys off the hook, he could hear someone coming down the hall of his building. He opened the door to see his son walking up to his door. "Wow, you sure are quick, for an older guy," said John.

"I still have my girlish figure for a reason, Dad." And before he let his father pass into the hallway, he added, "Are you sure you have everything?"

"I have my pills, I have my insulin, I have my clothes, and I have my ass," said John, "so, yep, I think I have everything." He patted his butt on his way out the door, and he turned the knob to make sure it was locked. "Let's roll," he said.

Marcus walked slowly alongside his father in his walker. "I think we need to stop and get you a walker that you can actually sit on," he suggested, "so that when you get tired, you don't fall down."

"This one was good enough for my grandfather," John said with a light chuckle.

"Stop arguing with me. We'll stop at the pharmacy on the way to the house and get you one from this century. The one you're using should be on the *Antiques Roadshow* or something."

"Okay, fine," John said.

Marcus and his father finally reached the door leading to the outside of the apartment building. There were three small steps, and then the sidewalk, and then a few feet from there would be Marcus's car. Marcus opened the door and let his father walk out onto the landing before he reached the first step. "Okay," he said. "You lean on me, and then we can get down these few steps."

"Okay, just give me a minute to get my balance." John was scared that he was going to tumble down the steps and find himself face-first on the sidewalk.

"Take your time," said Marcus. "Just lean on me."

John did as he was told, leaning against his son when he let his left leg down onto the step. It wasn't easy, but they made it to the sidewalk. John let out a big breath like he'd been holding it in the whole time he was descending the steps.

"Breathe, Dad, breathe. Don't pass out on me here."

"I'm fine, I just need a second."

"Take two or three." After two or three seconds had passed, Marcus said, "Okay, that's good. Now let's get going." Then, after seeing his father's face, he blurted out, "Just kidding!"

"Danny was right, Marcus," said John. "Your jokes are no good."

"Do you want to be left here, old man?"

"If I go, will your jokes kill me, or will the leg?"

"Neither," said Marcus. "I will."

"Pillow, please."

"You got it." Marcus walked John over to the car and opened up the door. He pushed the seat back as far as it would go, and he helped his father get his butt onto the passenger seat and then swung his leg around and into the car so that Marcus could close the door. With a lot of grunting, panting, and cussing from both parties, the leg was finally in place. Marcus threw everything in the back seat and secured the door, then ran to the other side.

Marcus climbed into the car and started the engine. He drove a nice luxury Cadillac, and he figured it was a good thing it was a larger car, or he would never have gotten his father inside. He sat there for a few seconds to catch his breath. Then he took his hand off the keys in the ignition and turned to his father. "Are you ready?"

"Do I have a choice?" asked John.

"Not really." Marcus pulled up to the stop sign, leaving his father's apartment complex, and he looked left and right, waiting for an opening to jump out onto the main road. His mind was racing. What on earth was he going to say to Danny when he got home? What on earth would make logical sense? He couldn't defend this decision other than to say that he was helping out someone who obviously needed it.

He pulled out to his left and headed down to the Walgreens around the corner to get his father a new walker. He didn't know how this was going to affect his relationship with Danny. He didn't even know if this was the right thing to do. But the one thing he did know for sure was that he had to do it. The knot in his stomach, or the lack thereof, told him more than anything that what he was doing had to be right.

LOOK WHAT I BROUGHT HOME

Marcus helped his father out of the car and up the few steps to the entrance to his own building. It was a bit easier going up than it was going down, for sure. Once they reached the top of the steps, Marcus put his key in the lock and opened the door to the brownstone. His condo was not far, and with this new walker, he was more confident that his father would survive the trek.

They walked the carpeted hallway slowly but steadily until they reached 2G. Marcus looked at his father and said, "Ready?"

"Do I have a choice?" asked John.

"Still no."

"Then, I guess I am."

They were both nervous and uncertain about what was about to happen. Danny could fly into a rage right then and there, or just wait until Marcus and Danny were alone to do it, but neither were prepared for the door opening up just as they approached it.

Danny looked at both of them in turn, and then looked down at John's leg. He didn't say anything other than, "Get your butts in here."

"How did you know we were out there?" asked Marcus.

"You two sounded like two bullhorns out there."

"Dad is a bit hard of hearing at times." Marcus was kind of relieved to not be facing the onslaught he'd been expecting. He was sure he would receive it later, though.

"So, John, how long are you staying at the D&M rehab center?" Danny asked.

"I guess that is kind of up to D & M?" said John.

"So, until you get better, I guess?" Danny was not curt or upset; rather, he just knew what had been placed in front of him, and he dealt with it. "Let me go put your stuff in the guest room," he added.

Marcus wondered if it would have been better to just deal with the meltdown now and get it over with. "Thanks, Danny," he said cautiously.

Marcus and his father watched as Danny disappeared around the corner. They looked at each other with what could only be described as pure confusion.

John sat on the seat of the walker and pushed himself into the living room. He was glad that the apartment was all hardwood flooring, which would make it so much easier to get around. He sat there waiting for directions.

After shaking the cobwebs from his brain, Marcus asked, "Will you excuse me for a minute, Dad?" He left the room in the same direction that Danny had gone.

John wasn't stupid—he knew that Marcus had gone to find out why Danny wasn't going bonkers over this. He would've probably done the same thing.

Marcus found Danny in the guest room putting fresh pillow cases on the pillows. He stood and watched as Danny just tidied up the room, as though Marcus wasn't even there. "Are we going to address this eighty-seven-year-old elephant in the room?" he finally asked.

"What's there to say?" Danny never raised his head.

"Please talk to me, yell at me, scream at me. Do something, but stop ignoring me." Marcus was ready for whatever was going to be thrown at him. He knew he deserved it.

"Marcus, you stupid ass, I'm not mad at you," said Danny.

"Why not?"

"Why should I be? We talked about this weeks ago, and we're not holding onto the grudges anymore. We're not feeding the hate and anger any longer. We talked about all that, remember? Do you want to forget about it and move on, or don't you?"

"I do, I really do," said Marcus, "but you are not mad at all?"

"I would have liked some warning, but in my heart of hearts I knew you were going to bring him home one day and ask if he could live with us," said Danny. "It was just in the cards, and not really that hard to predict. I didn't know you were going to have to break his leg to get him in here, but I'm okay with it as long as he behaves himself."

"I gave him that lecture on the way over here," Marcus said, feeling incredibly relieved that Danny was okay with this turn of events.

"So, who broke his leg?" asked Danny. "I mean, there must be hundreds of suspects." Danny gave Marcus a sly grin.

"No one broke his leg. He just fell in the kitchen. His leg bent the wrong way, yadda yadda yadda, and he tore a ligament, I think. He said he was like that for four hours before someone got him up and to a hospital."

"Holy shit." Danny winced in imagined pain. "That must have hurt like a son of a bitch."

"Yeah, it almost broke my heart to hear," Marcus agreed. "I felt so bad for the old dude. I could tell when he told the story that he realized how alone he was. And not just because he lives alone. I mean, *really* alone."

"Yeah, I get you. That must have been some eye-opening shit."

"I imagine it was."

"Let's get him in here so he can get settled and maybe take a nap or something," said Danny. "People his age love naps."

"Shit, then I must be his age, because I love some good afternoon napping, too."

In the living room, John saw a figure appear out of the hallway, and he saw that it was Danny, with Marcus close behind. He wasn't sure whether his welcome was worn out before it even began, or if he was going to get to stay. He was ready for both possibilities. "What's the word, boys?" he asked.

Danny cleared his throat and said, "The word is, John, that you are going to stay here until you get better, and then you can decide what you want to do. I'm not making you stay, but I'm not asking you to leave, either. I think you should stay here with us until you can get a clean bill of health from your doctor. That's what I think." Danny bent over and grabbed the few bags that were sitting next to John's walker. "Let's get you into the guest room, show you where the toilet is, and educate you on flushing and washing your hands."

"I'm okay with everything you said, Danny," said John. "Speaking of which, where is the bathroom? Old people have to pee a lot, or so my bladder keeps telling me."

Marcus gestured down the hallway. "Come on, Dad, I'll show you where everything is."

"Marcus, I am sure your father knows where everything is at," Danny joked, "and he should be the only one."

John cracked a smile. "I know where it's at, but it's just harder to find."

Marcus just stared in disbelief. He wasn't sure what was going on, but he knew at any moment that someone was going to pop out and yell surprise, because he had to be on some reality television show. It's the only possibility that made even a little bit of sense.

Danny and John got a chuckle out of watching Marcus. Then Danny pushed Marcus out of the way so that he could help John get to the bathroom himself, if Marcus wasn't going to do it. The two left Marcus standing confusedly in the living room alone.

When Danny made it to the bathroom, he opened the door and let John move slowly past. "Holler if you get stuck," he said.

"I'm not one hundred percent sure, but I think I can do this," said John.

Danny stood by the bathroom door in case he was needed. He didn't want to hear an old man peeing, but there was little choice in the matter.

Danny couldn't help but like this guy a bit. Even though he was once a homophobic, racist piece of shit, he was fun to joke with. He knew he shouldn't be feeling this way, but he just couldn't help it. All of his being wanted to hate this guy, wanted to have nothing to do with him, but he was literally like a totally different person now. He was jovial. He was empathetic. He was courteous. Danny just hoped that this was all really true, and not just some game John was playing.

Danny's daydream was disturbed by the flushing of the toilet. A few seconds later, he could hear John trying to get the door open, in spite of the walker being in the way.

"Do you need some help?" asked Danny.

"Can you push the door open, please?" John stepped back to give the door enough clearance. After the door was opened up and pushed against the wall, John had plenty room to get out then. "Thank you," he said.

"No problem." Danny stood there in case the old man needed some help, but it was obvious that it hadn't taken him long to figure out how to sit on the walker and push himself with the other leg. "Seems you got a walker that is perfect for this kind of injury," Danny added. "I need one of them for when I get tired after cleaning the house."

"Marcus just bought me this at the pharmacy on the way over," John said. "As soon as I get him to tell me how much it was, I'll make sure he gets it back."

"Don't be dumb, John, Marcus has more money than he knows what to do with," said Danny. "It's okay to let him spend some of it." They weren't really so well off as he had made it sound, but to those of John's generation, it was easier to accept help if you thought someone had money. It was just how they thought.

"I would still like to pay him back," John insisted.

"John, I'll add it to the bill when you leave," Danny said. "I'll write up the meals and the room and board, and my time, and a third of the electric bill, and I'll add the price of the walker on there, too."

"I can't tell whether you're serious or not, but you don't—"

"John, please stop being a jackass, pretty please," said Danny. "If we get to the point where we can't afford the light bill, I promise you'll be the first one we come to, okay?"

John said reluctantly, "Okay."

"Now, let's get you into your room and show you all the goodies."

"Goodies?"

"Yeah," said Danny. "Snacks, towels, and wash clothes are in the dresser. They're all in there if you know where to look."

Marcus walked up behind the two men. He didn't say anything or offer any help. He just stayed out of the way. He had seen Danny like this before. He knew that Danny loved taking care of people. He was a great host, whether it be at the dinner table or to an overnight guest. No one ever came closer to perfection, as far as Marcus was concerned.

Danny turned to see Marcus standing in the doorway. "John, here are the snacks in this drawer," he said, "and I'll put your clothes in this second drawer. The washcloths and towels are in the third drawer." Danny pulled the clothes out of the two plastic grocery bags and placed them neatly in the second drawer.

"Thanks," said John.

"Can I help you get in bed, or do you want to hang out in the living room for a while?" Danny asked.

"If you don't mind, I think I would like to close my eyes for a minute or two," said John. "I have to take my pain pill, and oh yeah, if the physical therapist calls tomorrow, can I give them this address to come to?"

"Of course." Danny pushed the drawers shut and helped John put his leg up on the bed to get a bit more comfortable. "Good?"

"I think so, thank you."

"You're welcome," said Danny. "Just holler if you need anything. Give me your phone." Danny held out his hand and John pulled out his phone from his shirt pocket, handing it to Danny.

"A flip phone, John, really?" Danny joked. He flipped the phone open, called his own phone number, and then added it to John's contacts. "Now I'm in your contacts, and if you need anything, you can call me if I don't hear you bellowing my name."

"Thanks again, Danny." John was extremely touched. All the fears and phobias and prejudices he'd had in the past, and all the anxieties he had about coming over there, were simply fading away. How could he ever have hated this person? He realized now just how deep his ignorance went.

"You're welcome," said Danny. "Have a good nap."

Danny walked out past Marcus and closed the door until it was mostly shut, but not completely. Marcus followed Danny out into the living room, past the couch, and into the kitchen. He was still kind of stunned. No matter how much they had talked about burying the past, Danny was actually doing it—or so it appeared. "What was that?" he asked. "*Who* was that?"

Danny didn't even look at Marcus as he continued to open up cabinets and the refrigerator, and then the freezer doors. "What?" he said innocently.

"Don't give me that shit, Danny. Stop fidgeting, please, and tell me what the hell that was."

"I thought we went over this."

"Please stop, Danny." Marcus had raised his voice, which he did not do very often, especially with Danny.

"What the hell do you want to know, Marcus?" Danny asked, exasperated.

"I want to know what that was," Marcus insisted.

Danny closed the last cabinet door more slowly and softly than the ones he'd been closing before. Then he turned to look at his beloved Marcus. He let out a sigh and said, "Okay, fine." Danny walked from behind the kitchen island and over to the table. "Sit, please." Danny waited as Marcus came over and sat in the chair across from him.

Marcus was a bit surprised, and definitely confused. What the hell was Danny about to say? Marcus assumed it would start off with anger or frustration, and he was ready for that. He'd been going over it in his mind while Danny and his father were playing in the bathroom. "Okay, scream and yell," he said now, "just get it over with."

"I don't want to scream," said Danny. "I don't want to yell. I don't want to fight. If this is what you want, I support you. I know you wouldn't have brought him here unless you wanted him here, and that's all that I need to know."

Nothing more was said, but after a few seconds, Danny realized that he had one last thing that he wanted to say. "Marcus, do you know what you're doing? I mean, do you really know what you're doing with John?"

"What do you mean?"

"What I mean is," Danny began, "that during the past few weeks, I've seen you happy. I mean *really* happy. The weight of hate seems to be lifted, and the look has done wonders for your complexion. I'm not going to tell you that what you're doing is wrong. It doesn't matter what I think anymore. It matters that you've found peace with it, and him, and that I will always support. I don't have to like him, or love him, or even want to talk with him. I just know that whatever the two of you have going on is good for you, and that's all I need to know. You should stop worrying so much about when I'm going to blow, because I'm not. And even if I do, that will be between him and I, and not you. Even if he's the greatest guy in the world, someone may still get upset with him for something. Just being an old fart gets some people upset." Danny finished with a big wide smile, indicating to Marcus that everything was fine.

Marcus outstretched his hand so that he and Danny's fingers could interlock. "Wow," he said. "I don't even know what to say."

"It's not that hard to follow the pieces," said Danny. "You two have talked like two sixteen-year-old kids getting ready to go to prom."

"I think you're overexaggerating a bit, don't you think?"

"Not really," said Danny with a shrug. "I hear you talking to him in the morning, and at least once at night. I'm not saying I don't like it. I'm saying it's making you happy, and because you're happy, I am too. Besides, I might even like the old fucker."

I WISH YOU LUCK

Johnny was glad to be away from Maryland, even if it was only just for a short while. He was actually more happy to be away from Nikki. He hated leaving her in the lurch, but he needed to do this, and his kids, David and Erica, were a hundred times more important to him than whether or not Nikki's feelings were hurt. It had been almost a month since he'd been down to South Carolina, and he had to admit that there had been a kind of peace down there that he never saw in Maryland. He assumed it was just from being around calming, pleasant people like Marcus and Danny.

He wanted to let Marcus and Danny know about his plans to move, but more importantly, he wanted some ceasefire between himself and Nikki. She was stuck in her pity party mode, and he was just getting sick of hearing how life was so hard for her. He needed to get away, and since Chicago was not his home yet, he decided to just sit back and sip mint juleps with his brother.

He couldn't do such a thing in Maryland, after all, not with his sister constantly knocking on his door and asking for handouts. His mind kept telling him that if he stuck with her, he was going to procrastinate until his whole life passed him by. The sooner he left town and sold the house, the sooner Nikki would have to leave.

Johnny knew in his heart that she only returned to Maryland to try to get the house from him somehow, or maybe just to stand there while he cashed the check. He knew all too well how low his little sister would stoop to get what she wanted. But the house was for sale, and there was a very good contract out on it.

He planned to hide out down in South Carolina until just before closing, and then he'd run up, sign a few papers, and never look back. He had spent the past few weeks throwing away or giving away practically everything in the house, and everything he wanted to keep was now in storage. He got a big smile on his face at the prospect that his life was about to change drastically, and Marcus gave him hope that maybe there was a rainbow in his future as well.

He was driving down Central Avenue toward Marcus's house, and when he saw the basketball court in the neighborhood, he remembered the games that he and his friends used to play where they used to live when he was a kid. He remembered so many things about South Carolina, too, but he couldn't say that all those memories were ones he wanted to relive. He watched as people walked their small dogs and big dogs and medium dogs on the bike trail, and he could see why Marcus lived there. It was serene, and quiet, and peaceful. He hoped that wherever he decided to live in Chicago, he could have visitors saying the same thing about his neighborhood.

He pulled up in front of Marcus's brownstone condo, and he looked over to see Marcus's Toyota sitting right in front of the building. If Marcus was home, then Danny was home, too. It was just then that it hit him—he figured that his father was probably in there, too.

He pushed off the steering wheel and took a moment to think. How in the world was Dad staying at Marcus's? It was unheard of to him. How could Danny be okay with it? How could Marcus be okay with it? He didn't get into it much with Marcus over the phone, but he did remember thinking for a moment that Marcus must have been joking.

Johnny peered up and through what would have been the guest room window. He had stayed there enough times over the years to know what the view was like when the window was open. He didn't currently see a figure staring out the window, only a pair of closed red drapes. He remembered those drapes very well. He had been staying there when Danny and Marcus had asked him to put them up for them.

How could this man be up in Marcus's house like nothing was wrong? His mind wandered to a big argument that he and his father once had, and he wondered if his father even remembered it. His father had been so hell-bent on him not becoming a cop. Johnny was young, but he remembered very clearly what had almost become a fist fight. His father always knew what everyone should do and how they should do it, and when, and to who, and why it was the right thing to do. But it had never dawned on him to simply ask what would make Johnny happy.

Now that he knew that his father was probably inside, Johnny had second thoughts about even being there. Truthfully, hanging out with his father was not the reason he'd driven nine hours. But then he looked in the rearview mirror and thought, "I'd better get out before I start talking to myself and answering, too." He grabbed the keys from the ignition and threw them into his shirt pocket. "Stop being a pussy, you pussy," he said aloud. He looked in the mirror again and shook his head with a sigh. Then he opened the door and closed it behind him, hearing the *chirp chirp* of his auto lock engaging.

On his way up the few steps to the buzzer, he reminded himself that he was there to see his brother, not his father. He knew that once the house was sold and once he'd gotten settled in Chicago, it would probably be quite a while before he would get back down this way. At his age, he didn't have too many more nine- and ten-hour driving trips left in him, and flying wasn't something he cared for too much either, so he knew that this was going to be the last time he would see his little brother for a while.

He pushed on the buzzer with the name "Jacobi and Edwards" next to it, and it was only a second or two before the buzzer on the door released the magnetic strip so that he could come in. He pushed the door open and took a deep breath before he was met by Danny with the door already open, awaiting his hug.

"God, you Jacobis just keep getting better looking as you all age," said Danny in greeting. "I wish I had that curse."

Danny let go and emphatically motioned him inside. Johnny walked past and saw Marcus sitting on the couch. Marcus took his wine glass and tipped it towards Johnny. Marcus handed Danny his glass of wine and asked Johnny, "Would you care for a glass after your long ride?"

"Sure," said Johnny. "I need something to wash down this road dust. I guess wine is as good as anything."

Marcus handed his big brother a glass of chardonnay. It was one of Marcus and Danny's favorites. "So, what the hell has been going on with you since you left? You left in such a hurry, I barely got to spend any time with you."

"I've been so busy—"

"I don't mean to interrupt," said Danny, taking his glass of wine from Marcus, "but where is your shadow?"

"You mean Nikki?" asked Johnny.

"Do you have any other shadows?"

"Thank God, I am down to zero shadows," he answered.

"Good for you, Johnny. Damn good."

"The last I saw her," Johnny began, "she was with some young guy, like in his forties. She said he likes older women. When she said that to me, I thought, 'Why would he want one that smells like the Great Depression, though?'"

All three cracked up laughing.

Johnny continued, "The last I saw, she had that 'I just hit the lottery' look in her eye, and I got out as fast as I could. I feel sorry for the guy who just wants a mommy, but he picked a mummy when he was looking for a mommy." Again, they all shared a laugh.

Danny said, "She hasn't lived well or taken care of herself at all. I had to vacuum away the skin she shed when she was here for dinner."

"Danny, that's terrible," said Marcus. "Stop being dreadful."

"Don't get me wrong, hon," Danny continued. "I love your sister, but I just love Johnny way, way more, is all." Danny raised his glass.

"Well, thank you, Danny, I appreciate that," said Johnny, "but if truth be told, I think you love even your pots and pans more than Nikki." They all three raised their glasses in unison and then busted out laughing once more.

Marcus continued, after the laughter died down, "So, what are you doing here? You were so cryptic on the phone."

"I'm selling my house and moving to Chicago," Johnny announced.

"Really?" Marcus was a bit surprised.

"Yep, really. I have a contract on my house, and as soon as it's sold, and the check clears, I will be Chicago-bound."

"So, why are you here, then?" Marcus asked again.

"I had to get away to get that boll weevil out of my ear. She was getting me to the point that I thought I was going to slap the shit out of her. She's so worried that me and my check aren't going to be around when she needs me, or *it*, I should say. So, I didn't say anything, I just up and left the house while she was gone, locked it up tight, and got in my car and ran down to see my baby brother."

"Wow," said Danny. He was at a loss for words, which was rare for him.

"I just had to get away," Johnny continued. "I spent about three weeks fixing up and hiring people to do things around the house, and the contract should go through in about three weeks or so. I guess I'll go back up a few days before closing and hide out in a hotel. I have the house almost completely empty, and except for a few hours cleaning the last little bit, I think I'm really done with that house."

"What if you run into Nikki?" Danny asked.

"That's what God made twenty-one-year-old kids for. One of my neighbors told me to call him and give him a key, and he'd get rid of everything, get everything cleaned up. It's definitely worth a few hundred bucks to me."

"Where are you going to live in Chicago?" Marcus asked. "Are you going to live with David or Erica?"

"God, no." Johnny took a sip of his wine. "I barely have a relationship with either of them. I could say they pretty much hate me for choosing my job over them. For so long, I took it personally, but I know that's Tina's words coming out of their mouth, and now it's my turn to fix it."

"Your turn?" Danny asked.

"Yeah, I could tell when I called my kids that the tone was, 'Yeah, what can I do for you, Dad?' It was something that broke my heart, but over the years, I just choked it up to them having their own lives, and now that I'm retired, I can't just sit around and *not* try to fix it. I can't blame anyone but myself, so I have to go up there where I can fix it, because I damn sure can't do it from Baltimore."

Marcus interjected, "You don't even have a place to live, though."

"The worst thing I can do is buy something sight unseen. I don't know the neighborhoods, and I damn sure don't want to accidentally buy something in a drive-by neighborhood, you know?"

"We get that." Marcus and Danny both nodded in agreement.

"I need to be there to change their minds," Johnny continued, "because I can't fight Tina's voice from hundreds of miles away. I have to talk to them face-to-face and tell them I was wrong, tell them I want to make it up to them. Right now, they don't want a damn thing to do with me."

"Are you sure about that?" John said, appearing out of nowhere and limping out from the hallway leading to the guest room.

Johnny wanted to yell, "Mind your own business, old man," but the reality was that this old man was now living in his most hated enemy's house, and if that wasn't a miracle, Johnny couldn't say what it was. "What?" he finally asked.

"I said, are you sure about that?" John repeated. "Are you sure they don't want you in their life? Are you sure they hate you? Are you sure they would not open up with a huge hug if you made the first step?"

"Marcus, I didn't know you had wise old Yoda staying with you," Johnny joked.

John Senior pulled out one of Anthony's very annoying habits. "You didn't answer my question, son. Are you sure?"

Marcus grabbed one of the chairs in the living room and brought it to his father. "Dad, sit down, please. You're pushing that leg too much."

John sat down and looked over at his oldest son, who was sitting there looking at his father with a quizzical expression on his face. Johnny didn't know whether to tell him to go fuck off or not, but it did make him think a bit. "Well, Dad," he began, "they never call, they never write, and I don't hear about anything that's going on in their lives, so what conclusion would you come to? I guess the apple doesn't fall far from the tree."

Marcus jumped in. "Johnny, I know you're hurting, but he didn't deserve that dig."

"He hasn't deserved it, Marcus? He has deserved a million digs, and maybe a million more after that. He has deserved a lot of things, and I'm sorry to say this to a guest in your house, but what the fuck, guys? Really?"

Danny had to say something. "Johnny, I love you to death, but you had one thing right—this is our house, and what happens under this roof is our business and no one else's."

John smiled and leaned forward in his chair. "Danny, thank you so much for coming to my rescue and being my knight in shining armor," he began, "but Johnny is right. He deserves to be pissed. We've said some really hateful things to one another over the past half century or so. He does have a right to be pissed. Pissed at me, and pissed at the life I helped put him in. He can be pissed all he wants, and he can stay pissed until his dying day if he wants. The one thing he does not have a right to do is sabotage my relationship with Marcus."

"Okay, fine," Johnny relented. "I'm sorry."

"I'm not finished. Not by a long shot." John leaned in to get Johnny's full attention. "I told you and your sister and your brother that I'm sorry. I can't change anything in the past, but I can try to change what is about to happen. I will not sit here for you or anyone else and become a victim of the past. If you hate me, and you choose to continue to do so, then I have to respect that, even though it tears my guts out. But I will not sit here and say I'm sorry to you a million times. I said it, and now the ball is in your court as to what you want to do with my apology. Marcus and Danny have graciously opened their house and their hearts to me, and I would never do anything—and I mean anything—to hurt them in any way. But I'll be damned if I am going to sit by and let you disrupt and diminish what we've worked for."

"You mean what *you* have worked for."

"No, son, what we *all* have worked for," said John. "You included. I took the first step, and I'm so glad I did. I was tired of living in a dark and dismal place, like the one I think you're living in. I think Marcus was too, or at least part of him was, because of me. Because of having to hate me. Every ounce of energy wasted on those things was an ounce of energy that couldn't be given to Danny and others in his life. That's on me, and I hope he never has to waste energy on that kind of emotion again in his life. And if I had even a small thing to do with that, I'm proud of myself and proud of him."

Marcus wiped his eyes with his shirt sleeve. "Thanks, Dad."

"You're welcome. I don't even know where all that came from."

Danny had a bit of mist in his eyes as well. "Well, wherever it came from, it was beautiful."

Johnny leaned back suddenly. "So, Dad, what you are saying is—"

"What I'm saying, son is that until you go up there, say you're sorry, and mean it, and ask them to please be part of your life, you're pretty much making your theories and perceptions of David and Erica become a reality. They want their father, but they just want to know that you think they're a priority. It's that simple, really."

"That's it, huh?"

"That's it." John was stupefied as to where all that came from, but the one thing he was sure of was that it wasn't only him who had said all of those things. He was definitely being helped by someone, or something.

Johnny holstered his anger and produced a genuine smile, because his father's words had given him a spark of hope. "Thanks, Dad. And I mean that."

"I know you do, and it makes me feel like a million bucks that I could help you."

Johnny looked around. "So, you've been here over a week, right? How is it living with two gay guys?"

John responded after pausing for a second or two. "They make me watch a lot of gay porn, but the food is out of this world." They all laughed, and it seemed as though Danny and John laughed harder than any of them. Johnny looked over at Marcus with his eyebrows raised, but Marcus just leaned forward and whispered in Johnny's direction, "Dad's been here over a week, and those two have gotten chummier than two old sweethearts. I tell them at least once a day to get a room. You would think they'd been best buds since college or something."

Danny turned to Marcus and Johnny. "Stop hating," he said.

"I'm not hating there, lovebug. I'm just telling Johnny the truth." Marcus motioned with his hand, indicating that Exhibit A was in front of them.

"The truth is, Johnny," Danny began, "your father is quite wittier than I would have thought. I haven't heard him say anything that made me want to put a rolling pin down his throat yet, and I give him credit for changing. I'm sure there are still some residual homophobic thoughts rattling around in that old attic of his, but as long as he keeps them in there and not out here, he's welcome."

John Senior interjected, "I *am* in the room, you know."

"Yes, we know, and we're still going to talk about you." Danny started laughing, and John took the joke in good fun. He wasn't the thin-skinned type, nor was Danny.

"Oh, okay." John just grinned and repositioned himself on the chair.

Johnny said in his father's direction, "So, you think you have it all figured out as to what I should do?"

"Not at all," said John. "I know how to make a cake, son, but if you don't want to follow my recipe, you might still end up with a cake."

Danny chimed in. "That was some weak shit there, John. I just told the man you were quick on your feet, and you come up with a cake analogy? I know how to change a tire, Johnny, but if you choose to do it with a stick instead of a jack, you could still change the tire."

Johnny grinned. "Oh, Danny, let's give him another chance. Maybe he has a really good cake recipe." He started laughing. "I'm just kidding, Dad."

"It's okay, son. I know you didn't mean to hurt your old man's feelings like you did."

"I'm sorry, but I—"

John waved his hand. "I was kidding, son. It takes a lot more than that to hurt my feelings. I'll give you my thoughts on what you should do. Whether you do them or not is up to you. If your gut isn't feeling it, then it probably isn't good for you."

"I'm listening," said Johnny.

Marcus rang in, "We're *all* listening."

John cleared his throat. "Well, I can tell you one thing for sure, and it's that I definitely don't have all the answers. In my whole life I've never had the answers. Even as a small boy, I struggled with doing the right thing according to everyone else. I don't know if your mother ever told you boys, but I was a very sickly child. Back in the 30s and 40s, the doctors were nothing like they are now. I never really had any relationships except with the doctors and maybe my mother. Have you ever heard this story?"

Marcus and Danny and Johnny all in unison pretty much shook their heads no, but they were clearly interested. Marcus leaned forward, as did Johnny and Danny.

"Well, I was a sick boy," John continued. "I had asthma, bronchitis, and a slew of other shit that kept me from being normal and healthy. My father and my grandfather on my father's side didn't do much to help the situation, either. They both smoked like chimneys. I couldn't be with either of them more than a few minutes before I lost my breath. Everything in the house smelled, or stunk, I should say, of cigarettes, which was one of the things that made my throat close up."

John looked back and pulled the memories from the far recesses of his brain. "I felt so alone, like no one in the whole world liked me, and that they only tolerated me, because the alternative was to tie me in a burlap sack and throw me in the river like a sack of kittens. I used to look out my window and wish I could be out playing ball like the rest of the neighborhood kids, but I couldn't. My father felt embarrassed having to go out and pick his son up off the street, half-dead and wheezing. It was just a lot easier to keep me locked up in my room with a few toys and a coloring book. We didn't have a television and a smart phone or an iPad, nothing really compared to what they have today." John stopped and glanced up at the faces staring back at him. They were old men, but their eyes were that of twelve-year-old boys hearing a ghost story around a campfire. "You asked me a question, Johnny, and my answer is this."

Johnny said quickly, "Finish the story first, and then we can fix my life. You tell me one good story in my life and you want to stop in the middle? I don't think so, Dad."

John was almost brought to tears by his son's words. "You two feel the same way?" he asked, pointing to Danny and Marcus.

"Finish the damn story, John," said Danny. He wanted to hear how it ended, even though he pretty much saw the ending sitting in front of him.

"Fine, where was I?" said John.

"Sickly boy, blah blah blah." Danny smiled.

"Right! Um, sick boy, in room, got it. Well, after a while of being treated like a leper from friends in school, and my dad, and my grand-dad, I began to act out. I fought in school, until I started wheezing, that is. I argued with the teachers, which back then was like spitting on them. None of the stuff that kids get away with now was tolerated back then. You would be missing a tooth or a jaw if you told one of your parents you hated them in my day." He stopped himself.

"What's wrong?" Marcus knew the answer, but he didn't want to open that wound up now that it was finally healing.

"Just memories, is all," said John. "Well, anyway, I acted out, and the only person on the planet that could get me to be normal, so to speak, was my mother. My father didn't know what to do with me, my grandfather even less, and I didn't know what to do except hate everyone on the planet. I cried ten times harder at my dog dying than when my dad died, or when my granddad died. I was sixteen when my dad died, but I didn't really feel anything. It was just like one less person to remind me I was weird."

"I hear you," said Danny. "So, when did you finally snap out of it?"

"I guess when I met Betty. God, she was such a loving woman who didn't care about my weirdness, about how I didn't have many friends. She used to call me the psycho loner. It was one hundred and ten percent true, though. She was the one person I'd ever met who I really thought a lick about. She was pretty and she was kind and she wasn't like anyone else."

"So why didn't it rub off on you, John?" asked Danny.

"Good question. She tried, but I hated everyone but her. I loved being around her, but everyone else, though, they didn't get much respect from me, except maybe my mother. I didn't want to hate the world, and I didn't want to be this oddball that no one really talked with. I just was. After I had kids, I thought maybe I would be better, that maybe I would be able to do what my father had been unable or unwilling to do for me, but it seems my abnormal ways just wouldn't let it be so."

"Why, Dad?" asked Marcus.

"I don't know, son. I really don't. I couldn't get past the hurt, I guess. I know it's a cop out, but it's the only way I can describe it. After you kids grew up and left the house, I just felt like such a failure. I said I wasn't going to be like my father, but I was ten times worse. I worried about being embarrassed and what everyone was going to think of me. After you all were gone, it was just too late. After Peter and your mother died, and I saw the looks in your eyes, I just knew. You would be better off without my baggage."

"Horseshit!" Johnny wasn't buying it. "That is a load of pure horseshit!"

"Maybe so," John admitted, "but it was what I thought, or what I convinced myself to be true at the time. It was so much easier thinking that it was the acorn falling from the tree and that I had no way of changing my stars, and all that crap. Now I see you pretty much doing the same thing as I did, and I'm trying to tell you something I needed to hear a long time ago. Put the pity party away, and just go to them. Don't expect anything. Don't expect hate or love or anything really—just go. Don't worry about what David is going to say or think, or Erica or Tina. Just go, and see what happens."

"Why did you wait so long to get so smart?" Marcus wished he'd heard all of this fifty years ago. He sure would have saved himself a lot of tears.

"Believe me, I'm not smart," said John. "My friend Anthony is the smart one. He helped me put this all into words. These are his words, not mine. I feel them, but was never able to say them properly, I guess."

Johnny wasn't sure what to think. "Just go and move up there and see what happens, huh?"

"Yep," said John. "You have to believe that your family loves you. You won't do it if you can't believe that your kids can get over the hurt. If they can't get over it, you have to respect it, but if they can, it would be worth all the fear and anger and anxiety, and especially the rage, that you are going to feel up to that moment."

"That moment?"

"Johnny, there is going to be a moment when your kids unleash the most hateful and hurtful words upon you. If they haven't already."

"They've both said some of both to me," said Johnny. "But they're right. I did choose my job over my family one too many times. I can't deny that, and I can't deny that I should've been there for them instead of saving some junkie with a needle sticking out of his arm."

"I'm sure that junkie you saved feels just the opposite, as do their families." said John, even as he could feel his son's pain and anguish.

"Still doesn't help."

"So, what are you going to do?"

"I'm going to take what little time I have left, and what little money I have, and move to Chicago and try and fix my mistakes," said Johnny. "They may wait until my dying day to forgive me, but I have to try."

"I wish you the best of luck, son. I really do."

"Thanks, Dad." Johnny couldn't have imagined this moment ever happening between himself and his father, and it gave him hope that one day he'd maybe have the same moment with his own kids.

Danny looked over at Marcus, and neither one of them had dry eyes. It was the moment that Marcus and Johnny had secretly dreamed of, Danny was sure. It was in that one instant that the anger, and the sorrow, and the bottomless gorge of regret seemed to dissipate a bit. Danny felt so honored to be a part of it.

WHERE HAVE YOU BEEN?

John sat and watched as his feathered friends pecked at the seed he threw down to them. It was odd, but he had really missed these birds. They were like old friends. Some of their markings made a few of them stand out. A green streak running down one wing, or a ring around their neck, or just a deformed wing tip. He saw that the leaves had started turning. The white oaks had bright red and yellow leaves hanging on its branches, and a good gust of wind was all that was needed to find them on the cobblestone path next to the hundreds of other leaves. John liked this time of year.

He watched as the same joggers as before whizzed past him. The same kids being walked to school, the same mothers hurrying past on the way back home, and the same dogs being walked. Everything was pretty much the same as in weeks past, except that a few of the shirts were long-sleeved instead of short-sleeved.

He looked around as if he hadn't been here in years instead of just a few weeks. He soaked in all the sights and sounds and smells, the squirrels running from tree branch to tree branch, and dogs being held back from running after them.

"Where the hell have you been, John Jacobi?" Anthony's voice was pure surprise. He seemed shocked to see John sitting in the seat that had been dormant for so many mornings. "I've been sitting here all by myself like a loser, waiting for you."

John looked up to see his friend coming down the cobblestone walkway, thermos in hand as always. This time, though, he had a light jacket on, a red windbreaker that John had never seen before. He had to admit that he was glad to see his friend. "I'm right here, waiting on you. Marcus said he stopped by a few times looking for you, but never saw you sitting here. Where have you been?"

"Why would I sit at an empty bench?" said Anthony. "There's no one to talk to on an empty bench. If I didn't see you, I went to another part of the park. So, what the hell happened to you?"

"I broke my leg, of sorts," John admitted. "I fell in my kitchen, and Marcus made me stay with him and Danny until I got better."

"Wow, that's big. Did they beat you? They should have beat you, you know."

"Yeah, I know. That aside, I couldn't believe it. He almost dragged me out of my house and took me over to the D&M rehab center. That's Danny and Marcus."

"Yeah, I gathered. I'm not one of your feathered friends."

"And did you help anyone else with life-changing advice while I was gone?" said John sarcastically.

Anthony said, "I helped a few squirrels with some marital problems, and a big dog who had a scratch he couldn't reach."

"I missed that," said John.

"What?"

"Wit. My son is a great guy, but quick wit is not one of his attributes. Danny, on the other hand, is a totally different story. He's more like you in that way."

"So, he's totally awesome?" Anthony joked.

"He's just a nice guy. A really nice guy."

"For a gay guy?" Anthony had to poke fun.

"No, just for a guy," John said.

"Well, look at you, making me all proud."

"Both of them are really great guys," John continued. "I wish I'd gone to them a long time ago."

"I'm sure they wish that, too," said Anthony.

"I did a lot of thinking about how lucky I am."

"Lucky how?"

"I don't think I would have ever gotten this close to them if I hadn't stayed with them. I think there would have always been that awkward wall between us."

"Did you thank God for breaking your leg?" Anthony asked.

"Really, Anthony, God again?"

"Why not?"

John looked up at the sky. "Thank you, God, for breaking my leg, and thank you, God, for having me move in with my son for the past few weeks. Thank you, God, for giving me so much pain, and of course so much fun on top of it. Thank you, God, for everything you do for me."

"Wow, that was so much easier than you thought, wasn't it?"

"That was easier than listening to you ramble on about how great God is," said John. "Do you ever get tired of singing that same song? That record has to be skipping by now."

"Never," said Anthony. "This song always makes me smile."

"I don't really believe in a God," John admitted, "but some of the things that have happened in the past few months kind of make me think. Why I met you, why I finally got the balls to confront my kids, why everything fell into place the way it did. How do you believe in something that can't be real? I mean, He can't be."

"Why not?" Anthony asked with a shrug.

"How can He be? How can something, some person, someone out in the universe that no one sees or hears or touches, be real?"

"I don't know," Anthony began. "I don't know how He came to exist, but how can He not be real when so many things happen every day that can't be explained? Science just isn't smart enough to explain it yet, maybe. Is that all God is?"

"Explain how all the bad things happen, and how the scriptures say one thing that totally contradict how people act," said John. "There is no one—no, there aren't *many* people out there who I would say are worth a nickel. So why keep us here? Why not wipe us out and leave the planet to the animals? They deserve it a hell of a lot more than we do. All we do is destroy things."

"You make a very good point, John. Why do we exist? Why not wipe us out? I guess it's like this," Anthony continued. "If your dad gave you a puppy or a goldfish and told you to take care of it and watch it grow and thrive, is it right if he comes back and takes it away because his idea of how to take care of it differs from yours?"

"If there was a God, I think He would get rid of all these bad people. He would get rid of all the people that made this world a shit hole."

"People like you, you mean?" Anthony said.

"Yeah, especially people like me."

"Then how could you have redeemed yourself like you did?"

"Okay, I've had enough," John said suddenly. "You Bible thumpers get on my nerves for this exact reason. You can't simply answer a question, so you throw out this bullshit until people either fall for it or get fed up and you move on to the next guy."

"Is that what you think I'm doing with you, John?" Anthony asked. "I'm trying to convince you of something? I'm not going to be happy until you are yelling Am-way at the top of your lungs and buying into the pyramid scheme?"

"I don't know, Anthony."

"I think you've got a screw loose, is what I think."

"Then explain it to me, please," said John.

"What do you want me to say to you? I can't explain it any other way. I believed because something happened in my life that I couldn't explain. I don't expect you to believe just because I do. I shared a few things that happened to me, and I thought it might help you with what you were going through, and screw you if you think it was anything else." Anthony needed to take a few deep breaths to calm himself. "I can't believe I'm wasting time talking to a dick like you. You haven't changed at all. You are still a narcissistic piece of crap trying to convince people you've changed."

John interrupted. "Shut the fuck up, please." After Anthony's surprised expression faded, John continued, "I *have* changed, you old prune, and I do appreciate your help with all of this. I want to believe that there was something besides dumb luck, but I just can't drink the Kool-Aid. I envy you for having it all figured out."

REDEMPTION

Anthony let out a hardy laugh. "You think I have it all figured out? I don't have shit figured out. I have faith because it's the only thing that makes me feel like I have a purpose. If I didn't, I'd be just like you were a few weeks ago, and *you* would still be like you were a few weeks ago. I have to believe it wasn't a coincidence that we met and that things happened the way they did, because otherwise I wouldn't have the balls to go up to someone I never met and get all in their business. I would be an introvert sitting over there sipping my hot tea and watching the world spin by."

"I'm sorry," John said.

"Don't be sorry, John. Don't be sorry if you don't believe in God. Don't be sorry if things don't work out with you and your kids. Be sorry for not helping someone who is obviously in need of a friend. My kids are in my life, and my faith lets me see the world with such vibrant colors. I'm so thankful that people such as yourself tell me how their lives have changed for the better, and that I had even a very small part in it."

"Thank you, God, I guess?" said John.

"That's who I thank," Anthony said. "You thank whoever or whatever makes you find some semblance of peace, even if it's just a painted rock."

"Well, I can't say I'm on your wavelength today, but maybe someday." John was being sincere when he said he wanted to believe. He wanted to feel like there was a purpose to things, but the truth was, at this moment, all he saw was a world filled with misery that no sane God would ever just ignore.

"That's all I ask, John. Maybe someday you'll be sitting in my spot. Maybe someday you'll find a person who needs some help."

"Maybe," John grudgingly admitted.

"So, let's change the subject," Anthony said. "How are you and the kids?"

John was happy to change the subject, and even happier to talk about something that had made him happier than he'd ever thought possible. "I love living with Danny and Marcus. They make me laugh so much. Danny and I have really hit it off, and Marcus and I have really become close, too. Even Johnny and I have become closer. He's getting ready to move to Chicago, and he calls me every day or so. And all sarcasm aside, all joking aside, I just wanted to say thank you, Anthony. I know we haven't known each other very long, but you've helped me out more than I could ever say."

"You're welcome, my friend," said Anthony. "I'm really happy for you and your kids, and glad that I could help, even if it was just showing you what an ass you were being."

The two sat there on the bench enjoying each other's company. They talked about John's kids, and Anthony's kids, and how things were going to be different. They laughed and talked and then laughed some more.

John knew that people would have thought these two old farts were mad, laughing as loud as they were. No one was staring or gawking, but in the back of his mind, he knew there were at least a few people who were thinking them odd. But for the first time in forever, John didn't really care what everyone else thought.

IT'S A DAMN SHAME

Marcus couldn't help but feel bad on his way home that night. He'd been working with Tom and the other volunteers for a few months, and he wondered how people could take on this much sadness on a daily basis. He had heard so many sad stories over the last few weeks, and it made his heart ache. He felt so bad for all of the boys he'd spoken with—Scotty, Andre, Eric, Andy, and a whole slew of others who just had the most heart-wrenching stories about their lives.

He knew he couldn't help them all in the ways that he would like, but it was very comforting to know that maybe, just maybe, one kid out of that bunch may go home tonight knowing that someone cared about them. Kids came and kids went at the club. He hoped for most, but feared for the rest. It was obvious the road that most of these kids were on, and he knew you didn't have to be white or black or Latino to go down the road that led nowhere. After all, it was a road he'd travelled for a while.

When he pulled up to his house, he parked his Cadillac on the street and put it in park, but he left the engine running. He wasn't ready to go inside and face Danny and his father. He had to get his face on. Right now, in the dim light in the car, the rearview mirror showed him a man who had lost control. A man who cried all the way home. He didn't want to be that guy tonight. He had brought his work home to Danny on too many occasions already. Danny had helped Marcus with words of wisdom over the years, and ever since Marcus took this job, he had given many more. He knew it broke Danny's heart to see him in such anguish and sorrow over these kids' stories and to not be able to do a thing about it. It wasn't his job to fix these kids, he would say. It was his job to guide them in the areas that they needed guidance on, nothing else.

MICHAEL L. TYLER

Marcus couldn't shake the story he had heard earlier that day at group. Sometimes sitting in at group was like taking a beating all its own. He listened to a young boy tell the story of watching his little sister get killed by a car while he was too afraid to help her. How he just left her there and didn't help. The detail of how it felt watching your sister say her last words until her eyes became hollow and there was no life left in them was enough to make anyone cry. Marcus wanted to cry for the boy, but was it any worse than the kids who were beat or raped or abused in all those other ways?

It was hard for Marcus to hear these stories and not think of his own childhood, when he too had fought off thoughts of doing violence to others, as well as to himself. There had been many a night when he knew that one knife and one bath later, it could be all over with. It was such a simple solution. You just had to take a nice hot bath and just lay there while the life drained out of you. How hard could it be to just lay there and go to sleep?

His mind wandered to all the kids who may have done just that. How many kids he hadn't seen in weeks who might be contemplating, or had achieved, that easy task.

Marcus wiped away the tears streaming down his face. He was an emotional person, and he had empathy for everything from a kid living on hard times all the way down to the field mouse that just wasn't quick enough to escape a predator. He told himself to grow up and stop laying this shit on Danny's feet three nights a week. It wasn't fair to Danny, and it wasn't fair to himself to take on such a burden. It wasn't fair to the kids, either.

Marcus took a tissue from his console and tried to wipe the tears from his face. He popped the door open and looked at himself once more in the rearview mirror. Once he'd gotten himself looking presentable, he stepped out onto the sidewalk. He let himself inside his building and wiped his face once more with his sleeve before heading down the carpeted hallway toward his condo. He knew after going into the kitchen and getting himself a nice relaxing glass of wine, he would start to feel better.

Danny saw Marcus come through the door and knew that it was another one of those nights. It was evident in the way he walked, the way he held his head, and most definitely the way he was headed to the wine cabinet. "Rough night?" he asked cautiously.

"Could have been better," Marcus admitted.

"Feel better now?" Danny came over and gave Marcus a hug from behind.

"I do. I don't know why I do it to myself, but I just can't help myself." Marcus pulled his favorite bottle out from the small fridge containing the special bottles of wine, usually from trips they'd taken in the past.

Danny held onto him while Marcus poured himself a glass of his favorite wine. "It's obvious why you do it," Danny said from behind Marcus. "You're a caring and loving person. That's why."

"Don't make me laugh," said Marcus. "I want to stay sad. I want to hate myself because I can't help these kids."

Danny spun him around so that they could be facing one another. He pressed his fingers to Marcus's lips to silence him. "Stop it, Marcus. Stop beating yourself up. You are a great person, a fabulous person, but you can't help the whole world. You have to be okay with helping the ones you *can* help, and be satisfied with that. Do you understand what I'm saying?"

"Yeah, I do hear you, I swear," said Marcus. "But I don't want to be some whiny bitch who comes home every night and cries on your shoulder. If I can't hold it together, then I might as well quit." He didn't want to quit, but it wasn't reasonable to keep doing this to Danny.

"Stop!" Danny exclaimed. "The only time you're being a whiny little bitch is when you keep saying things like that." Danny knew that Marcus kept his heart on his sleeve. It was one of the things that he loved most about him. "You love being there for those kids," he continued. "You love being a small part in helping them through things, so, no, you are not going to quit, but you're not going to think it's all on you, either."

"I know, but—" Again, Marcus was quieted with a finger to his lips.

"You are going to come home and tell me all about your day," said Danny. "The good stories, the bad stories, and the triumphs and the defeats. You and I are going to deal with them all. Do you hear me?" Marcus nodded his head up and down with Danny's finger still on his lips. "I'm not going to get upset because you're helping too many kids, or that I'm tired of hearing the horror stories. I'm going to get pissed if you keep trying to keep things from me that affect you so deeply. If you can't do that, then maybe you should stay outside a bit longer and do a better job at fixing your face."

Marcus pushed Danny's finger away and pulled him close. "I love you, you know that?" He pressed his lips to Danny's. "Everyone should be as lucky as me."

"If everyone was as lucky as you, then who would we make fun of when we go out to eat?"

As always, Danny made Marcus feel better. He just had a way about him that made Marcus feel as though everything was going to be fine.

"How's Dad?" Marcus asked.

"He's fine. I took him a sandwich a little while ago, and I told him I would holler when dinner was ready. Go in there and get cleaned up, and tell the old man to get his ass out here. By the time he gets out here, dinner should be on the table."

"You two seem to be bosom buddies here lately, always cracking each other up."

"I look at it as community service. Now go get ready." Danny pushed away from Marcus and went over to the stove where his soup was slowly simmering.

Marcus smiled and headed down the hall to get his father.

WHAT DO YOU WANT TO WATCH?

Danny and Marcus were sitting on the couch before the glow of the television. Marcus leaned his head on Danny's shoulder as they watched the news, which was about the only thing on television that both of them could stand to watch. The reality television and the home fix-up shows were just too much to absorb, and the crime shows and the violence weren't something they cared to watch. But even the news wasn't much better these days, as both would attest to.

John came out of the hallway and found the two relaxing on the couch. There was a time that the sight of two guys lying against each other would have made John feel uncomfortable, but after living with these two for the last month, and seeing things a bit differently now, he came to just see it as normal.

"What are you watching?" he asked.

"Right now, the news," said Danny. "There weren't any good movies on, and the gay porn doesn't come on HBO until after midnight." Danny couldn't help himself. Messing with John was like an illness that there was no cure for.

"Until then, I'll keep you company, if that's okay." John walked over to the other chair opposite the couch. His conservative views were very different from his son's and Danny's. He couldn't understand how the Democrats thought it was okay to save the whole wretched world, but his son couldn't believe anyone would have any other desire. He knew that politically, at least, they were the north and south poles.

"Anything wrong, Dad?" Marcus said, looking up at his father.

"No, just couldn't sleep," said John. "I guess I've just been thinking about how alone it's going to feel once I go back home next week. I think I'm excited to get back home and get into my routine, but I just wanted you two to know that I will miss you, and that I really appreciate your hospitality." John relaxed and leaned back into the big loveseat.

"We will miss you too, John," said Danny. "I mean, I'll have to go back to Marcus's idea of a joke, and that's going to hurt me more than you know." Danny wondered if John was fishing to stay longer, or maybe even forever. He had to think whether he hated the idea or not, and having to think about it gave him his answer.

"Screw you, fella." Marcus punched Danny in the arm.

"Sorry, babe, but your jokes are about as funny as a fungal infection." Danny dodged the second punch that he knew was coming.

John enjoyed the banter and the obvious love that the two shared with each other. More than anything, he felt he would miss that the most. "You two kids behave."

"Okay, Dad." Marcus leaned back on Danny's arm and fluffed up his shoulder as though it was a pillow.

John wished he had had that kind of relationship with Betty. She had known that the best way to keep John happy was to agree with him, but after living with these two, John now knew that you could disagree and still have a deep love. He felt as though there was something in this house that made the outside invisible. He wished he had done this decades ago. He just wanted to blurt out how sorry he was, but he kept his mouth shut and watched the news with his two sons.

"Did you want to watch something, John?" Danny asked. "I mean, I'm sure we can find a cowboy and Indian flick, or a John Wayne movie where he dies at the end."

"No, thank you," said John. "I just came out of my room to stretch my legs. I think my leg is finally starting to feel better. The more I walk on it, I think, the better it feels. I don't bounce back anymore like I did when I was fifty. Between the physical therapy and the occupational therapy that I've had the last few weeks, I think I'm in better shape now than before I fell down like an idiot."

"John, no one falls like an idiot, except maybe after a few drinks. You're definitely an idiot, but you fell like a guy who is almost ninety years old, and that's allowed."

"I know I said this before," John said, "but you two really saved my life. I wasn't sure about it when I first got here, but I've had the time of my life with you two. You both are great people, and I just wanted you to know how grateful I am."

"Thanks, Dad," said Marcus.

"Yeah, thanks John," echoed Danny.

"The one thing I didn't tell you was what I was thinking when I laid there for four hours on that kitchen floor. I thought a lot about dying. I thought about them finding my body with mice nibbling at my toes. I really did think that. I was almost sure that I was going to die in there. I didn't have my phone, and I was in such pain that I really couldn't yell loudly enough for anyone to hear me. I think after hour three I was looking at life a whole lot differently than I was before I cooked that egg."

"But you're okay now," said Danny. "You don't have to think about that kind of stuff now. You know now that you aren't alone." Danny was trying to make him feel better, but it was obvious he had something to say—or better yet, something to share.

"I am now," John agreed, "but the truth is that I would never have known this. I would never have had the closeness that the three of us have now. Hell, I think even Junior has softened up a little towards me."

"I think he likes you more than he lets on," said Danny. "I think he, like the rest of us, are ready to put it to bed, ready to bury the crap and move on to something better. I think he needs to think more about fixing his own shit, rather than worrying about how much he does or does not hate you."

"I'm really happy for him. I mean, really," John said sincerely. Then he leaned back and continued watching the television. He looked around and, in the dim light, he could see all the things around the house that made these two who they were. Pictures of places they had been, and Knick knacks that symbolized memories from each of those places. He saw pictures of Danny and Marcus smiling in different locales. They were smiling on top of a snow-covered mountain, they were smiling on top of a rock-covered mountain. They were smiling at a wedding or smiling at a local shop. John figured that after you accumulated all these pictures, you must be so proud of yourself seeing all these wonderful places and having someone you couldn't wait to share these experiences with.

John wished he had seen these places. He wished that he had taken Betty to all of them. He wished he'd taken his boys to places like Germany or Italy or France or London. Not just two states over to visit Aunt Laura, because she had money, and maybe if he visited her enough, he would find his way into her will. John smiled at the thought of how that had worked out. The old bitty had left everything to the church. *Stupid old cow*, he thought. He wondered how on earth someone could give all their money to people running the biggest con job in the world. John thought some of the worst people on the planet were involved in organized religion. Preachers molesting kids and staying in ten-thousand-dollar-a-night hotel rooms on the church's dime. He always knew Aunt Laura was daft, but he never dreamed she was outright idiotic.

"What are you thinking about, Dad?" Marcus asked suddenly.

"Huh, what?"

"You looked like you were doing some serious thinking."

"Just thinking about your Aunt Laura," said John.

"I haven't thought about her since I was a kid. Why are you thinking about her?"

"Just thinking about a lot of stuff, I guess. When you get to be my age, thinking is about all you can do. The back don't work, the legs don't work, the peter don't work."

"One step too far, Dad," Marcus groaned. "Always one step too far."

"Yeah, but that's where they keep all the good jokes," John said with a laugh.

"Yeah, Marcus," Danny chimed in, "everyone who loves to joke knows that's where they keep the good ones. Oh, I'm sorry, I meant to say everyone with a good sense of humor. I guess that's why you don't know about that place."

REDEMPTION

"Leave Marcus alone, Danny," said John. "He has a great sense of humor."

"See, Marcus, now *that* was funny."

"You two better stop picking on me," Marcus said, even though he clearly enjoyed having a third in their banter sessions.

"Are you serious, or were you trying to tell a joke?" Danny mussed up what was left of Marcus' hair.

John just smiled with contentment. He was genuinely happy there. These two men were in their sixties, but if you didn't know any better, John would swear they were much, much younger.

"You two are getting on my nerves," said Marcus. "I'm going to bed. And you, you and your boney ass elbow have given me a bruise on my arm."

"Do you want me to kiss it and make it better?" Danny tried to grab Marcus's arm, but Marcus was already on his feet. "Don't go to bed mad."

"I'm not mad," said Marcus, "but I *am* tired. It's almost midnight. You two can sit out here and tell jokes about me all night if you want, but I don't have to sit here and listen."

"Okay," Danny relented. "If we come up with any good ones, I'll let you know."

"Don't bother, Danny. I'm sure I've heard them before."

John stood up along with Marcus. "I think I'm going to go to bed, too. I'm kind of beat myself. I'll see you kids in the morning." John shuffled past Marcus and Danny and into the hallway that led to his bedroom. He stopped to take one last look at them.

"See you in the morning, Dad," said Marcus.

"See you in the morning, John," echoed Danny.

"Goodnight, kids." John disappeared around the corner and down the hall.

Danny stayed on the couch. "I will be in in a while, babe. I have to take the dishes out of the dishwasher first."

"Okay, babe. Don't stay up too late."

"Be in soon."

HE'S WHAT?!

Danny stumbled out of the hallway and into the living room. He was speechless, his face void of color. He had to call someone. He had to get the phone. The phone was in the kitchen. He found his way blindly to the kitchen, and before picking up the phone, he leaned up against the counter to collect himself. Then he picked up the receiver and dialed 9-1-1. It seemed like several minutes before someone picked up. Finally, the operator said, "9-1-1 operator, what can I help you with?"

Danny had to bring himself back to the here and now. "I have an elderly man not breathing, and I need an ambulance." He wasn't sure any of this was real.

"Okay, please give me the address," the operator continued calmly.

Danny gave his address. "Please get here as fast as you can." He held the phone away and then brought it back. "Tell the ambulance drivers to buzz 2G." He then hung up the phone.

The kitchen door swung open and John said, "What's going on? Are you okay? What's wrong?"

"He's gone!" Danny exclaimed.

"Who?"

"He's dead, John, your son is dead!" The emotions that were swirling around in his head, taking him in like an undertow. He was about to drown.

"I don't understand," said John, his face blank as reality set in. He pulled one of the chairs out near the breakfast nook and lowered himself into it, shocked.

"Doesn't matter, John, Marcus is gone," said Danny. "He's dead." He couldn't hold back the onslaught of tears being held back by pure disbelief.

REDEMPTION

"He can't be. He can't be," John kept saying.

"He is, John. He's in the same position that I saw him in when I came to bed last night. His face is ice cold. He didn't die a few minutes ago, John. He has been dead all night." The tears began falling to the kitchen floor like rain. *How could this happen?*

John looked around the room and for the first time since he'd woken up here, it wasn't bright like it had been every other morning at this time. This room was always cheerful and teeming with love, and the aroma of a delicious breakfast was always warming it up. There was nothing better than coming down this time of morning and having a cup of coffee waiting for him when he threw open the swinging door. He could always count on a few jokes from Danny, and a few pretend gasps from Marcus. Now he looked at said swinging door. He would never be able to look at it the same way again.

John looked at Danny with the kind of sadness he had never felt before. He didn't get up and go to him and hug him and console him, but it wasn't for the reason he would have thought. He wanted to, he wanted to very much, but he didn't know what to say. He didn't know how to do anything at the moment. He figured he was still processing his own grief.

Danny looked over at his father-in-law through blurry eyes and just wondered what was going on, and why wasn't John's face covered in tears like his was? *Is he just too manly to cry? Is he that uncaring?* Danny watched John until his mind was shaken by the buzzing of his intercom bell. He stood up and pushed the swinging door open, leaving John there with his dry, hard-hearted face.

John just looked out the window and saw the light shimmering on the back of the building. He'd never noticed how much light came through the kitchen this early in the morning. He'd never noticed the graffiti written on the opposite wall. He didn't notice what an ugly color the next building was. It was eerie how such a beautiful day could be so ugly and so dismal. To John, it was like a rainy, overcast, cold day, not the sunny day that everyone else was seeing. It wasn't fair. This couldn't be happening. Just when his life seemed to be going in a different direction, a direction

MICHAEL L. TYLER

he was proud of—just when he no longer had to fake the smile on his face. *It's just not fair.*

John could hear the commotion in the other room. He could make out voices, and even though he wasn't there, he could see it as plainly, just as if he were standing there at the doorway. He could see the stretcher being wheeled past with the sheet over his son's face. He could see the paramedics walking past Danny and asking if he needed anything. He saw it all. He saw them wheeling Marcus down the hall towards their ambulance. It was so vivid, he could almost swear he wasn't sitting in the kitchen all alone.

A few minutes later, he saw the door swing open. Danny walked past him, and he knew that John was hurting, but it was not even in the same universe as the pain that he was feeling, and he wanted John to know it. "I have some calls to make, John, so I think it's best to get your own coffee."

John could tell that Danny was on the verge of screaming and tearing the whole apartment apart. He didn't want to approach him. In this fragile state, Danny would snap him in two. "Is there anything I can do to help?" he asked. He didn't know what else to say. "Do you want me to call anyone?"

"Thanks, John, but I would like to just be alone, if that's okay." Danny *did* want to scream and yell, and break things, and go on a rampage and destroy everything he could until he felt better.

"Did the paramedics say anything or see anything that might be a cause, or—" John fumbled over a bunch of words, trying to make a coherent sentence.

"They said it looked like a heart attack, but only the coroner would make that determination." While Danny looked up numbers in the book near the phone, he took a deep breath and exhaled slowly before continuing. "They're right. He said last night I bruised his arm, but I think he was having a heart attack then. I think he went to bed, and just went to sleep forever. No pain, just fell asleep."

"Everyone should be that lucky," said John. "It's the way everyone should go out of this world." John was still fumbling for something to say that didn't sound stupid, uncaring, or insensitive. "I'm going to go in the other room and let you make your calls. Danny, if you need me for anything, to make calls, or just to talk, please let me know." John figured coffee wasn't that important this morning, and he left it behind. Today was not going to be like any other day.

"Thanks, John, I will." Danny went back to writing numbers down on his pad. He had to call Johnny and Nikki and Tom, and the worst of all, the Lansing Funeral Home, and the slew of friends that they both had. Everyone was going to be crushed. No one was going to believe that Marcus was gone. Hell, *he* didn't even believe Marcus was gone, and he was the one who found him.

As soon as Danny touched Marcus that morning, he knew without knowing. It was weird, but no one alive is that cold, and he knew just by touching Marcus' cheek that his husband, his best friend, his everything, was gone. He got up and kissed his forehead and knew that life had changed, and not for the better. There were moments in life, and everyone had them, that you will never forget no matter how much time goes by.

A flood of memories from the previous night and all the nights before rushed over him, all the way back to the day they'd met. He remembered Marcus's laugh, and the way he held his hand, and the way he smiled, and the way he helped so many people. Marcus was always the one guy who would sacrifice himself to help someone else. It infuriated Danny, but at the same time, it had made him so proud.

Danny shook the cobwebs away and started making the calls. He would start with Mr. Lansing at Lansing Funeral home. He had been to too many of his friends' funerals, or friends of friends, but he'd never dreamed he'd be the one in black.

NOT TODAY

John slowly climbed out of the cab. Everything was slow today, especially this time of morning. He walked down the cobblestone path to where his bench was waiting, and where his feathered friends were waiting. The closer he got, the more he wished that Anthony was there waiting for him, too, but this early in the morning, there was no one there but him and a few birds. It was a dismal, misty day. The only ones who thought today was a great day were the flowers and the trees, he figured. The clouds were ready to open up, he could just tell. The humidity and fog were signs that everything was going to be soaked in a matter of hours or maybe minutes. For a brief moment he thought maybe the rain would drench him, and that he would get sick and die, and then this pain in his heart would go away.

It was obvious to everyone else that today was a day to stay inside and watch television or clean the house or play cards with your significant other. But staying inside today was the last thing he wanted to do. He wanted to cry, he wanted to scream, he wanted to yell to the heavens that it wasn't fair. He wanted Anthony to and sit down with his stupid tea and his stupid face and his stupid advice. He wanted to hear that everything was going to be fine, so that he could then tell him to go screw off.

When John finally reached his bench and plopped down, resting his old bones, it was as if every bird from a mile around flew in for the feast that was about to ensue. John pulled the bag out of his windbreaker and set it down next to his thigh. He grabbed a generous handful of seed and threw it down, spreading it across a wide area. The birds ate as though they knew that at any moment the downpour would start and they would be soaked, along with the old man feeding them.

REDEMPTION

John looked around and saw only one or two people braving the on-coming storm. Anthony was not one of them, though. John had to admit it that Anthony was probably at home, sitting and watching the television, sipping his stupid tea. It was something that he wished he could be doing, too, but being home with Danny right now was not where he thought he should be.

It was obvious watching Danny around the house the past two days, his friends coming over to help with everything, that John's place was not there. It was obvious that Danny didn't want him there as well. He was sure that after the funeral he was going to leave Danny alone, so that he could grieve in peace.

John threw down another healthy helping of birdseed to his friends. He watched as the pigeons and the cardinals and the finches pecked at the tiny seeds that had gotten lodged in the cracks of the cobblestone.

As he watched his feathered friends fight over the meager scraps that were disappearing almost as fast as he could throw it down, he couldn't help but think of times gone by. He remembered not the long faraway thoughts, but the recent ones held in the highest regard. He remembered Marcus helping him to his feet so he could be carried off to stay with him, the look on Danny's face when he sat down to their first dinner when all three were eating some spaghetti or linguini concoction that Danny had whipped up. It was a tense dinner, but by the end of it, they were all laugh-ing as though they were old friends who hadn't seen each other in quite some time. He could hear Marcus's laugh as if he were standing behind him. Danny's voice, too.

John remembered the night when they all had cigars on the balcony, talking about what a great city this was, and how everyone was so nice. He didn't believe in everything that Marcus and Danny believed in, but he did believe in *them*. He believed in two people—not just a man and a woman—who could find love. He knew firsthand that it was definitely possible to find love outside the man/woman relationship.

His mind flooded with warm memories of the past few weeks with Marcus. He had never dreamt that the two of them would ever be talk-ing, and even harder to believe was that they would be laughing with one another. Now that he was gone, it almost seemed as though it had all been a dream. And he so wanted to be back in that dream. He didn't want to be out there with the thunderclouds and the rain and the depression and the heartache. He wanted to be laughing and smiling and joking again.

John looked up at the grey clouds about to burst, and wished with all his heart that he could believe in some higher power like his friend did. He wanted to find that peace, but all he felt was hollowness. He didn't curse God, or even hate Him, really. He knew in his heart that the last few months were his own heaven on earth, and he needed to realize that, and also realize that he didn't even really deserve those two months. He wanted so much to be mad, but at who, at what? It was so hard to try and find some sense as to why this happened. He missed his son so much.

John watched as the tears fell, the waterworks hitting his windbreaker like rain drops, and they seemed unstoppable. He couldn't control the convulsive spasms wreaking havoc on his body as he sat there alone and sobbed.

THE VIEWING

Danny watched as more and more people arrived at the funeral home. The room where Marcus was being viewed was becoming a full house. He could only imagine what the actual funeral was going to be like. There were so many people walking around, and so many people offering their condolences. Danny was touched at the number of individuals that had showed up. He knew they had friends, but Danny never thought in his wildest dreams that this many people would have come. Danny thought it must be upwards of a hundred people circulating around.

Danny scanned the room and saw Johnny sitting near the casket, looking as though he had lost his best friend. He wanted to go over and put his arm around him and tell him that everything was going to be okay, but tonight, Danny had a hard time believing that himself. Nothing was going to be okay. Nothing was ever going to be the same.

Danny looked across the room and saw what looked like the whole Boys Club standing around talking to each other. There must have been forty or fifty boys there, and it amazed him just as it made him feel such a welling up of pride for the man he'd lost. No wonder there were so many people there tonight. Marcus had always gone out of his way to help anyone who needed it, whether he thought they deserved it or not. Danny's heart ached at the loss he was feeling at the moment. His chest felt as though it had been slammed by a sledgehammer.

A boy came up to Danny and extended a hand. "Hi," he said. "This is my little brother Andre, and my name is Scotty. Mister Marcus was the best, and we just wanted to say how sorry we are." Scotty did know that Marcus was gay, and yesterday it might have meant something, but today, at this moment, he could have cared less. He got what Mister Marcus had always been saying about everyone having a story and everyone having their own kind of pain to deal with.

"Thanks, Scotty," said Danny. "I am really glad you could come."

Danny didn't believe in the hereafter, or reincarnation, but he wished with all his heart that he did. If he did, then maybe, just maybe, he could believe that he would see Marcus again someday, and maybe, just maybe, he could get through the rest of this life he was going to have to endure.

"Mister Marcus was so cool," Andre said. "He always had time to play a game of pool with me, or show me how to shoot a shot, or help us in group, or just listen, you know?" Scotty's little brother couldn't hold the tears in any longer. He turned to shed his tears away from his big brother's gaze.

"Thank you, Andre," said Danny. "He loved you all, too. He spoke of both of you more than once."

Danny was approached by scores of kids throughout the evening, offering their apologies and sympathies. It was nice to see such love for someone you thought to be your whole life. It was heartwarming to hear all the stories that Marcus had shared with these kids. There were times that one kid was on the verge of doing something very stupid, and Mister Marcus helped out with this or that, and stories of how Mister Marcus kept them from doing drugs, or kept another kid from robbing a liquor store, and so on and so on. The stories warmed Danny's heart.

Danny mingled and shook hands and talked about things that Marcus had done to help this person or that person. Marcus had always loved helping people. Whether it be a ride to the store, or to help a person cross the street, it seemed to Danny as though everyone whose lives Marcus had touched had shown up there tonight. His eulogy seemed to be writing itself.

Danny felt a hand on his arm, and when he swung around, he saw that it was Johnny. "Hey, Johnny."

Johnny didn't know what to say, other than he was so deeply sorry. "It was a loss to anyone who knew him, that's for sure."

"I agree with that," said Danny. "You can tell by the amount of people here tonight."

"This is nothing," said Johnny. "There are a ton of people outside still. They're coming in and paying their respects and leaving, but some are staying outside and just swapping stories. I've noticed a bunch of people just standing by the casket for a minute, shedding a tear and then just leaving. I've seen dozens of people do that. I've been watching people do that for an hour. Marcus must have helped a lot of people. You must be very proud of him. I know I am."

"So proud. I can't tell you how much." Danny wanted to change the subject before he turned into a blubbering fool. "Where's Nikki?" he asked.

"Oh, she and her new boy toy are around here somewhere. She's leading him around with a collar and a leash and acting the clown. She's so happy that someone is taking care of her that he could look like the elephant man and she wouldn't care."

"Is he that hideous?" Danny asked.

"No, actually he's young and not bad looking," said Johnny with a shrug, "but don't ask him what two plus two is. He might start to look constipated."

"That bad, huh?"

"That bad is right." Johnny placed his hand over his mouth. "I really should stop. I shouldn't be so mean. I *am* trying to be a better person and all."

"How is it going with David and Erica?" Danny was happy to talk about anything besides how much Marcus was going to be missed. The last few days of sleeping alone had brought him nothing but tears and insomnia. Waking up in the middle of the night and seeing an ocean of empty space in the bed was all he had to look forward to. His whole body ached so much that it was really hard at times to even take a deep breath.

"David and I talk about once a week or so. I still haven't found a place in Chicago. I'm living out of my suitcase right now at some Airbnb. The landlord has been helping me find a place nearby, since I like the neighborhood and it's close to the kids. Erica has been a bit standoffish, though. Let's just say she is a carbon copy of her mother."

"She'll come around, but you have to not push too hard."

"I know, I have to be patient, but I'm not getting any younger, and she isn't getting any more forgiving," said Johnny. "All I hear about are things that happened thirty years ago, and I can hear her mother talking through Erica. Everything Erica says are the same things I heard from my ex when we split up, almost word for word."

"Be patient." Danny didn't have any words of wisdom to share. "You could be in the same boat as your sister, living any life that gives you a hot meal, instead of the one you want to live. Start with David and—" He was cut off.

"He is here tonight, I almost forgot. He really liked Uncle Marcus. He thought Uncle Marcus was cool."

"Tell him Uncle Marcus *was* cool," said Danny. "He was the coolest."

Danny was nudged again, but this time it was a grown-up and not a kid, as so many times before had been. It was John this time, looking to be well over a hundred years old and a victim of the same insomnia that Danny was. "Hey, John. How's it going?" he asked.

"Just wanted to come over and talk to you guys, because if I have to shake one more hand, I think mine is going to fall off." John smiled weakly to let the two of them know that he was just kidding. He looked over at Johnny. "Hey, Junior."

"Hey, Dad. Can you believe all the people here?"

"I know," said John. "I've met some of the nicest people here, and the stories I've been hearing about how Marcus helped this guy or this kid or that kid out. I never knew how many people really relied on Marcus to stay sane, among other things."

Danny blurted out, "Marcus was a lot of things to a lot of people, but the thing he was most was a true friend. That's why you see so many people here. He wasn't phony with people, and he helped out whoever had any issue, no matter what. No matter his own fears and pain, he always put others first." Anyone could hear in his tone and in his words the pain and the restraint he was exhibiting to keep from lashing out at anyone and everyone. "Excuse me," Danny said, leaving the two standing there alone.

John said, "I wish I could do something for him."

"You can," said Johnny. "Just be his friend, and be there if he wants to pour his heart out, or if he wants to pound his fist into the wall. Just be there."

"I keep telling him that very thing. I'm still staying at his house, but every time I try to talk to him about moving home, I feel like I'm running out on him. I don't want to be there if he wants to be alone, but I don't want to leave him to drown in his thoughts twenty-four seven either."

Johnny couldn't believe he was saying the words, but they came out as plainly as ever. "You're doing the right thing, Dad. You need to stay as long as he needs you, and you will know when the time comes when you aren't needed anymore. Give him time, and if he yells or screams or kicks or punches, let him get it out, because it's coming. It's definitely coming."

"Yeah, I know," said John. "Being around him is like being around a powder keg. He just exudes this aura of someone getting ready to implode. I don't know what to do except say 'what can I do?' And I sound so lame saying it." John was also hurting, and wanted to kick and punch and scream, but he had to hold it in. He had to wonder if his and Danny's relationship could survive without Marcus.

"You don't really have to say or do anything," said Johnny. "You just have to be there. You have to be available, and if you do that, if he needs you, he will reach out."

John knew that his son was right. "I know," he admitted. But John was confused about their relationship now. There were times he wanted to run back to his apartment and deal with his own pain, crying into his own pillow and letting Danny do the same. There were times, he hated to admit, when he really didn't care about Danny's pain and Danny's feelings. He had lost his son. He had lost the one chance he had to make things right, and without Marcus, he knew that nothing was ever going to change. He didn't get another chance to fix things. It wasn't fair.

Johnny looked at his father's face and it was obvious his mind was a million miles away, and it was also obvious that whatever he was thinking about did not include conversation. He politely lost himself in the shuffle of people walking around the room.

John realized then that he had some things he wanted to get off his chest. He made his way through the sea of people and up to the casket. He waited until the kid was done talking to his son, and then moved to position himself. He looked down and saw Marcus looking almost lifelike. He wanted to grab him and shake him awake.

John put his hand on his son's hand positioned on his torso. It was cold, but it felt so good to touch him. "You know, I'm going to miss you more than words can describe. You changed my life. I need to thank you for so many things you know? You changed me into a decent human being. I can't put into words how thankful I am to you for all you've done for me. I can't put into words how much I'm going to miss you. I just found you and now I have to say good bye. It's not fair!" John sucked in a gulp of air, and swallowed as much of the pain as he could. After pushing back the tears, he continued. "I'm so proud of you. I'm so in awe of the amount of people you've helped, including myself. How do I get you to understand how I will miss you every day of my life?"

John didn't say another word. He just sat there and stared at his son, and thought about how life was so unfair. He thought about how it was nothing but cruel from day one until the last. How could any God ever think that this kind of pain was good for us? The truth was that it proved to him once and for all that there could not be a God, and if there was a God who believed in this kind of cruelty, it was a God he wanted nothing to do with. He always left one percent of doubt just in case, but the way he felt right now, there was no room for that one percent anymore.

After a second or two more of the pity party, John snapped himself out of his daydream and realized that he was standing there by himself. He needed to sit down. He could feel his back starting to bother him from so much standing. He was usually okay after a few minutes of sitting, so he scanned the room for a seat where he could rest for a few minutes and take the weight off his back. When his back started yelling, he had to listen.

John came upon a nice cushy seat in the corner next to the flowers. There was a small kid sitting in it, but as he approached, the boy jumped up so that John could have the chair. "Thank you," said John as he lowered himself onto the seat.

REDEMPTION

The boy just smiled. "You're welcome." Then he disappeared into the crowd.

John looked out at the sea of people. There was almost too many people to even stand and not be nudged or jarred by an elbow. He was glad to not be in that melee. He just leaned back and took the pressure off his back. He felt ten times better than he had a few seconds ago. After a few moments of rest, he would be okay to mingle once more.

John only knew a small fraction of the attendees. He didn't even really know his son, and that made him so incredibly sad. He wanted to hear each and every story that these people had to tell. He wanted to hear how Marcus helped so and so with a flat tire, or how he kept so and so from doing drugs, or even how he was the shoulder to lean on when a shoulder was all that was needed. He'd heard quite a few of these stories, but it was obvious that there were so many more.

John marveled at the spectrum of people in the room. There were obviously kids from the wrong side of the tracks, and these boys were just as welcome there as any of the people who showed up in fancy, expensive suits. Some people were obviously friends of Danny and Marcus's. And then he saw one person who stuck out from the crowd. He couldn't believe it. There was Anthony standing next to the casket, paying his respects. He knew Anthony must have heard, but the fact that he had come out to pay his respects, even though they were not longtime friends, really made John feel a new kinship with the man. He watched as Anthony stood there, obviously reciting a prayer.

John got to his feet. He wanted to tell Anthony how touched he was that he had come. He didn't move fast with his bum leg, so by the time he'd pushed and shoved his way to the casket, Anthony had left. He spun around, and after looking for a few seconds, he found Anthony heading towards the back where the door opened to the main hall. He didn't want to wait until tomorrow to thank Anthony. He wanted to say it now.

He pushed and shoved again and made his way to the back door. He entered the main hallway and it was then that he saw Anthony heading toward the main entrance. "Anthony!" he yelled, but he wasn't loud enough to be heard over the people talking in the hall. More pushing and more shoving, and then he finally made his way outside.

Once outside, he looked around but didn't see Anthony. *Damn it*! he thought. John walked past the few people who were smoking near the entrance to the funeral parlor to look on the side of building and maybe get a glimpse of his friend. And as he went around the corner, Anthony was standing there as if he had been waiting for him. "Jesus, Anthony," John said after gasping loudly. "You scared the shit out of me."

"I'm sorry, my friend. I didn't mean to scare you."

John put his arm up against the building's brick wall and took a few deep breaths. "I can't be scared like that at my age." But after he caught his breath, he continued, "I just wanted to thank you for coming out and showing your respects. It was very nice of you."

"I came here to make sure Marcus got home," said Anthony.

"What does that mean?" John was obviously confused.

"I wanted to make sure Marcus got home. It's why I'm here."

"Got home?"

"Yes, John," Anthony said without emotion.

"You're not making any sense. You don't even know Marcus." John was trying to piece it together, but a perplexed expression on his face was all that he could muster.

"Silly man," said Anthony. "You thought you were the main character in this story?"

"I still don't understand," said John.

"I wanted Marcus to go home with peace in his heart, and thanks to you, he has it. And with work, my friend, so will you."

John didn't understand what Anthony meant, but it led him to one path of questioning. "Do you think you're you some kind of angel or something?"

"No, John, I'm no angel, believe me," said Anthony. "I've done my share of things that I wish I could take back, believe me. I'm just a simple man who was lucky enough to find a purpose. Hemingway said it best: 'The two best days in your life are the day you are born and the day you figure out why.' I was lucky enough to be shown why I was here."

REDEMPTION

"To take dead people up to heaven? Really? You have to be messing with me, right?" John was incredulous.

"John, I told you that there are tons of people in this world that need help," Anthony said. "We all decide whether to help them or to not help them. You needed help, and your son needed help. I ended up helping you, but my whole being says that my purpose, the reason I was here, the reason I met you, was to help Marcus."

After a pause, Anthony continued. "John, we all walk this earth to feel a purpose, to feel anything besides misery and pain and regret. That empty feeling you've carried around for so long John—it's time to fill it with something besides regret and despair. Marcus was helped by you, and yes, he was also helped in more ways than you could ever imagine. He found a purpose thanks to you, and those kids in there would never have met Marcus without you. They would never have benefited from knowing him. Get to know them John, and others like them, and help them the way Marcus did. You don't have to *be* him, just be a guy who is willing to help another human being, even ones sitting on a park bench. That's what this is all about, John. Love thy neighbor, help thy neighbor. Whatever you heard me say, please remember those two things, and you will be just fine."

John looked on, searching desperately for the words that he wanted to come out of his clamped shut mouth. Half of him wanted to look behind the man before him and see if there were any wings, and the other half thought this guy, or himself, to be plum crazy. "So, was all that stuff you told me at the park just made up?" he finally managed to say. "The shit about your grandkids and the refrigerator? That was just bullshit?"

"John, you were never told anything that wasn't true," Anthony said patiently. He could see that John just wanted to go straight to negative, but he tried to veer him away. "John, stop looking for answers anywhere but right in front of you. If you're loving your neighbor, and helping them, you will believe in yourself. That's just the next progression, trust me. I'm not trying to convince you of anything, John. What I'm telling you is how to find that peace in your heart you've been so desperately seeking. You will never find it watching television or sitting at a park with your impression of the world being so dismal. You have to be okay with putting yourself out there, and maybe finding hurt or ridicule. But the reward is beyond imagination."

John's face said it all. No words, just a look of disbelief and confusion. A million questions swirled around his head like lottery balls. *Who, or what was this guy?*

"John, we all have to die someday," said Anthony, "but did your life mean something to someone, did it have a purpose? We need to control what we put out in the world. We need to hope it's enough to make our lives matter."

"I don't understand a thing you're saying."

Anthony chuckled lightly. "Your past is like a shadow that always follows you. Whether you choose to remember or forget that past, whether you choose to forgive or not forgive yourself, and others, or help or not help anyone else, all of these are choices. You can choose to shine light on them, face them, and then those shadows will disappear."

Anthony took a second or two to find the right words to say it another way. "If you ask any astronaut who has looked down at a tiny speck of life in a cosmic sea of emptiness and darkness if we are not a miracle, they will all tell you the same thing: 'How can it not be?'"

The look on John's face indicated that Anthony was speaking a completely different language.

Anthony sighed and continued. "There are a room full of people in there, John, who can testify to whether Marcus mattered. Just remember that it is your actions and deeds that get his attention, not the denomination you choose to put in the collection plate. Tell Danny that Marcus will be there waiting. Tell him, please. I have to go now, John, my ride is here. I will so miss your sense of humor."

John blinked an eye and his friend was gone from in front of him. He was several feet away by now, walking through the parking lot, and never looking back. John wanted to respond to that last statement, but before he could formulate a reply, Anthony climbed into the passenger seat of a car, and it drove off. Before he could even think, the car had driven off and was out on the main road, and he couldn't see the car, nor his friend any longer. He looked around fiercely from left to right, looking for something or someone—or probably more aptly, looking for answers.

He rubbed his eyes, but all he saw was a bunch of cars parked in the parking lot and people mingling as though they had not a care in the world, nor did they act as though they had even seen Anthony. Did he just have the conversation he thought he had? Whether he did or didn't, he knew at that moment that his mind was different somehow, as was his whole world. An overwhelming sadness washed over him, because he just had a gut feeling that that was the last time he was ever going to see his friend.

He turned around, blinked a few more times, confused and perplexed. He didn't really know how to rationalize to his brain what he'd just seen. His brain alleged and assumed he had just seen Anthony pretty much say that he was some sort of messenger of God, or something, brought here to take his son home to heaven. *How in the hell was that possible?* he thought to himself.

He shuffled and stumbled his way back to the main entrance to the funeral parlor and found himself face to face with Danny. He didn't know what to say.

Danny said, "Where were you? I've been looking for you." After he saw the ashen look on John's face, Danny became a bit alarmed. He didn't want a medical emergency tonight of all times and this place of all places. "What the hell is wrong with you? John, you look like hell."

"I look like I just saw a ghost," said John. "I think that's a better analogy."

"What does that mean?" Danny gently pushed John out of the path and over near the huge flower pot in the corner, a few steps away. He had John sit on the marble bench near the pot. "What are you talking about? Are you okay?"

John shook the cobwebs out of his head. "I don't know. I feel fine, but I don't think I will ever be fine again." John put the second 'fine' in air quotes.

"What the fuck are you saying?!" Danny was getting tired of the cryptic dialogue.

John looked at Danny and just said, matter-of-factly, "Marcus is in heaven."

"Have you been drinking, John?"

John began to laugh. "I'm sorry, because I can't believe I'm saying this, either."

"What are you saying, though?" Danny asked. "Just tell me what the hell you saw."

"I saw my friend Anthony outside," John began. "He said he was here to take Marcus home, and then he told me to tell you that Marcus will be there waiting for you when it's your turn, and then—poof!—he just walked away. There, and then not there."

Danny looked at his father-in-law and didn't know what to make of anything he was saying. He wasn't a drinker, and he didn't seem to be having a stroke or some sort of a delusion. Whatever happened to him, though, was enough to shake him, which had never been an easy task. Danny could tell by his almost white complexion that John had seen something, and whatever it was, it had really messed him up. "You're not making any sense, John," he said finally.

"Tell me about it. I think I just saw my refrigerator."

"What!" Danny was trying to keep his voice down but still be heard, but this conversation was worrying him, and frustrating him, too.

"Never mind, I'll tell you later. Let's just say that everyone sees that one thing in their life they will never ever be able to understand, and I might have just seen mine."

Danny turned to see all the people still milling around. It reminded him more of a cocktail party than a funeral. He appreciated everything and everyone who came, but the truth was that he was tired, exhausted. He wanted to go home. "Are you ready to go home, John?" he asked.

"Whenever you want me out, I will go," said John.

"I mean *our* home," Danny clarified. "Are you ready to go home?"

"I'm confused. I have a home, and as soon as you don't need me, I'm going to go back to it."

Danny put his hand on John's shoulder and uttered the words that at one time he would've thought impossible. "John, if anything you have just told me is true, even a little bit of it, I have a lot of catching up to do if I want to see Marcus again. Marcus had a habit of finding family wherever he went. He didn't always have family, and so he had to make it himself. And he was good at it. I don't intend to explain to him how I let his father live out the rest of his life alone and without family. I don't think Marcus would want either of us to live that life." Danny helped John to his feet. "Let's go say goodbye to Marcus one last time, and then go home. I think we both need some sleep."

John, still a bit confused, although secretly elated at the prospect of living full-time with Danny, followed Danny to the door that led back to the viewing area. Once inside the viewing area, he turned left and then right and took a last look at the mass of people that his son had helped and befriended, and called family, and he felt a swell of pride that he'd never felt before, never before thought possible. He had a million questions, maybe more, but he knew that Danny was right. If he wanted to see Marcus again someday, he too had a lot of catching up to do. He grinned at the thought. Whatever he had just seen, real or delusional, if nothing else, it had showed him that he had to stop saying 'why is this happening to me?' constantly. It had showed him mostly that he had a long way to go, and a very short time in which to get there.

30 DAYS GONE BY

John walked the cobblestone walkway a bit differently than the last time he had come. The park felt a bit more desolate, as if he was walking in an area that he had never been in before. It had been a month, but it felt like so much longer. He chalked it up to him being there just a bit earlier than usual.

Danny had dropped him in front of his apartment so that he could check on things at his apartment, like mail, and things in general, and tell the complex that he was putting in his thirty-day notice. He hoped that it was the right move, but he was still a bit anxious about the decision. He was plagued with thoughts about the possibility of things going wrong and Danny kicking him out. He would be totally screwed, and he knew it. The two had gotten along really well without Marcus the past month or so, but as he knew all too well, that could change in an instant.

He had an hour or so to kill before the front office was open, so he had come down to tell his old friend—the bench—that he missed him, and would miss him greatly in the future. Danny said he would bring him over from time to time, but John knew that it wouldn't be the same as being this close, when he could come at any time he liked. It would be hard for John to give up his routine, and even more so the possibility of ever seeing Anthony again.

John looked around and could see that the formerly green leaves on the trees had mostly changed to bright reds and yellows, and just the hint of some cool air was coming their way. He was anxious to see if his bench was still where he left it, and anxious to see if maybe, just maybe, his friend Anthony might drop by. As he inched his way along, and he inspected everything a bit more closely, it seemed as though not much had changed, other than a few brighter colors on the trees than he had remembered, and maybe a few more dead leaves on the ground.

As he approached his bench, he had to admit that the teaming life around him wasn't quite what it had been the last time he was there. He saw an occasional jogger whiz by, but the multitude of life, both human and otherwise, seemed to be diminished. He put his hand on the back of the bench to steady himself. "Good to see you, old friend," he said aloud. "Have you seen Anthony, by chance?" John actually hoped that invoking his friend's name might make him pop up.

He sat down, and as usual, the muffin he'd grabbed from the corner store was set down next to him on the bench. But it felt different, somehow. Like he was intruding in some way. He looked up several times, but saw nothing, or no one, that he wished to see. "Stupid old fool, he's not coming," John muttered to himself. He grabbed the seed out of his brown paper bag and began to sprinkle a light dusting onto the ground to see if maybe his feathered friends still remembered him. After a few seconds, he looked around, but he didn't see anything that even resembled a bird. He assumed they had all flown a bit further south to somewhere in Georgia or Florida, probably.

After a minute or so, though, a lone bird came down and started pecking away at the ground. John remembered this bird because he had the bit of white right near his left eye. John's heart rejoiced upon seeing an old friend. It didn't take long to see another, and then another, come down to pay their respects. He was elated to see them, and wished he could convey his thanks somehow. He threw out another generous handful of seed and took one last hopeful look around, but he saw nothing but strangers, and the cold emptiness of missing Marcus crept back in. He wished he had had more time with him, more time to get to know him and more time to say that he was sorry, more time to make up for the things he had done and said. He knew it would haunt him for the rest of his days, and he knew that no matter what Danny said, or what John Junior said, it would never be enough, because this was one wrong he would never feel was righted.

He had reflected on that last night with Marcus so many times. They had had such a great night. They laughed and they joked, and it felt like maybe, just maybe, he was going to die feeling like he had done what he could to fix things between them. He had always lived his life feeling that it was his duty to make sure his kids had food and clothes and a place to stay that was warm and dry, but now he wished he had done so much more. He wished he had listened to Betty and was their friend as well as their father, instead of feeling hurt and betrayed because they didn't see the things the way that he did. He had been so angry at them for so long, and it tore him up inside knowing that some wrongs would never be able to be undone.

John looked up to the sky. "I am so sorry, Marcus," he said. "I wish I could have had more time with you, son." John kept looking up as tears fell down his cheeks. He was not an emotional man, but it felt good to talk with Marcus, even though he knew he was talking to nothing, but that faint possibility kept him talking. He had talked with Marcus and Betty almost every day recently. He was so sorry for the things he had done, but it was obvious to him that he was to live with the guilt and regret and the sadness for the rest of his life. It was his penance, and he had to accept it.

John was suddenly shocked back into reality by the feeling of a hand on his arm. He wiped his eyes and looked up at the blurry figure before him. "Are you okay, mister?" said Sammie, the young boy with the limp, shy and sheepish.

"Uh, I am," John stammered. "I am fine, thank you." John was amazed and honestly stunned by the boy's obvious concern. Maybe there were a few kids who hadn't been eaten up by insensitivity and narcissism after all.

"We thought you were dead. I saw you on my way to school every day, and then one day you weren't there anymore."

Sammie's mother chimed in from behind him. "Excuse Sammie, but he was very excited that you weren't dead."

"No, I'm very much alive," John confirmed. "I'm just having a good cry."

"Why are you so sad?" asked Sammie.

"I'm just missing someone, that's all."

"Mom thought that since we didn't see you for such a long time, that maybe you had died."

REDEMPTION

His mother jumped in once more. "Sammie, don't be rude. What I said was that it was possible that the gentleman had passed away."

John smiled. "So, you thought I was dead, like Sammie said?" He looked over at Sammie and gave him a big smile. "Well, I'm very glad you stopped by to say hi this morning, Sammie. It made my whole day."

"You're welcome," Sammie said. "But my mom told me not to, because you were a stranger."

"Well, as of now, Sammie, we are officially not strangers. My name is John, and you can call me Mister John, if that's okay with your mom." John and Sammie both looked over at her for approval. To both of their delight, she nodded.

"My name is Patty," she said, "and it is very nice to meet you, Mister John."

"You too, Patty. You have a very nice boy there."

"Yeah, he's a great kid. He cares so much about everyone."

"Sammie, maybe one day, when you have more time, you can feed some of the birds, and I can tell you their names."

"They have names?" Sammie asked, his eyes widening.

"They sure do," said John with a smile.

"Is that who you're always talking to?"

"No, I say hello to them, but that's about all." John thought it funny to imagine having a real conversation with a blue jay or a cardinal.

"Then who do you keep talking to?" Sammie insisted.

Sammie's mother clearly didn't want to make John feel uncomfortable. "Sammie, it's time to go to school," she said, reaching for his hand. "We had better get going. Say goodbye to Mister John."

But John was more perplexed than uncomfortable. "Can I ask Sammie a question before you all go?"

Patty nodded, and John leaned back to think for a moment. He wanted to make sure that he phrased the question in just the right way. "Sammie, this is very important," he began. "When you came by in the mornings, did you ever see a man sitting on that side of the bench? He usually was dressed pretty nicely." John pointed over to the other side of the bench where his friend had sat almost every morning.

Sammie giggled. "No," he said. "You were always talking and laughing to yourself, and Mom told me to not bother you."

"Thank you, Sammie." John's face had turned pale, as if all the blood had run out of it all at once.

Patty could tell that John was needing some time alone. "Come on, Sammie, let's get you to school. Talk to you later, Mister John." She seemed to have just realized in that very moment that John realized he was an old man, a sick man, who talked to himself. Her heart went out to him, but she knew that there was nothing she could do for him.

John watched as the mother and son slowly walked away. He could tell that Patty was lecturing Sammie on something he had said as they walked hand in hand, and John knew exactly what was being said, even though he was far out of earshot.

John silently waved to Sammie as the boy gave the old man an emphatic wave behind him in return. He was beyond dumbfounded. Everything that he had taken a month to logically explain and rationalize and justify to himself had just disappeared. *Was he going crazy? Had he imagined the whole thing? Was it even real?*

John looked down at his feathered friends who had returned after his newfound acquaintances had left, and the biggest, broadest smile anyone could have ever seen bloomed brightly across his face. He thought himself daft. He must be crazy, he thought to himself, but nonetheless there it was, that one percent was growing by leaps and bounds. He looked up to the sky with a tear running down to his jawline, and silently, and most sincerely said, '*thank you.*'